"You return in  deputy minister. "A theatrically, pleased with his news, wanting to extract the maximum from it. "You're going to be elected to the Central Committee, Pietr."

Orlov, shocked, didn't respond. The Central Committee! The inner sanctum, the cornucopia of power. Except he didn't want power anymore. Once maybe, but not now. Now he wanted freedom.

There was no doubt or uncertainty about what he intended doing—there couldn't be. But when it was all over there would still remain the regret at how he'd had to deceive his friends. And an even deeper regret that there was no way he could attempt to apologize or explain. He could do nothing. Nothing except hope that in some way, somehow, Sevin would come to understand. Orlov doubted the man would though. How could he? How could anyone?

He said honestly, "It's difficult to express myself."

THE LOST AMERICAN

Look for this other TOR book by Brian Freemantle

THE VIETNAM LEGACY

THE LOST AMERICAN

BRIAN FREEMANTLE

TOR

A TOM DOHERTY ASSOCIATES BOOK

THE LOST AMERICAN

Copyright © 1984 by Brian Freemantle

First printing: November 1984

A TOR Book

Published by Tom Doherty Associates,
8-10 West 36 Street,
New York, N.Y. 10018

ISBN: 0-812-58250-0
CAN. ED.: 0-812-58251-9

Printed in the United States of America

*For Dudley and Elian,
with love*

I pray you, do not fall in love with me,
For I am falser than vows made in wine.

—Shakespeare, *As You Like It*.

CHAPTER ONE

Housework had become important, a time-filling ritual, and Ann moved dutifully through the apartment, vacuuming carpets already vacuumed, tidying things already tidied, and dusting where no dust had had time to collect since the previous day. She tried to concentrate on what she was doing, but by now the ritual had become mechanical as well as dutiful, just as so much else had become mechanical. She'd expected the uncertainty, of course; the doubts even. For there to have been any other reaction, after what had happened and where they were, would have been more unsettling than the feelings she now had, because it would have been unnatural. But it should have gone by now. Lessened at least. Not gotten worse.

She stopped the vacuum abruptly, the movement a physical correction. Only *some* things seemed to have grown worse. To think everything had would be to exaggerate, and it would be wrong—dangerous—to exaggerate; certainly not the way to settle and adjust, imagining things to be worse than they really were. The hostility from the other wives had definitely disappeared. Eddie insisted that it had never existed in the first place, dismissing the impression as her confused response to the trauma of the divorce and the reaction of her family and the abruptness of the Moscow posting, but Ann knew she wasn't confused. They *had* been hostile. She'd rationalized the attitude; she understood it, now that she'd lived in Moscow for two years.

The Western diplomatic community in the Soviet capital was an enclosed, insular and claustrophobic existence, the same faces appearing at the same receptions and parties with the same small talk and the same gossip. She'd been a subject of that gossip, and maybe she still was. After all, she was the woman half her husband's age who'd wrecked a happy marriage. And if she'd done it once, she could do it again. Especially in the unnatural circumstances in which they lived, crammed together in constant contact. Bloody hypocrites. She'd seen flirtations and guessed at affairs, and those she hadn't guessed had soon been reported to her on the gossip mill. At least she and Eddie had been honest. Refused to lie and instead confronted all the consequences: the bitterness and the recriminations and the nastiness— God, the nastiness!—which was more than any of them were doing.

Ann abandoned the unnecessary dusting and sat down, arriving at another ritual, the increasing (daily, almost) reflection on what that honesty had cost. She told Eddie and Eddie told her that each had expected what had happened, but she knew that wasn't true. She certainly hadn't anticipated her family's reaction. She knew they'd be upset, obviously; they couldn't be anything else. But she'd thought they would have accepted the situation by now, not gone on behaving like some parody of Victorian rectitude, practically refusing to acknowledge her existence. Whenever her mother wrote, which was only in response to Ann's letters, never initiating any correspondence herself, there was always the line: "Daddy sends his regards," but Ann knew that her father had done nothing of the sort. And what father sent his regards, for God's sake? No, it wasn't a parody of Victorian rectitude; it *was* Victorian rectitude. And it was hurtful and unnecessary and cruel. It was one of the reasons—one of the main reasons—why she was so miserable.

She looked across the room at the drinks tray and then at her watch and then at the drinks tray again and decided against it, pleased at her control. Quite a lot of women started cocktails at four, but she hadn't, not yet. And she wouldn't, Ann determined. That would be giving in, and she didn't give in. She hadn't given in to her family or to the unpleasantness of Eddie's divorce. . . . Ann stopped, examining the word. Had Eddie's divorce been unpleasant? Of course it had, on the surface. The tight-lipped meetings with the lawyers and the financial arrangements and the division of property, the dismantling of years together.

But there hadn't been from Ruth anything like the sort of reaction that had come from Ann's family. And from Ruth it *could* have been expected. She was, after all, the abandoned wife, saddled with two bewildered sons and an empty house and empty memories, wondering where she went wrong, although Ann knew Ruth hadn't gone wrong anywhere. She hadn't had affairs and she hadn't drunk and she hadn't failed and she hadn't, when Eddie announced he'd fallen in love with someone else, railed against him or fought him or hated him. Eddie said he'd imagined her behaving just as she did, because that was the sort of woman Ruth was, but Ann didn't believe that either. She had been surprised, and she knew Eddie was as well. No sneers and no reproaches. It was Ruth who initiated the letters more often than not, always chatty, always friendly. And always "love to Ann." The discarded wife could send love to the woman who had replaced her, but the best her father could manage was regards, and that a lie, Ann thought bitterly.

She returned to the beginning. The honesty had cost them both a lot. So had it been worth it? Another part of the ritual. Of course it had been worth it, she decided in familiar reassurance. She loved Eddie as much—more—as she ever had, and she knew he loved her. It was just Moscow. If it been any other posting to any other embassy, they could have had outside friends and outside interests and driven a hundred miles out into the country on Sundays when they'd felt like it, and Ann was positive everything would have been all right. She made another mental pause. Everything *was* all right between her and Eddie. Which was all that mattered. Moscow was important to Eddie's career, vitally so. All she had to do was endure it as philosophically as she could and ignore her bloody stupid family, as they were ignoring her, and wait until the next posting.

She supposed Langley was a possibility after Moscow. Ann decided she'd like that. Eddie was almost certain to be upgraded, perhaps as high as G-15. He had a lot of experience and was respected because of it. If he got G-15, they'd probably be able to afford something in Georgetown. But maybe not, what with the support he paid Ruth and the kids. If not Georgetown, Alexandria then. She liked that almost as much. It would be wonderful to be in Washington. There'd be the concerts and the plays at the Kennedy Center. And New York was only an hour away on the shuttle, so they could see the Broadway shows whenever they wanted. And they'd drive out into the country and go to restaurants and not have to wait three hours for service and make friends with people they wanted to be friendly with, not those forced upon them by some restricted, hemmed-in environment. Moscow was an unnatural existence, so it automatically followed that she should feel unnatural in it. Endure it until the next posting, she thought again. That's all she had to do.

It had turned five before she took the first drink while she began preparing dinner, and she made it last until Eddie came home promptly at six, which was another ritual. He kissed her and held her tightly and she held him tightly back, needing his closeness. He *did* love her and she loved him; just endure it, she thought.

Ann fixed his drink and made another for herself and said, "Steak. That okay?" At least they were able to eat well, having easy access to the embassy concessions.

"Wait until I can teach you how to cook a steak outside." Eddie Franklin was a tall, heavy man of casual, almost slow, movement. He spoke slowly too, the Texas accent pronounced. His slowness, frequent references to cookouts and range riding, and his tendency to dress in jeans and sports shirts for the more casual parties, conveyed to some the impression of country-boy stolidness, which was intentionally misleading. Franklin was one of the highest-regarded officers within the Central Intelligence Agency, already at supervisor rank.

"I'm looking forward to it," said Ann honestly. "How was your day?"

He grimaced. "Average. Yours?"

"Average," she said. Liar, she thought. She added, "Betty Harrison called, suggesting lunch. But I said no."

"Why not?" asked Franklin.

Because I lunched with her yesterday and two days before that and I'm lunching with her tomorrow, thought Ann. She said, "I was busy here in the apartment."

"Nothing for you in the bag," he said. All their overseas correspondence arrived in the diplomatic pouch.

"I wasn't expecting anything," she said. Father sends his regards, she thought. "You?" she asked.

Franklin reached into his briefcase and took out the letter, still sealed. "From Ruth," he said unnecessarily.

"Let's open it," said Ann. They'd made each other several promises when they married. One, practically a cliché, was no secrets, and that extended to the letters between him and Ruth. Franklin interpreted it by never opening his first wife's letters at the embassy but always waiting until he got home.

She refilled his glass and decided, after a moment's hesitation, against having a third herself while he opened the letter and read it. "She's taking the boys to her folks' place in Maine for Thanksgiving," he reported. There was a few seconds' silence and then he said, "Paul's grades aren't good; his teachers are apparently disappointed. John's neither."

Ann wondered if the kids' poor performance was because of the break-up, and knew he would be wondering too. He missed the boys. His guilt—the guilt he sought to minimize despite the agreement about no secrets—was as much for abandoning them as it was for abandoning Ruth.

"Ruth's been dating," he said, still reading the letter.

"Guy called Charlie Rogers. Someone she knew in high school. Friend of the family apparently."

"How do you feel about that?" she asked, wishing immediately she hadn't.

Franklin frowned up at her. "Pleased for her, of course," he said. "What else should I feel?"

"Nothing," she agreed at once. He could have made an argument out of it if he'd wanted to. Thank God he hadn't. She was still nervous about arguments in their relationship.

"She's sent some pictures." Franklin studied the prints for several moments and Ann stared at him, alert for his facial reaction. There wasn't any. "Here," he said, offering them to her.

Paul was the older, fourteen in two months' time. John was nine, dark-haired like Ruth. Paul had his father's blondness and would be big too. Already he had to be almost five feet. She guessed they'd posed specially for the photograph to be sent to their father; their lips were barely parted in reluctant indication of a smile. They were standing against Ruth's car in the driveway of the Rosslyn house. If Eddie got the headquarters posting he expected, he'd be very near them, Ann realized, able to see them. Would the boys accept her? Ruth had—or appeared to have—despite the strained tightness of the initial confrontations and the immediate aftermath of the divorce. There'd been only one meeting with the children, and they'd treated her then like the enemy she was. Well, it was all she could have expected. She hoped the attitude would change with time.

"Is John wearing braces on his teeth?" she asked, passing the pictures back.

Franklin stared down and said, "Difficult to tell. Ruth doesn't say anything about it in the letter."

He held it out for her to read, another part of their no-secrets agreement. Ann hesitated, appreciating the gesture but reluctant to take the paper from him. It *was* part of the pact between them. And he always read her letters from her mother, although more out of courtesy to her than for any other reason because they were so damned stiff and formal. Nevertheless, she felt the embarrassment of prying when it came to Ruth's correspondence, a feeling that was probably illogical considering that she'd taken the woman's husband. There was, of course, the other reason. To want to read the letters from his first wife could have indicated a jealousy. Ann was confident she didn't have anything to be jealous about, not with Ruth. It was only to be expected that Eddie would still have some feeling for her—love, even, of a kind. But not the kind that was any danger to her. So there was no reason for jealousy and no reason, therefore, to do anything that might hint she felt that way. Like reading her letters. "Later," she said. "I have to fix dinner first."

As soon as they started to eat, Ann realized the steaks were slightly more overdone than he liked, but Franklin didn't complain. "Sorry," she said, not wanting him to think she didn't care.

"It's fine, really," he said. "John Ingram has got his posting."

"Where?" she asked. Ingram was Franklin's counterpart at the British Embassy, the resident for Britain's M-16.

"London," said Franklin.

Lucky John Ingram, thought Ann. London was where she'd first met Franklin when he'd been attached to the embassy there, liaison attaché with the British. "I'll miss them," she said.

Lucinda Ingram had been one of the few wives to accept her almost from the start; she was a bustling, no-nonsense woman, one of those who didn't flirt. She drank a bit, though never beyond control. Lucinda's going would mean she was losing her closest friend.

"The farewell party is next Saturday."

Same faces, same small talk, she thought. "When did they hear about the move?"

"Today apparently."

Lucinda hadn't called. She'd only be hearing about it herself tonight, Ann supposed. "I must buy her something. A farewell gift," she said.

"That would be nice."

"Maybe something from the gold shop on Gorky Street." There was little in the way of a gift obtainable in Moscow.

"John asked me to look out for their new man."

"Who is it?"

"Someone called Brinkman. Jeremy Brinkman."

"Wonder if he knows what to expect," said Ann. A new arrival was always lionized, a fresh face with fresh stories and news from outside their confines.

"John doesn't know him."

"Is he pleased to be going?" Lucinda's attitude had always been that Moscow was a stepping-stone assignment for her husband and, as such, had to be enjoyed by a careerist's wife.

"It's a promotion, so I think so," said Franklin. "I don't know that he likes the idea of being stuck in London."

Dear God, just for the chance, thought Ann. She asked, "Will he be?"

"He's not sure."

"How long has he been here?"

"Three years," said Franklin.

Three years, Ann thought. Endure it. She said, "Thought about where you'd like to go next, apart from back to Langley?"

Instead of answering, Franklin said, "What about you? Where would you like to go if you were given the choice?"

Anywhere away from this damned place, Ann thought. She said, "I don't care where I am just so long as it's with you."

He reached across the table for her hand. "I love you," said Franklin. "I love you very much."

"I love you too," said Ann. "Very much."

Pietr Orlov traveled on a diplomatic passport, which meant he was able to bypass the frustrating delays and formalities at the Sheremetyevo airport. It meant, too, that his incoming luggage and freight were spared any customs examination. He stood watching the dour-faced inspector in head-bent consultation with the official from the Foreign Ministry, guessing they both would be resentful of his ability to bring so much back from America. Orlov hoped it wasn't too much, but he wanted it to look right. Someone recalled to Moscow after two years in New York would surely bring back the maximum he was allowed.

The check completed, the Foreign Ministry official came over with the manifest. "Welcome back," he said.

Six months, calculated Orlov. Longer, if necessary. Like returning with the maximum allowance, everything had to look exactly right if Natalia were to be protected. And Orlov was determined she would be. He had loved her once even if he didn't now, not in the way that he should love his wife anyway. He was going to take every precaution to keep her safe. Harriet was as insistent about that as he was. A year then, if it had to be. Orlov hoped it wouldn't be as long as that.

He didn't think he could exist for a year without Harriet.

CHAPTER TWO

Jeremy Brinkman entered the Foreign Office from Parliament Square, guessing that this, his final meeting before Moscow, would be the waste of time all the others had been, self-important officials in mahogany chambers lecturing about do's and don'ts and what was expected and what was not expected. Brinkman knew all about self-important officials who disdained changing governments and considered themselves—perhaps rightly—the true governors of the country. His father, who was one, had been a good teacher in all things, particularly about what was expected from the son of a Permanent Under Secretary whose father had been a Permanent Under Secretary before him and whose family service to the country—the country and the crown, not some passing political fancy with its cant and hollow propaganda—stretched back earlier than that.

Brinkman knew, too, that he could fulfill the expectations.

But his way. He'd proved that he didn't need to rely upon the family connections—not unless there wasn't any other way, in which case it would have been stupid to ignore the advantage. He'd proved it by getting into Cambridge on a scholarship so that the family money was unnecessary. And by getting his rowing blue, something else they couldn't use their influence to obtain. Any more than they could have bought or manipulated his Double First in history or the ninety-eight-percent pass mark for the Foreign Office entry examination, although his father had hinted that help was available had the mark been borderline, still not fully aware of his son's unshakable intention never to do anything borderline in his life. But on his own: his way. Which was why Brinkman had applied to the intelligence service, purposely selecting a department far away from his father's sphere of influence but not so entirely removed from the Foreign Office—to whom MI-6 were responsible— that there wasn't a final safety net if he lost his grip on the high trapeze. Not that he expected to, because Jeremy Brinkman was supremely confident, to the point of having people misunderstand the attitude as arrogance. Brinkman knew he wasn't arrogant, because he knew everything about himself. Just determined. And properly, necessarily, confident.

His selection of the country's intelligence service had annoyed his father, of course. Sir Richard Brinkman found no difficulty in ignoring Britain's most recent spy scandals and thought the idea preposterous that a chap would read another chap's mail or doubt the loyalty of anyone who had been to a recognizable handful of good and proper universities. He accepted the existence of such a department but more from the historical precedent of its formation during the reign of Queen Elizabeth I than for its practical necessity. He certainly didn't consider it something with which the Brinkman family should become associated.

So he'd argued with Jeremy repeatedly, not in any gesticulating, shouting manner but in the level, measured tones of a Permanent Under Secretary at the Foreign Office intent upon persuading someone with less experience of the obvious error of a mistaken judgment. Sir Richard hadn't raised his voice or changed his calm demeanor even when he realized that his son couldn't—or wouldn't—accept the logical argument. Between them now there existed the sort of unspoken, unannounced truce that sometimes develops between equally strong and equally implacable foes who know that continued fighting is pointless but that fresh strategies are necessary.

Jeremy Brinkman smiled at the analogy as he walked along the now-familiar, hushed corridors. Moscow had created the strategy for him. He was regrouping, far away from any intrusion the old man might make. His smile faded, however, as he arrived at the designated doorway and handed his appointment chit over to the waiting security guard. At least he *hoped* he was far enough away.

There wasn't any formal introduction because that wasn't the way these interviews were conducted, but Brinkman knew the man's name was Maxwell and that he was number three on the Moscow desk and the one who would, after analysis and checking, receive his reports. Maxwell waved him to a chair and offered cigarettes, which Brinkman, who didn't smoke, refused. Maxwell took one, lit it, and said, "Shouldn't, I know. Filthy habit."

Brinkman smiled politely but said nothing, waiting for his superior to lead. There was a protocol about everything in the Foreign Office and Brinkman knew every bit of it.

"Finished the rounds?" Maxwell had a rough, hello-me-hearties voice. If the tie the man was wearing designated a rugby club, then Brinkman guessed he knew all the barroom songs.

"I think so, sir," said Brinkman. "It seems a lot of advice is necessary."

"Civil servants, justifying their existence," said Maxwell.

Brinkman decided he liked the man. "What's the proper briefing?"

"If it were thought necessary to give a lecture, you wouldn't have been selected in the first place," said Maxwell gruffly. "As it is, you've jumped over quite a few heads."

Father's influence? wondered Brinkman at once. But that didn't follow. Unless Sir Richard had accepted that persuasion was impossible and decided instead to get the best possible posting for his son. Probing, he said, "I'd hoped I'd got it on merit."

" 'Course you have," said Maxwell. "How else?"

Very early Brinkman had learned the advantage of apparent ingenuous honesty. He said, "It doesn't seem to be any secret within the department that my father is attached to the Foreign Office."

"Hasn't made any sort of approach to me," said Maxwell, and Brinkman believed the man. Maxwell went on, "You got it because of your ability with the language and your pass marks and your general aptitude in all the examinations and tests."

"Thank you," said Brinkman.

"Which don't mean a damn on the streets. Not much anyway," said Maxwell. "Give me common sense compared to a ninety-eight-percent pass mark in an examination and I'd choose common sense every time."

"I understand," said Brinkman too glibly, regretting it as soon as he spoke.

"No, you don't," said Maxwell. "There's no way you can, not yet. But I think you will. Every assessment and aptitude test you've taken repeats the same characteristic— you're fast on your feet. Cunning was one word used, though not unkindly. And you don't make mistakes, not twice."

Brinkman felt the burn of embarrassment at the compliment. He wished he could think of a proper response. Knowing it was insufficient, he said, "I'll try."

Maxwell shook his head. "You have to do better than that. I don't want you making any mistakes, not even once. Classrooms and mock-these and mock-thats can never properly equip you for the real thing. You're going to a sensitive place: *the* most sensitive place. I know you're ambitious; that's another finding of the aptitude tests and psychiatrists' reports. I'm glad. Someone without ambition isn't any good to me. But use it properly. I'm not expecting—no one's expecting—sensations: no Khrushchev-like denunciations of Brezhnev or Andropov at secret Politburo sessions. I want steady, practical work. I want the analysis to be correct and I want the assessments to be in accord with the facts as best you can obtain them. Don't ever take a chance to impress me or anybody else. You got that?"

"Yes, sir, I've got that," said Brinkman, knowing he had to. He didn't intend taking any chances; not stupid ones anyway. But if one came that wasn't stupid, he was going to grab it like a drowning man snatching at passing driftwood and show everyone—Maxwell and his father and *everyone*—just how good he was.

"Ingram's staying over to ease you in."

"That's kind," said Brinkman. He didn't want to be eased in by anyone, picking up cast-off contacts like second-hand clothes, but it wouldn't have been politic to say so.

"He's done a good job there," said Maxwell. "He won't be an easy act to follow!"

"I'll do my best," said Brinkman. Modesty, like apparent honesty, was another thing he practiced.

"Do more than that," said Maxwell in his hearty voice. Brinkman wondered if he took the part of Santa Claus at the department Christmas party. "This could make or break a career, you know."

"I know," said Brinkman. He knew it was going to be the former, not the latter.

Maxwell stood, ending the meeting. He offered his hand and said, "Good luck."

"Thank you, sir," said Brinkman, modest still. Luck wasn't going to have anything to do with it.

The lovemaking was good, as it always was, because he was experienced and unselfish, knowing how to bring her up and then keep her there so that she had orgasm after orgasm and even then didn't want to stop but kept pulling at him, urgently demanding. When they finished, Ann still clung to him, wanting his nakedness next to hers. After a long time she said, "Eddie?"

"What?"

"Why not?"

"You know why not." He sighed, confronting a familiar argument.

"I don't think that's valid."

"I do."

"Dozens of men your age have children. You're only forty-five, for Christ's sake!"

"And you're only twenty-six. And when I'm sixty—if I live to be sixty—you'll be only forty-one."

"So what?" she said, exasperated. "If we had a child now, he or she would be eighteen or nineteen when you're sixty. And of course you're going to live beyond that." Ann wanted a baby for all the natural, proper reasons, but there was another one as well. A baby would occupy her completely, take away the aimlessness of her life in Moscow.

"We'll see," he said.

"You're avoiding it."

"I said we'd see."

Ann recognized the note in his voice and knew it was time to retreat. "I want a baby, Eddie," she said, firing a final salvo. "I want a baby very much."

CHAPTER THREE

Farewell parties were usually the best. There was a purpose to them, an actual reason beyond the usual excuse of escaping from one set of four walls into another. There was the official affair for Ingram at the embassy on Morisa Toreza, but the bigger gathering was at Ingram's own apartment in the official diplomatic compound off Kutuzovsky Prospekt. It wasn't limited to the British but included all of Ingram's friends from the other embassies as well, and this was the party Ingram assured Brinkman he would find most useful. Ingram was a small, rotund man given to quick, fussy movements. He wore glasses with large, round frames that made him look like an owl, an owl in a hurry. Toward Brinkman, Ingram's attitude was very much that of mentor to pupil. Brinkman resented the patronizing attitude but indicated no sign of doing so.

Brinkman, who was taking over the Ingram apartment,

arrived late from his temporary accommodation at the embassy, looking proprietorially around at the smoke-filled, noisy rooms and hoping there wouldn't be too much damage to get fixed afterward. He knew the smell of smoke would last for days.

A temporary bar had been set up along a wall immediately adjacent to the kitchen. Ingram stood beside it, urging people to take fresh drinks, blinking around in happy contentment at being the object of attention. His wife bustled back and forth from the kitchen, ferrying food to a separate table near the window. Lucinda remembered Brinkman from their brief embassy encounter. Taller than her husband and not so obviously excited as he was by all the fuss, she wore flat-heeled, practical shoes and a day dress instead of the cocktail creations all about her. Brinkman identified Lucinda Ingram as the sort of woman whom, in another time at another place, the natives would have instinctively addressed as *mem-sahib*.

It was she who saw Brinkman first, standing just inside the door. She smiled and beckoned for him to come farther in. As he started through the crush, he saw her speak to her husband on her way to the kitchen and at once Ingram looked in his direction.

"Come in, come in," urged Ingram, thrusting through the crowd to meet him. He cupped Brinkman's elbow with his hand and propelled him toward the drinks, and Brinkman wished he hadn't. He didn't like that sort of physical contact. Brinkman chose scotch, frowning as the other man gushed an overly large measure into a tumbler and gave it to him without ice or water. Brinkman took it but didn't drink.

"Quite a crowd," he said.

"More to come yet," said Ingram. "More to come. Lucky to have made a lot of friends."

"Certainly looks like it."

Briefly the owl settled on a perch. "Important that some of them become your friends too," said Ingram.

"Who, for instance?" asked Brinkman obediently.

"Australians are useful, although not for the obvious reason. Get a lot of playback from Canberra on what's happening in Peking. . . ." Ingram smiled, a man about to impart a secret. "No reason to consider yourself limited by the boundaries of the country you happen to be in, is there?"

"None at all," agreed Brinkman. He decided that irritating as Ingram might be, he wasn't a fool.

"Canada is important too. By the same token. Ottawa was the first to recognize Mao way back. So there's a lot of playback through here: analysis requests on how something or other emerging in Peking will be viewed in Moscow. It's a worthwhile tennis game to watch."

With China the subject, Brinkman thought ping-pong would have been a more appropriate metaphor. He said, "Anyone else?"

"The French are pretty good but they're an awkward bunch of bastards, all give and no take. Always a one-sided affair, dealing with them."

Only if you let it be so, thought Brinkman. "Sounds typically French," he said.

"And there's the ace," said Ingram.

Brinkman followed Ingram's look. On the far side of the room, actually leaning against the wall, was a tall, loose-limbed man. He wore an open-necked plaid shirt and jeans and appeared to be feeling the heat, from the flush on his

face; the fair hair was disordered, falling forward over his
forehead.

"Name's Franklin," said Ingram. "Eddie Franklin. Been
the CIA resident here for a couple of years. Hell of a
guy."

Brinkman looked at Ingram. The open admiration surprised him. "In what way?"

"Every way," said Ingram. "Straight as a dye, first of
all. He'll help if he can, but if it interferes with anything
he's doing, or if he can't because of orders from above,
he'll say so straight out. There isn't a member of the
Politburo he can't quote chapter and verse about, going
back as far as their grandfathers, and his political judgment
is superb."

"Like you said, a hell of a guy."

"It doesn't end there," said Ingram, enjoying the lecture.
"Technology is the name of the game. That's what the
Russians want, to catch up with us. But with America
most of all. And technically Franklin's got a mind like a
computer. He actually *understands* all of it. Do you know
what the joke is?"

"What?" asked Brinkman politely.

"That Washington doesn't bother to send in the electronic people any more to sweep the embassy and the
apartments for bugs. Because Eddie Franklin knows more
about it and can do it better than any of them."

Brinkman looked idly about him. There were a hundred
places in the room where listening devices could be
concealed; there always were. The jabber of this crowd
would nullify anything tonight anyway.

"Franklin's the man to watch," said Ingram.

Brinkman wondered if the Russians were doing just
that. "I'll remember," he said.

"Why not meet him now?"

"Why not?" agreed Brinkman. Before leaving the drinks table, he put as much water as possible into his scotch and sipped it. Still not enough, he thought. Ingram had already opened the introduction by the time Brinkman crossed the room, and the American was smiling toward him invitingly.

"Hi," said Franklin. "Welcome to fun city."

The handshake was strong but not artifically so. "This usual?" asked Brinkman, gesturing back into the room.

"Better than usual," said Franklin. As Ingram, his mission completed, eased back toward the bar, Franklin asked, "How are you settling in?"

"Not at all at the moment," admitted Brinkman. "Living out of a suitcase at the embassy and going everywhere with a map in my hand."

Franklin smiled at the self-deprecation, as he was supposed to. "Takes time," he said. "Actually didn't like the place in the first few months. Thought I'd made a mistake in accepting the posting."

"And now?" asked Brinkman.

"Moscow's a good place to be," said the American. "It always has the attention of a lot of important people."

An ambitious cowboy, very rare, thought Brinkman. "Hope I don't fail them."

Franklin smiled again at the modesty. "Takes time, like I said. It's a difficult place to get the feel of and put a handle on." The American paused and then said, "Difficult for the wives too. Not enough for them to do."

"Won't be a problem for me," said Brinkman. "I'm not married."

Franklin looked around the room and said, "You must meet Ann."

He waved and Brinkman turned to see a slim, dark-haired woman coming toward them, smiling uncertainly. She'd taken trouble with her clothes, which her husband hadn't. The turquoise dress was designed to show both the slimness of her waist and the fullness of her breasts. She wore a single-strand gold necklace and only the minimum of make-up. She was much younger than Franklin, Brinkman realized at once. As Franklin made the introductions, he put his arm around his wife's shoulders, and Brinkman wondered if the gesture were one of possession or comfort. He isolated the accent as soon as she spoke.

"English?" he asked.

"As roast beef and Yorkshire pudding," confirmed Franklin.

"Birkhampstead, actually," said Ann.

Brinkman saw she had small, even teeth and the apparent habit of catching her lower lip between them, like a guilty child frightened of being caught out.

"Long way from home," said Brinkman.

He thought she paused momentarily. She said, "We all are." The smile this time was more open than before. "It'll be good to have a new face among us," she said. Why was she being like the rest? Ann thought, angry at herself. At once came the contradiction. Why not? She *was* like everyone else.

"I'm looking forward to it," said Brinkman. But not to parties like this, where the biggest ambition seemed to be who could get to the bottom of a whiskey glass quickest, he thought. His own glass was still practically full.

"You must come and dine with us one night," said Ann. "It'll be good to be able to talk to someone so recently from home."

"I'd like that," smiled Brinkman. London thought Ingram good, and Ingram eulogized Franklin. Until he found his own roads to follow, the American was obviously the person to travel with.

The arrival of the British ambassador, making his duty visit, was the signal for the evening's formalities, which broke up Brinkman's contact with the Franklins. There were short speeches, carefully guarded of course, praising Ingram as a colleague and friend whose companionship would be sadly missed. Ingram's blinking grew more rapid with the praise. Lucinda stood alongside, her expression making it quite clear that she considered it all justified. The ambassador presented the decanter set with matching glasses, and Ingram assured those who had contributed toward it that he would always treasure it as a reminder of happy times in Moscow, which he was going to miss both as a city and as a place where he'd made many wonderful friends, people whom he and his wife sincerely hoped would remain in contact. There was the predictable attempt at a joke, which fell flat, and the predictable ribald shout from someone in the crowd, and Brinkman wondered why these things were inevitably so embarrassing. The presentation broke up, as they normally did, in the uncertainty of people not knowing what to do. Brinkman smiled at the ambassador's approach.

"Sorry I haven't had time to properly welcome you yet," said Sir Oliver Brace.

"People seem to have been doing almost nothing else," said Brinkman. At the embassy gathering there had been the briefest of introductions; the formal interview was arranged for the following week.

"Son of Sir Richard Brinkman, isn't it?"

"Yes, sir," said Brinkman, feeling the stomach-sink of dismay.

"Harrow together," said the ambassador. "Damned fine bat. Still play cricket?"

"Not any longer," Brinkman replied.

"Everyone treating you all right?" demanded the man. "No problems?"

"Everyone has been extremely kind," said Brinkman.

Brinkman's nominal cover was as cultural attaché, but in veiled reference to his true function, the ambassador said, "Tricky place to be sometimes, Moscow."

"I was fully briefed before I left London, sir," assured Brinkman. Dear God, don't let this red-faced man with his clip-speech mannerism adopt the role of surrogate father, he thought.

"Any problem, you let me know, you understand?"

"Of course, sir," promised Brinkman. There *had* to have been contact with his father. The head of Chancery was the diplomat with whom intelligence officers customarily dealt, specifically to spare the ambassador any difficulty if things went wrong. And that was the person with whom he would continue contact, determined Brinkman. Damn his busybody, interfering father!

His duty done, the ambassador moved away toward the door. Brinkman looked about him, unsure of how to make his own escape. Although it was Ingram's party, Ingram had made it very clear that Brinkman shared in it too for the advantages it might have. Near the table where Lucinda's food had been—which was now a messy, destroyed surface—a space had been cleared for dancing and a few couples were making desultory attempts to follow the music. There were obvious invitations from two women who caught his eye and smiled hopefully, but Brinkman chose to misunderstand, smiling back but remaining where he was. The cigarette smoke, thicker now, stung his eyes and the long-held drink was warm when he sipped it. He looked around for Franklin and his English wife, but they appeared to have left.

Because politeness demanded it, he asked Lucinda Ingram to dance, and because politeness demanded it, she accepted, appearing reluctant to follow his lead and pushing him around instead like a busy shopper maneuvering a cart through a crowded supermarket. There was the formalized conversation about how glad he was to be in Moscow and how much she was looking forward to returning to London, which she hadn't seen for a long time because before Moscow their posting had been Beirut, and before that, Lima. Lucinda promised that the apartment would be properly and thoroughly cleaned after the party and asked if he wanted to retain their maid, and Brinkman thanked her and said yes, he did. They were both relieved when the dance finished. He walked over with her to Ingram, who stood stiff-legged beside the drinks table, pink and smiling. Brinkman decided it wouldn't be long before the owl fell out of the tree.

"Thanks for the party. And for everything else," said Brinkman.

"Remember what I said." Despite the obvious intake, Ingram was still very clear-voiced.

"I will."

"Stay close to Franklin and you won't go far wrong," insisted the other man as though he feared Brinkman hadn't understood.

"I will," promised Brinkman emptily. "I will."

"What did you think?" demanded Ann.

"About what?" Franklin emerged from the bathroom, wiping the toothpaste residue from his lips.

"Our new arrival."

"Seemed a nice guy."

"Betty Harrison decided he was gorgeous."

"Betty Harrison's got hot pants."

"Think Brinkman will fill them for her?"

"Seemed a cautious guy to me," said Franklin. "Hardly touched his drink all night and spent most of his time looking around making judgments."

"Poor Betty Harrison," said Ann.

"I could be wrong."

"You're usually not."

"There's always a first time," said the Texan, switching off the light.

Ann lay waiting in the darkness, but she felt him turn away from her.

"Good night," she said.

"Good night."

CHAPTER FOUR

Pietr Orlov was well aware that when it happened, there would be reactions beyond the official ones, the vilification and maybe the physical pursuit. There would be bewilderment among those who knew him, incredulity that, having everything—and well knowing he had everything—he would abandon it. Incredulity, too, at the reason for the abandonment. They'd have understood ideology or greed better.

At the time of his departure from New York, Orlov had been the Soviet ambassador to the United Nations. But that had been a misleading description, belying his function and status within Russia. A more correct title would have been Ambassador Extraordinare and Plenipotentiary of the U.S.S.R., because that was the role he properly performed. It was Orlov who had been summoned back from New York personally to brief the ailing Brezhnev on the likely

Western reaction to the Afghanistan incursion. And Orlov again upon whom Andropov—ailing also—had depended for advice in determining the Russian propaganda response to the positioning in Europe of the American cruise missiles.

So much, reflected Orlov, entering the Kremlin complex and heading toward the section of the Foreign Ministry. So much and yet so little. He wanted so much more: so much more that only he—no one else, perhaps not even Harriet—could or would ever understand. Maybe Harriet would come to understand in time. Orlov hoped to God or whatever controlled the destiny of man that it wouldn't have to be as long as a year before he had the chance to start making her understand.

He hesitated at the very moment of entering the office of Yuri Sevin, suddenly envisioning Sevin's future reaction. The deputy minister was one of the minority, someone who knew him well, and therefore Sevin's first thought would not be pragmatically nationalistic but personal. He would shake his head and find words difficult, and when they came, they would be mundane and ill-fitting, like "Why? Why—how—did he do it?" Sevin was a friend first, colleague later, someone whom Orlov had known for more than twenty years and who had been his constant supporter—and, when the occasion demanded, an undeterred and unfrightened advocate—here in the politically backbiting jungle of Moscow while he had been far away and exposed in New York.

Not only Natalia to protect and by whom to do things properly, recognized Orlov, but so much to time exactly right.

Sevin came forward, arms outstretched, tears already starting down his face, a bear of a man with the emotions of a rabbit. "Pietr," he sobbed, joyfully. "Pietr!"

Orlov allowed the bear hug—what else from a man of Sevin's size—and the tear-smeared kisses on either cheek and a further bear hug as though the first had been insufficient. And then he underwent the arm-stretched examination; it was as though he were being searched for physical flaws and contamination caused by his prolonged exposure to the West. Yes, there is what you would regard as a flaw, dear friend, thought Orlov, but not one that's visible.

"Yuri!" He grinned. "Yuri, it's good to see you."

Sevin led him away from the desk, impatient—embarrassed, almost—at the indication of rank and power coming between them. They went instead to the windows overlooking the Alexander Gardens. There a low table between the chairs and the couch was already set with vodka and caviar. Sevin, the considerate host, had even included a samovar beside the couch. Orlov stared at it, wondering how long it had been since he'd seen one.

"Pietr!" said Sevin once more. "How good it is to see you. Really *good*."

"And you," said Orlov.

There was no doubt or uncertainty about what he intended doing—there couldn't be after all the planning—but Orlov knew that when it was all over and he was happy, and when the fear had diminished, there would still remain the regret at how he'd had to deceive his friends. And an even deeper regret that there was no way he could attempt to apologize or explain. To attempt it now—to take someone he considered his closest, dearest friend into his confidence—would be suicidal for him. And to attempt it later, in some guarded, hopefully disguised message, could be murderous to Sevin. So he could do nothing. Nothing except hope that in some way, somehow, Sevin would come to understand. Orlov doubted that the man would though. How could he? How could anyone?

"You return in triumph, Pietr," declared the deputy minister at once. "Absolute triumph."

"That's good to know," said Orlov, trying to overcome his discomfort.

"You didn't need me to tell you that," his friend rebuked gently.

"Sometimes it's difficult to judge from so far away."

"You never made a misjudgment, never," praised Sevin. "It's an impressive record. One that's been rightly recognized as such."

"I'm flattered," said Orlov.

"You will be," predicted Sevin. He paused theatrically, pleased with his news and wanting to extract the maximum from it. "There'll need to be formal votes and resolutions, of course. But they're just formalities. The decision's unanimous. You're going to be elected to the Central Committee, Pietr."

When Orlov, shocked, didn't respond, Sevin said, "Congratulations, my friend. You've earned it."

The Central Committee! The inner sanctum, Orlov realized: the cornucopia of power. Except he didn't want power any more. Once maybe, but not now. Now he wanted freedom; freedom and Harriet. Would Sevin have been his sponsor? Obviously, because Sevin was allowed to be the bearer of good news. In ancient Rome it was a custom to sacrifice the messenger bearing bad news, and this was going to become bad news soon enough. He said, honestly, "It's difficult to express myself."

The old man smiled, pleased, but misunderstanding his friend's difficulty. "It needn't stop there, Pietr. You're a chosen one, a star being groomed. I'm too old and so are at least six others on the Politburo. But you're not. You're still only forty-four—practically juvenile—but you've had more international experience than most of them put together. All you need is two years, three at the outside to show the proper understanding and appreciation of domestic problems, and there won't be anyone who could stand in your way."

Leader! thought Orlov in a sudden oblivious-to-everything-else mental lurch. The euphoria leaked away as quickly as it came. He didn't want to be leader, and he didn't want to be a deputy, and he didn't want to be married to Natalia, and he didn't want to be in Moscow. All he wanted was Harriet. He said, "It's an overwhelming prospect. Everything's overwhelming, in fact."

Sevin laughed at his friend's difficulty, pouring large measures of vodka for them each. He raised his glass. "To you, Pietr Grigorevich Orlov. People are going to know of you; know of you and respect you and fear you. You're going to break the mold of stagnating, senile leadership in this country, finally sweeping away the blanket of nepotism that's smothering our leadership and our progress."

From the hyperbole, Orlov guessed Sevin had rehearsed his speech. People *were* going to know of him, Orlov thought sadly. But not for the sort of reasons that Sevin imagined.

Sundays were always difficult. Every other day of the week had its regular, fixed commitments around which everything else revolved; even Saturdays. But definitely not Sunday. Sunday was a do-nothing day, without a peg upon which Ruth could hang her coat. She hated Sundays. They were a constant reminder.

She'd fallen back on the Smithsonian, as she had so many times before, but halfway around the science exhibition the boys' boredom became too obvious, so she decided to cut her losses and run, taking a cab up to the Hill, to the American Café.

Paul, maybe because he was the elder of the two and saw it as his role, led the attack when it came to ordering drinks to go with the hamburgers.

"Bloody Mary," he said.

"Don't be ridiculous!" refused Ruth, too vehemently and in front of the waitress; she could have turned everything aside had she treated it as a joke, she thought. With no other choice now but to continue, she said, "You know you can't have a Bloody Mary. Don't be silly!"

The child reddened under the gaze of the patient, amused waitress who'd seen it all before. Damn! thought Ruth.

"I want a Bloody Mary," insisted Paul.

Ruth outflanked him. To the waitress she said, "My son is not yet fourteen. What non-alcoholic drinks do you have?"

"Sodas or shakes, tea or coffee."

"Assholes!" said Paul.

Both women heard him but pretended not to.

"Sodas or shakes, tea or coffee," recited the waitress again.

"Nothing," said Paul, denying himself so as to deny them as well.

"Coke," said John. Belatedly he added "Please." Because of the braces, it came out as a lisp.

After the waitress had gone with their order, Ruth said to Paul, "Okay, what was all that about?"

"Nothing," he said, his head lowered to the table, regretting it now as much as she did.

"You made a fool of yourself," said the woman

nervously, trying to reinforce her position so as to prevent it from happening again. "You made a fool of us all."

Paul said nothing.

"I'm waiting for an apology."

The boy remained silent.

"I said, I'm waiting for an apology."

"Sorry," said Paul, voice soft and his lips barely moving.

"And you'll apologize to the waitress when she comes back," said Ruth, building on her advantage.

"I think she's a bitch!" blurted John.

Ruth turned to the other boy, looking bewildered from him to the departing waitress.

"Not her!" said John with childish irritation at being misunderstood. "The woman daddy's with. I think she's a bitch."

"You don't know anything about it," said Ruth, which was a mistake. Since the divorce, both boys had attempted the role of guardians, and she realized as she spoke that she was diminishing their efforts.

"We know everything about it, for God's sake!" snapped Paul, anxious to recover from his previous defeat.

"I know that," said Ruth, striving to maintain a reasonable tone of voice. "I know you're affected as much as I am—maybe even more—and I'm sorry, John, that I said you didn't know anything about it. That's not what I meant."

"What, then?" asked the younger boy.

"I meant that there are some things that occur between grown-up, adult people that are difficult for younger people. . . ." Ruth hesitated, not wanting to cause further friction ". . . Grown-up and adult though those younger people are, that are difficult for them to understand."

She trailed to a stop, realizing how awful the attempt had been.

"Like going to bed together, you mean?" asked John, anxious to prove his worldliness.

"That," conceded Ruth cautiously. "But that's not all of it. Not even the important part of it. There are lots of other things as well."

"Didn't you go to bed with Daddy?" demanded Paul, determined upon vengeance.

Ruth felt herself blushing. "That isn't the sort of question you should ask me," she said desperately. "But you know the answer anyway. Of course I went to bed with Daddy."

"Then why did he go to bed with her as well?"

"I don't know," said Ruth, an admission as much to herself as to the children. "I really don't know."

"I hate her," said John fiercely. "Don't you hate her?"

"No," said Ruth. This, at least, she had carefully rehearsed. "No, I don't hate her. And I don't hate Daddy."

"I don't understand you!" protested Paul, exasperated. "How can you not hate her?"

Not easily, conceded Ruth to herself. "Hate doesn't achieve anything," she said.

"What will, to get Daddy back?" implored John, who had tears brimming in his eyes when she looked at him.

"I don't know, darling," she said soothingly. "Not yet I don't know."

"Will you?" he asked with trusting anxiousness.

"I don't know that either," said Ruth honestly.

The return of the waitress stopped the conversation and Ruth smiled up at her gratefully. Remembering, she said to Paul, "Don't you have something to say to this lady?"

There was a moment when Ruth thought he would refuse, but then he muttered, "Sorry."

Why was it, wondered Ruth, that sorry had been the most familiar word in their vocabulary for so long now?

CHAPTER FIVE

Brinkman settled in carefully, cautious about his assessments, cautious about making friends, and cautious about his new colleagues. Realizing it was the traditional practice—something upon which they depended, in fact—he bought from the departing Ingrams their car and their specially adapted stereo unit and a few pieces of kitchen equipment. He moved in the day after they left Moscow.

The place was clean and tidy, as Lucinda had promised—she'd even left a welcoming vase of flowers in the main room—but it was not clean enough for Brinkman, who had the maid do it all over again while he was there, watching to ensure she did it properly. She was a bulged, overflowing woman named Kabalin, who muttered something under her breath when he told her to clean once more and who appeared surprised when Brinkman, who hadn't heard what she said, continued the instructions in his perfect

Russian, intent upon stopping any insubordination—even whispered protests—before it began. He knew she would spy upon him, officially of course; that was one of the standard warnings. Probably steal too. Which was why it was important to establish the proper relationship from the beginning. It wouldn't affect the spying but it might lessen the theft if she realized at once that he wasn't a weak man prepared to tolerate laxity.

At the embassy Brinkman remained polite, even humble, grateful to people who identified the various departments for him, courteously introducing himself to the head of each and joining the various embassy clubs and organizations that existed to relieve the tedium of Moscow. Most important of all, he never indicated that because he was an intelligence officer, which most of them knew even though they shouldn't have, he considered himself in any way superior to them or beyond the rules and regulations they had to obey. During the official welcoming interview, the ambassador asked to be remembered to his father and repeated the invitation to call upon him personally should he encounter any difficulty. As at the Ingrams' party, Brinkman thanked the man politely. At a subsequent meeting with the head of Chancery, whose name was Wilcox, Brinkman let the offer be known, apologized for the intrusion of his father and assured Wilcox—quite honestly—that he had no intention of ever going over the man's head. It let Wilcox know he didn't want any special favors. And by being open about it, Brinkman took out insurance against Sir Oliver mentioning it to Wilcox himself.

Brinkman did not seek out the Westerners whom Ingram had recommended, wanting the approaches to come from them and not from him, which would have put him in the role of a supplicant.

The Canadians bit first, at a reception marking some Commonwealth event. Brinkman was picked out of the English contingent by Mark Harrison within thirty minutes of his arrival. Harrison was a heavy man, florid through obvious high blood pressure. Relaxed in his own embassy, he wore a string tie secured at the throat by a heavy clasp. There was the settling-in conversation, which by now Brinkman felt he could recite in his sleep, and then the restaurant-delay conversation, and then the restriction-of-travel conversation. Harrison let the talk drift into generalities, although Brinkman suspected that the man wasn't dealing in generalities at all. They discussed the apparent relaxation under the new Soviet regime, and Harrison asked Brinkman whether he considered it a genuine desire for friendship with the West or motivated by some inner Soviet requirement of which they were unaware. The seemingly innocuous question sounded the warning bell, but Brinkman answered casually—and untruthfully—that the impression within the Foreign Office immediately prior to his departure from London was that there was some desire from Moscow for a relaxation in tension.

Harrison then asked whether trade approaches in recent times supported the relaxation theory. The question lit another light; Brinkman replied, again casually, that he'd always found it ironic that relationships between East and West had for so long existed on two seemingly contradictory levels, opposing rhetoric at conference tables and necessary trade agreements upon which each side was dependent beneath that. Brinkman discerned Harrison's disappointment and wondered if it would be possible to impress Maxwell at this early stage.

Before they parted, Harrison suggested that Brinkman dine with him and his wife sometime. Not knowing if it would be necessary to maintain close contact with Harrison over whatever it was he was talking about but deciding to take out insurance if it were, Brinkman seized upon the invitation, saying he'd be delighted to accept and asking when. Trapped, Harrison fixed dinner three nights away. Brinkman hoped he would have discovered more by then.

It was easier, in fact, that he had expected. The trade counselor at the British Embassy, a man named Street, was immediately forthcoming to Brinkman's approach, impressed by Brinkman's earlier modesty and anxious to help a newcomer with the proper manner. There hadn't been any unexpected trade approaches during the preceding six months. In fact, the only thing that had caught his interest was a query a month earlier about the availability of British-owned bulk carrier ships. Brinkman pressed further, persuading Street to pull the file. When they examined it, there was a tighter definition; the inquiry had been specifically about bulk containers, not carriers.

Ingram had been a meticulous keeper of files; better, in fact, than regulations required. And from the date of the ship inquiry, Brinkman knew he had only the preceding month to check. Hunched in the intelligence-records room in the embassy basement, it took Brinkman less than an hour to find what he thought he was looking for, but meticulous as he was, he merely marked it as a possibility and continued on through the remaining records. There had been three more notes from Ingram, the last two definite confirmation of what earlier had been simply supposition from intelligent reading of Soviet publications. Wheat production was the perpetual problem of Soviet agriculture, something that bad weather, inefficiency and government changes seemed always to conspire to bring hugely below the required norms. No admissions were ever made of course, but Ingram had picked up the indications from reports in *Izvestia* and *Pravda* from the growing areas on the steppes, a prelude to the personnel shift within the Moscow ministry, which Ingram had noted and properly connected.

From his meeting with Mark Harrison, Brinkman thought he was able to make further connections. Predictably, he was cautious. In his message to Maxwell in London he reminded the controller of Ingram's earlier assessments—cleverly sharing credit if credit had to be given—and then said he interpreted an approach to the trade section of the British Embassy as the beginning of a widespread Soviet chartering effort to transport wheat from the West. Indicating that he was in no way politically naive, Brinkman said he was well aware that such trade was not unusual—in fact, it continued all the time—but that he believed from sources within the Soviet capital that Moscow was spreading its purchasing this time, moving away from the traditional suppliers, the United States and, to a lesser extent, Argentina.

His belief, he said, was that a substantial agreement was being negotiated with Ottawa to make Canada a greater trading partner than it was at present. Taking a chance, but not much of a chance, Brinkman wondered if the Canadian agreement didn't indicate a desire in Moscow to protect itself from any possible trade embargo by the United States if relations between the two countries worsened despite the surface indications of apparent friendship. He concluded by saying he believed the Canadian agreement was not yet fully resolved and that Ottawa was concerned about entering into a commitment that unquestionably would annoy its neighbor to the south unless there was a positive assurance from the Soviet Union that transportation facilities existed to move the wheat.

The congratulatory message arrived from Maxwell two days later. A simple check with Lloyds of London had revealed the Soviet chartering operation, not just of British vessels but of others which, although foreign, were being insured through the British firm. There was a second message from London, from Ingram. It was of congratulation, but Brinkman knew it was also a message of thanks for having been generous and mentioning his earlier work. And he knew then, satisfied, that he had an ally in London, where it was always useful to have allies.

The Harrisons' dinner party was a small affair: the Canadian military attaché, called Bergdoff, his wife, and an analyst from their economic division, a hopefully smiling, shy girl named Sharon Berring, who had been invited to balance the numbers. Brinkman was an accomplished raconteur when the occasion demanded, and he decided it did now. He monopolized the conversation, the anecdotes usually deprecatingly against himself, enjoying their enjoyment of his newness in the city, always withdrawing when either Harrison or Bergdoff made a contribution so that his monopoly did not become irritating to the other men. He was equally attentive to the three women, although toward the end of the evening he devoted more time to Betty Harrison in her role as hostess. He escorted Sharon back to her apartment and refused her invitation for a final drink by convincingly pleading pressure of work the following day so that she was not hurt by disinterest, and he said he too hoped, as she did, that they'd meet again soon. The following day, with his note of thanks to Betty Harrison, he sent flowers. He sent smaller bouquets to Mrs. Bergdoff and Sharon Berring.

Betty Harrison telephoned Ann at midday. "Fabulous, darling," gushed the Canadian. "Absolutely fabulous. There hasn't been anyone like him in Moscow since I got here."

"Flowers?" queried Ann. In Moscow it was neither cheap nor easy to make such a gesture.

"To all of us. My arrangement was bigger, of course," said Betty, who had made a social coup in being the first to have Brinkman at her table.

"Guess he's going to be in demand," said Ann.

"Believe me, darling," said Betty, "I'd like to make a demand any time!"

Brinkman's invitation to dine with the Franklins arrived two days later.

Orlov found everything about the subterfuge difficult, but most difficult of all was Natalia, far worse than he had anticipated and rehearsed. Natalia had remained in Moscow during his New York posting—frequently, guiltily, he wondered if things would have been different if she hadn't—so it was to be expected there would be a strangeness between them. He prolonged it as long as he could, but above all he needed to avoid her suspicion even though he trusted her, so finally the coolness had to end. She was anxiously eager because she loved him, thereby creating another plateau of guilt, and then there was another too because although he didn't love her and although he loved Harriet, he found it surprisingly easy—embarrassingly, shockingly easy—to make love to her. She made it obvious that it had been good for her. It had been good for him too, a further reason to despise himself.

"I missed you," she said. She was still breathing heavily from their lovemaking and there was a catch in her voice.

"I missed you too," he said, hating himself for the necessary lie. It had seemed so easy in New York—even necessary if she were to be protected. He hoped that one day she might come to guess why he was doing it—but it wasn't easy now. It was degrading and obscene, and it wasn't fair to her. They had made love with the light on because Natalia was a sensuous woman who liked it that way. Orlov looked sideways at her. She detected the glance and turned toward him, smiling, glad that a barrier had been removed, and Orlov knew she would expect to make love regularly now. She was an attractive as well as a sensuous woman, beautiful even, with a long red hair that cascaded over the pillow and the freckles that went with such coloring faint upon a diminuitive nose and high, refined cheekbones. She was careless, pleasured by nakedness, the sheet thrust aside because she wanted him to see her, firm-limbed, her stomach naturally flat. Her breasts were firm too, jutting upright despite their weight, and Orlov felt a surge of excitement and shifted so the bedclothes covered him, wanting to hide the physical evidence of it. Was it possible to love two women equally?

He'd avoided the obvious way out. Defecting in America would have been easy, but he wanted to spare Natalia the retribution that would quite illogically have been exacted against her for having married a traitor. He wanted to divorce her and distance her from any harm. Wasn't that love? Of a sort, he supposed. Responsibility, he thought, seeking another word. Guilt, the most familiar one. Beautiful, he thought again; more beautiful than Harriet if he were to make a brutal, objective comparison.

Had Sevin been right? Had he been brought back by a

powerful, inner caucus to finish some final training and then emerge as a contender for the ultimate position? *You're going to break the mold of stagnating, senile leadership in this country. . . .* Over-dramatic words, certainly. But Sevin had never been personally over-dramatic. He wouldn't have made the promise, disclosed the plan, if it hadn't been the truth. Orlov looked again at Natalia and thought of how well she would fit into the role of First Lady. He remembered that day at the Ministry when Sevin had made the announcement and the phrase that throbbed through his head like an ancient church chant: *so much, so much, so much. . . .* Stop it! Orlov thought abruptly. He had to stop it. He was having doubts and there weren't any. He'd gone through all that. Through all the heart-searching and uncertainties and recriminations. He was going to divorce Natalia and spare her any possible harm, and then he was going to make his contact, and then he was going to go to America to a new life with a woman who consumed him and for whom he was prepared to make any sacrifice.

"I love you so much," murmured Natalia beside him.

Orlov closed his eyes and said, "I love you, very much."

"Make love to me again," she said. "Make love to me a lot."

Orlov turned toward his wife, aware of how easy that was going to be and hating himself for that, most of all.

CHAPTER SIX

Brinkman was pleased with his initial success but not complacent about it. Improperly created foundations could be washed away in the first rainstorm; and he hadn't created proper foundations yet, just a minimum impression in London and a minimum impression within his own embassy. The first layer, then. It was time to build up, to withstand gales as well as rain. Brinkman calculated his building precisely, with stop-watch finesse, arranging the lunch with Harrison on the day he was later to dine with the Franklins so that if there were any later comparison—he didn't, after all, know how close the two were—he would be seen to have been scrupulously honest.

Brinkman slotted himself into second place during the lunch conversation, as he had at the Harrisons' embassy, referring in almost an aside to their conversation that day and offering the information about the chartering as though he

were unaware of its full significance. Brinkman admired
Harrison's professional reaction, or rather lack of it, enjoying an encounter he was dominating despite his apparent
secondary role. It became an exercise in comparative
tradecraft, Harrison pecking at the bait until he considered
he had enough and then withdrawing with some inconsequential small talk to digest the forage, and Brinkman
setting out bait one grain at a time, not wanting the man to
glut himself and realize afterward how he had been spoon-
fed. The encounter ended with Harrison's invitations—more
fulsome than the first—to further social gatherings.
Brinkman's role was still demonstrably that of an overawed new arrival grateful for the advice of someone more
experienced; someone who would—more eagerly next
time—drop the valuable hints, confident now of an ingenuous playback.

Brinkman went to the Franklins' bearing gifts. Remembering Ann's apparent interest in clothes, he had obtained
from London *Vogue* and *Harpers* and Harrods' catalog—
although not quite the current ones, which would have
shown he was trying—and apologized for his presumption.
He explained that he'd brought them from London and
read them and thought perhaps she might be interested.
Franklin's gift could wait until later. Ann thanked him
sincerely, and Franklin, the cosseting husband, thanked
him too as he poured their drinks. Sharon Berring arrived
within fifteen minutes, and Brinkman noted the liaison
between the Franklins and the Harrisons. He was mildly
amused, not offended, correctly recognizing the effort to
which they had gone.

The Canadian economist was more relaxed with him the
second time, actually offering stories of her own, some of
which were genuinely funny. Brinkman trotted out anec-

dotes he hadn't recounted at the Harrisons', enjoying
Sharon's laughter. When he began a story about life at
Cambridge, Ann cut across him.

"You were at Cambridge?"

Brinkman nodded. "King's," he said.

"Girton," she said, matching colleges like playing cards.

Ann became animated at the link, even more excited
when she realized that despite their different periods at the
university, they had shared three common tutors. The
discovery was fortunate because it enabled Brinkman to
include Franklin and Sharon in the conversation, recalling
fresh stories about the academics that were amusing even
to the American and the Canadian.

As Ann chimed in with a tale of her own, Brinkman
studied her. Her appearance at the Ingrams' farewell party
had been misleading. Her blouse was fuller and her skirt
longer, and she'd been wearing a shawl before dinner,
although she had taken it off now. She wore flat-heeled,
pump-type shoes too. Altogether, it was the undergraduate
style that had been emerging just about the time he was
leaving the university. The style didn't end with the clothes.
The walls of the Franklin apartment were draped with
carpets—even a shawl in a small alcove—and there were
miniature icons, miniature samovars, and at least three sets
that he could see of *matroyshka*, the traditional Russian
doll, one of which lifts from the other until a whole family
is disclosed. Like a dozen university rooms he'd known,
festooned with the adventures of foreign explorations.

He talked again, the words prepared and easy, his mind
readily able to consider something else. He'd been passingly
aware of the age difference between Franklin and his wife
at the Ingram party, but now Brinkman considered it again.
Franklin was in good shape and his size further diminished

the difference between them, but it was ten years, maybe more, Brinkman recognized.

Franklin's attitude toward Ann, the arm-around-the-shoulder protectiveness Brinkman had noted at the first meeting, betrayed the newness of the relationship. It was the period before they had had time to come to properly know each other—like couples know each other in the fullness of years—so that it was, instead, a time of proud possession, as of the icons on the wall and the rings on the fingers. How, wondered Brinkman, had a cowboy-booted Texan—and he'd bet a week's salary a paid-up Republican—become involved with a shawl-wearing English girl who—he'd bet another week's salary—had chanted outside the American Embassy in Grosvenor Square in protests? None of his business, recognized Brinkman. His business was an unimpeded, unobstructed career, not the intimacies of some-one else's affairs. Unless those affairs affected that career.

Sharon maintained her part of the conversation, her genuinely amusing talk disclosing a considerable ability as a mimic, mostly applied to people whom the Franklins knew among the Western community in Moscow. Although they were unknown to him, Brinkman responded politely. She was a pleasant dinner-table companion.

Franklin was a generous host; another bottle of wine was opened when the previous one was only half empty, and Brinkman quickly found that the way to avoid his glass being constantly refilled was not to make room in the first place. By the time the meal ended, both Sharon and Franklin seemed drunk, although Ann appeared to be in better control.

Sharon unsteadily helped the other woman clear the table while Franklin poured brandy, a brief moment when the two men were alone.

"Maybe we should get together soon, by ourselves?" offered Franklin.

"I'd like that," said Brinkman. Had Ingram openly asked the American to protect him? It was unlikely but not unthinkable. Brinkman hoped not.

"When are you free?"

"Any time," replied Brinkman generously. How could he maneuver the conversation around to the wheat discovery? He wanted to show the intelligence to be his, which meant he had to speak tonight; tomorrow Harrison would be bustling between the Canadian mission on Starokonyushen-nyr and the United States Embassy at Chaykovskovo, eager to impart it as his revelation.

"What about Thursday?"

"Thursday's fine," said Brinkman.

"You haven't been to our embassy yet?"

"No."

"The cafeteria is never going to make the *Guide Michelin* but occasionally it has its moments."

"Sounds fine." Seeing the opportunity, he said, "Just call if anything comes up."

"Of course," said Franklin. "Can't imagine anything will though; it all looks pretty quiet at the moment."

"I'm not so sure," said Brinkman.

"Why not?" Franklin's head came up and the relaxation seemed to leave the large body. If Franklin were as drunk as Brinkman suspected him of being, the man had an impressive ability to recover—practically before one's eyes.

Brinkman told him disjointedly, the same way he had told Harrison, wanting each man to imagine that he was testing out his impressions and theories. Franklin listened expressionlessly and sleepy-eyed and at the end said laconically, "Interesting. Certainly worth thinking about."

Brinkman knew that the American was doing more than just thinking about it, just as he knew that after he left tonight, Franklin would take advantage of the time difference between Moscow and Washington and go back to the embassy and send a report. Which meant Ottawa and Washington would hear of things within a time frame that for all intents and purposes was simultaneous, and that London—because of their advance knowledge—would be able to offer confirmatory help as soon as the requests came from both capitals. And that Franklin and Harrison would be grateful to him and wouldn't hold back from helping him in the future. Which was just the way Brinkman wanted it to be.

The coffee was good—imported—and the brandy too, but Brinkman was conscious of Franklin's impatience. Conscious too that the American resident had stopped drinking. To make it easy for him, Brinkman soon excused himself, declining Ann's insistence upon another coffee or another drink, but agreeing to another meeting soon because there was so much about Cambridge they hadn't talked about.

Brinkman escorted Sharon home again and once more refused her invitation to a final nightcap, risking offense this time by not even pleading pressure of work. She was an amusing girl and an intelligent, witty companion, but she might also become an encumbrance, imagining something more than properly existed in a casual, one-night stand. And Brinkman didn't want any sort of encumbrance.

Back at the Franklins' apartment Ann was startled at her husband's announcement that he had to return to the embassy. "What for?"

"Something's come up."

She looked at the telephone and then back to him. "Nobody called."

"Something I forgot to do today. Just remembered."

While the agreement was for no secrets in their personal relationship she accepted the fact that because of what he did, his work was sacrosanct. It was just that it had never happened this way before. "How long?" she asked.

"Not long," he promised. "Just a cable to send."

"Hurry back."

"Sure."

She tried to remain awake, actually taking another brandy she didn't want and staying up for an hour. Then she went to bed, intending to wait there, but she fell asleep, so deeply that she wasn't aware of his return or of his easing quietly in beside her.

He could make out only the vaguest outline in the darkness—the jut of her chin, and her nose, and the swell of her breasts, rising and falling rhythmically in the darkness. He loved her so much, Franklin thought. So very much. Everything that had happened was worth it to have her as his wife, he determined. Just as he determined they would always stay together.

"How heavy?" asked the embassy doctor, bent over Ann's case notes.

"Very heavy," insisted Ann. "I've flooded for the last three months."

He looked up at her. "There's no indication of high blood pressure."

"Need there be?" she asked. She knew the answer because she had already checked.

"Not necessarily," conceded the doctor. "If you're going to stop using the pill, what are you going to do?"

"I don't know," she said.

"What about a coil?"

"I tried it in England," lied Ann. "It hurt; it was always uncomfortable."

"A diaphragm then?"

"I've never used one."

"It's your responsibility," he warned. "You have to remember to use it."

"All right."

"You sure about the pill?" asked the doctor, still doubtful.

"Quite sure," said Ann.

CHAPTER SEVEN

The cafeteria of the American embassy was on the ground floor in an annex at the rear of the main premises on Chaykovskovo. The walls were festooned with posters of American scenes: aerial shots of the Grand Canyon, and Mickey Mouse at Disneyworld, and the Statue of Liberty, all reminders of home. There were some framed pictures too, outdoor scenes, and around some hung forlorn streamers, forgotten residue of some Christmas or Thanksgiving. The menu prices and payment, Brinkman saw, were in dollars; another reminder of home. He chose steak, knowing it would have been flown in. As Franklin had warned, the place would never have achieved a listing in the *Guide Michelin* but it wasn't bad either. Both drank coffee.

"Able to abandon the map yet?" asked Franklin.

Brinkman frowned, momentarily not understanding, then

remembering his casual remark the night they had first met at the Ingrams' party. "Just about," he smiled. Franklin had a remarkable memory.

"Like Moscow?"

"I can see its limitations but they don't worry me, not yet. So yes, I like it," replied Brinkman honestly. Wanting to match the other man's recall, he said, "I think it's a worthwhile place to be professionally; always has the attention of a lot of important people."

Franklin grinned at him, awarding him the point. "That wheat thing came out right," said the American, giving him another.

"Ingram did the groundwork," said Brinkman. The two men had been friends and might still be in touch. It was unlikely they would discuss something like that even if they were, but Brinkman decided it didn't hurt to be generous.

"Half an assessment isn't any good," said Franklin.

Brinkman began to smile, imagining further praise, but then stopped, suspecting that Franklin meant something else. "What's yours?" he asked.

"I think there's more to switching the wheat purchasing to Canada than finding alternative supplies. That's too simple."

Franklin was being objective, not critical, Brinkman decided; and he hadn't committed himself too strongly to London, he remembered, relieved. Wanting to show analysis in his question, Brinkman took a chance and said, "You think the shortage is serious?"

Franklin nodded and Brinkman was further relieved. "We *know* it is," he said. "Got a playback from Langley. Our spy satellites go over the wheat-growing areas. They're a disaster."

"Famine proportions?" probed Brinkman, staying on safe ground.

"Practically, in some areas. The harvest was bad last year so there isn't any stock for them to fall back on."

It was repayment time, Brinkman realized; he hadn't expected it so soon. Deciding it wasn't a naive assumption, he said, "Which puts Serada on the spot."

"The whole Politburo," expanded Franklin, "but Serada most of all, I agree. He's shown bad leadership from the time of his election. There have been changes within the Ministry, sure, but they're just cosmetic and don't matter a spit within the Politburo, where Serada's critics are. And he has plenty."

"Enough to be purged?" Brinkman tried to avoid showing any excitement and thought he'd succeeded.

"Difficult to be positive," replied Franklin cautiously. "But it could happen. Serada came from the Agricultural Ministry. He was supposed to know all about it. Agrarian reforms were the first things he introduced when he got the chairmanship."

"So he's directly responsible?" asked Brinkman, another safe question. He did not want any more of his meal but continued eating to disguise his feelings.

"Right in the firing line," agreed Franklin. "So we're going to see some defensive play."

Brinkman didn't understand and searched desperately for the right question. "Can he manage it?" he pursued.

"Maybe," said Franklin, pushing his plate away. "Maybe not."

Come on, for Christ's sake! thought Brinkman. He wanted it *all*. He said, "It'll have to be something pretty dramatic."

"I think it will be," said Franklin. "Predictable but dramatic."

But I can't bloody well predict it, thought Brinkman. Unable to manage anything better, he asked, "Could support swing back to Serada if he gets it right?"

"*If* he gets it right," qualified Franklin. The American hesitated, appearing unsure of whether or not to continue. Brinkman sat with apprehension burning through him, hoping it wasn't showing in open perspiration on his face. Then Franklin said, "The Canadian deal has two sides in my opinion. It's to relieve the shortage here, certainly. *And* for insurance if the United States uses its supplies as a weapon. Serada's gesture has to be dramatic, like I said. It has to be dramatic and it has to be convincing to everyone here—the Politburo and those poor bastards who are starving out there in the boondocks. What's the usual move of a dictatorship when there's an internal threat?"

Brinkman drank from his coffee cup to give himself time. Usual, the man had said. What the hell was usual? "Create an external one," he said, his stomach knotted at the fear of getting it wrong.

"Exactly!" said the American, and Brinkman put the cup down. Franklin went on, "The Soviets are paranoid about war. They lost twenty million people fighting Hitler and have never forgotten it. Neither should we forget how it affects their thinking. If Serada can stir up a war threat, he's home and dry."

Franklin was mad, thought Brinkman. Up to now everything had been logical and acceptable, but now the man was running off into fantasyland. And then it came to him. He said, "So you're guessing Geneva?"

"Right the first time," congratulated the American. "I

think Serada is going to make a whole bunch of public proposals to the disarmament conference, proposals he knows damned well will be unacceptable to the United States. Say something like he's prepared to go there personally to negotiate and sign a treaty and actually invite the president to meet him there. We'll turn it down because we'll have to. And the president will announce he's not going. Serada will be able to tell the Politburo and the Russian people and anyone else who'll listen to him that he made a genuine gesture for peace but America, the warmongers, rejected it. And then, in protest, he'll break off the Geneva conference. My guess is that he'll actually *hope* we'll use wheat as a weapon. If we do that, he can say it's America causing the starvation, not his half-assed policies.''

It was good, conceded Brinkman, bloody good. A neat, intricate jigsaw puzzle with all the bits in place, even the awkward ones all the same color. ''It's a fascinating scenario.''

''It's the way I'm reading it,'' said Franklin.

The American gestured for more coffee and Brinkman took some too, content to let Franklin run the encounter. The ace, Ingram had called him, Brinkman thought it was a pretty good description. He asked, ''Who succeeds if Serada goes?''

Franklin grinned. ''The sixty-four-thousand-dollar question, as they've said too many times. It's Russia's perennial problem, a gang of old guys at the top. Gushkov is a contender but he's seventy-two. Chebrakin has the support of the military, which is always a factor. But he's seventy. Didenko is the youngest at fifty-nine. But he's spent most of his administrative life out in the provinces and hasn't had any international experience at all; never even been out of the country. I'd put Yuri Sevin down as an outsider, but my guess is he wouldn't take it. His reputation is that of a kingmaker, never the king.''

''Anybody's guess then?''

''If I were asked to make it, I'd risk a buck on Chebrakin. But only as a caretaker.''

''Until Didenko gets the experience?''

''Maybe,'' said Franklin. ''Maybe someone we've never even heard of. I've a gut feeling that we might see changes that will take us all by surprise. . . .'' Franklin grinned again. ''But that's all it is, a gut feeling. And gut feelings make bad intelligence.''

If Franklin were right, thought Brinkman, he couldn't have been posted to Moscow at a better time. He realized too that the American had repaid him in full: with interest. He said, ''Would America suspend the wheat sales to get Serada back to the conference table?''

''Not if we've got any sense,'' replied Franklin. ''It's a myth that we supply all that much anyway. And what we do supply could be replaced. As a gesture it would be more to Russia's propaganda advantage than a serious threat to them.''

He'd include that in the file to London, Brinkman decided. It would show impressive political acumen: maybe even be transmitted from London to Washington. He experienced a warm contentment and satisfaction. He said, ''I'd like to return the other night's dinner. Have you and Ann over to my place.'' In fact, thought Brinkman, he wanted Franklin to be a frequent guest; *very* frequent.

''We'd like that,'' accepted the American. ''Ann has lots more she wants to talk about with you, about England." The American paused then asked, "Found the bugs yet?"

"I haven't seriously tried," replied Brinkman, who'd searched but found no listening devices.

"Light fittings are a favorite," said the American. "Keyholes too. When they swept the apartment of our trade attaché last time, they found one in the flush handle of the john."

Brinkman laughed. "What did they do?"

"Took it out," said Franklin. "The Soviets know from the maids when there's an official sweep, and because it's official, anything found is removed. We don't touch anything we find ourselves. Indicates we might have something to hide and they'll only put another one in anyway. Better the ones you know than the ones you don't. If you know where they are, you can just avoid them."

Remembering Ingram's praise of the other man's electronic ability, Brinkman said, "Found all yours?"

"I think so," Franklin answered casually. "Score's up to five so far. I play them a lot of Brubeck."

"I prefer classical," said Brinkman.

"I guess they do too," said Franklin.

Brinkman's report to Maxwell in London was lengthy and it took a long time to encode, so it was late when he got back from the embassy. Despite the time, he spent three hours making a detailed search of the apartment, concentrating on the spots suggested by Franklin. He found three devices, two in light fittings.

Four days later the Soviet leader appeared publicly on state television to announce his new disarmament proposals for the Geneva conference. Washington responded not with rejection but with caution, issuing a communiqué stating that the proposals would have to be studied in depth before any proper response could be given. Brinkman received another cable of congratulation from Maxwell.

Ruth accepted Franklin's apology that there was nothing really worth buying in Moscow for Paul's birthday, but she still wished he'd sent something instead of enclosing an impersonal check. Trying for something different, she took both boys on one of the cruise trips along the Potomac, on a boat where it was possible to eat. Afterward they went to the Biograph in Georgetown because it was showing a movie Paul particularly wanted to see, and even though they had the big tubs of popcorn, she took them later to the French restaurant on the opposite side of M Street.

"I'd like you to write to your father when we get back, to thank him "

"What for?" demanded Paul belligerently.

"Your present," Ruth replied carefully. She wouldn't fight with him, not on his birthday.

"Twenty lousy bucks!"

"Stop it, Paul," she said evenly. "He's your father and he loves you, and it made more sense for him to send you the money to buy something you really want than trying to guess."

"If he hadn't run out on us, he wouldn't have had to guess, would he?" asked the boy.

"He hasn't run out on you," said Ruth, maintaining her control. "He divorced me."

"Isn't that the same thing?" asked John.

"No, it's not," she said. "I've told you he loves you. And he does."

Paul took his father's check from his pocket and studied it. "He can go stick it up his ass."

"Stop that!" said Ruth, her voice rising for the first time. "I will not have you use language like that in front of me."

Abruptly Paul tore the check in half and then in half again, letting the pieces fall into the ashtray between them.

"That was stupid!" said Ruth.

The boy looked up at her. "So's not having a father."

CHAPTER EIGHT

Orlov had been born in Georgia, in the port of Poti. He'd tried—prompted by his anxious mother and aided by blurred, already fading photographs—to recall his father, and he said he could because he knew it was important to his mother, but truthfully he could not. He could remember the anguish though, the immediate crying, and afterward, for several months, the long days and nights the woman had spent in her room by herself, refusing to emerge and for days even to eat, although it was not until some years later that he came to know what Leningrad meant and realized that the mourning had been for his father's death during the Nazi siege.

The death meant that Orlov was brought up almost entirely by his grandfather—a fierce, mustached man—and his timid grandmother. Orlov knew now that the bellowed talk and the guffawed laughter and the belly-slapping and the drinking were covers for an inferiority, the man's inner fear. But as a child he had lived in permanent awe of his grandfather, imagining him the bravest man who ever lived. Certainly that was how Orlov considered him after that day on the sea, although now Orlov recognized that what had happened had occurred through stupidity and their survival through luck.

The old man had been a fisherman so he should have known better, even though when they sailed, there had been no hint of the storm, not even a cloud in the sky. He'd taken them too far out in a little coastal dory, and he'd ignored the clouds when they appeared, first a bubbled line on the horizon and then, with such frightening quickness, churning out over the sky and blotting out the sun. The old man had reacted then, of course, but the wind was already too strong, tearing at the full sail he first attempted and threatening to overturn the boat so that he had had to trim sail practically to pointlessness. He'd roared and shouted, creating his own noise to give him courage, and made Orlov take the tiller while he rowed, the effort against the heaving waves as futile as maintaining the sail. The old man had shown some seamanship, Orlov supposed, keeping their constantly swamped head into the wind, and despite his age—he must have been nearly seventy—he had never flagged throughout the long night, bailing the water to keep them afloat.

The storm eased by early morning so that they put more sail on, but when they were in sight of the harbor, the sea played a trick, as the old man should have known the sea often did, suddenly trapping them in a confluence of currents and eddies and tidal shifts. They'd spun helplessly, tiller and sails and oars useless, caught in a sort of whirlpool that Orlov had thought was going to suck them down. Which was how he felt now.

Everything was happening too suddenly, with the unexpected quickness of that childhood storm, and he hadn't anticipated any of it. He'd known his position and the esteem in which he was held. If it had been less, the danger to Natalia would not be so great. But not in his talks with Harriet nor in his own private considerations had he anticipated how quickly he would be caught up in events upon his return to Moscow. He'd expected a transitional period, a time when he would be spared from the Ministry to settle back into the country, a time when he had intended as kindly and as painlessly as possible to formally separate and divorce himself from Natalia. But it hadn't happened that way. There had been the need to attend the Kremlin practically from the first day, and now he felt trapped as inexorably as he had been that day long ago in the spinning water. Trapped by the ambition of a trusted and dear friend and by his relationship with Natalia, from whom he should have been distancing himself and with whom, instead, he was increasingly resuming the complete and normal married life that had been interrupted by his posting to America.

That day at sea the spinning had stopped as suddenly as it had begun and the sea had flattened into an unnatural calmness, enabling them easily to get back to shore. Now Orlov, caught between two different sorts of tempest, couldn't imagine a way that either would blow itself out.

On the morning before his election there was a meeting with Sevin, an unnecessary preparation for his appearance before the Central Committee but an indulgence the old man required and which had to be allowed.

"This is it!" said Sevin enthusiastically. "This is the beginning. . . ." At once he corrected himself, given to flamboyance in his speech. "No," he said, "definitely not the beginning. The final, well-deserved end."

Outside the window, in the open gardens, Orlov could see people moving, tourists mostly. He envied them their minimal anxieties of where to eat and where to stay and whether or not they could afford either. He said, "I've been surprised by the quickness."

"I didn't intend it should be so," conceded Sevin at once. "No one imagined how quickly Serada would fall; not even me, and I've been here since Stalin."

"Serada hasn't fallen yet," qualified Orlov.

Sevin gave a dismissive shake of his hand, a gesture almost of irritation. "It's inevitable. Everyone knows it. Even Serada himself."

"I'm not sure I'm ready," said Orlov, still looking through the window so that his back was to the room. How could he stop the spinning?

"Don't worry," soothed his friend from behind. "It seems rushed at the moment because of the circumstances. None of us anticipated how bad the harvest would be, as I said. Your election today won't arouse any suspicion. It'll be as a non-voting member and merely establish your presence. When Serada goes—as he will—it won't be you who's proposed. No one will even consider you."

"Who?" asked Orlov, turning back into the room.

"Chebrakin," disclosed the older man. "He has seven of the Politburo committed, and I'm one of them. The military too. We'll let them all exhaust themselves this time, let them make their promises and threats to give an old man his moment of glory. But that's all it will be, a moment. Chebrakin is a diabetic and there's a liver malfunction too, just like Andropov's. I'd estimate a year, eighteen months at the outside. That will give us all the time in the world to bring you up to full membership and plan the strategy; and supposedly a supporter of Chebrakin, I shall be on the inside, able to forestall any opposition before it has time to become established."

Faster and faster, thought Orlov desperately; he actually felt dizzy. "What if you can't forestall the opposition? What if a stronger faction emerges with someone else?"

Sevin laughed at the question, enjoying being able to prove his manipulation. "I'm not your only supporter within the Chebrakin camp," he said. "Afansasiev and Visko have aligned themselves too. When we switch to the opposition, that gives us the majority. Didenko has only the backing of two anyway. The rest will come with us when they see the way it's running."

"It all seems so easy," said Orlov emptily. "So prosaically easy."

Sevin shook his head positively. "It hasn't been and it won't be. There'll be a fight. There always is. But we're well prepared. . . ." He paused, smiling. "I've admired you and your ability from the moment of our first meeting," he said. "Do you know what my ambition is?"

"What?" asked Orlov miserably.

"This is my final effort," said Sevin in tones of confession. "I've spent a lifetime here in government. I've survived purges by megalomaniacs and wars by megalomaniacs, and I've made or unmade scores of ambitious men who espouse communism and aspire to the crown of the czar. But no more. This is the last time." The old man hesitated at the final revelation. "I want to live to see it," he said. "I want to be there, in the great hall, when the announcement is publicly made and you are declared leader of the Soviet Union, Pietr Orlov. I want to be there and know that this country, after all the mistakes and the stupidities and the disasters, can at last be properly guided at least partway in the right direction."

Why, oh, why did Sevin have to put it in terms of dying or living?

Two hours later, Sevin by his side as sponsor, Orlov was elected a non-voting delegate to the Central Committee, representing the Moscow area.

The reply arrived, as Ann had anticipated, exactly three weeks after she dispatched her last letter to her mother. The replies always arrived like some strictly controlled calendar notation. Which they probably were. Her mother was that sort of methodical woman.

Ann read the letter carefully, deciding as she did so that the news her mother had written could have come from *Newsweek* or *Time* or any other of the publications they received from the embassy. It wasn't a letter at all; it was three sheets of widely spaced writing showing nothing but the performance of her mother's duty, a duty as perfunctory as subscribing to a charity or stopping the milk when going away for the weekend or putting the cat out at night. Why did she bother, Ann asked herself. Why did she continue with this ridiculous charade of maintaining contact with a family so stupid and so traditional and so behind the times that they'd probably even discussed cutting her out of their will? Damn their will, she thought. Damn their will and damn them and damn bothering to write any more.

The last line of the letter was the inevitable "Your father sends his regards." Damn his regards best of all, thought Ann.

CHAPTER NINE

The evening was an undoubted success, but not because of the effort Brinkman put into making it so. And he made every effort, bringing in everything through the embassy concessions and cooking the beef to perfection and entering triumphantly with the Yorkshire pudding and enjoying Ann's obvious delight and Franklin's appreciation of the remark at their introductory meeting, which was why he had done it. He accepted their praise of his ability as a cook, knowing it to be deserved. It was something he actually liked doing but he made the deprecating remark that if he hadn't learned, he would have starved at university. Able to talk more fully on this occasion, he and Ann found mutual acquaintances who had overlapped at Cambridge, which provided the subject for a fresh round of chatter. Franklin sat quite contentedly silent, not understanding talk of the Long Vac or the intricacies of punting or the rituals of picnics beside the Cam.

After the meal Brinkman served perfect coffee and left the brandy open between them on the table, playing the overture from *Swan Lake* on the second-hand stereo. That led the conversation to the ballet. Brinkman said he was very fond of it and Franklin admitted honestly that he found it boring.

"One of the few good things about living here," said Ann.

"Do you go often to the Bolshoi?" Brinkman asked. Her obvious disappointment with the city registered, but he decided against pursuing it.

"Not as often as I'd like. Eddie's not keen."

"Let's choose carefully and take him sometime and educate him," said Brinkman. He felt sufficiently comfortable with the American to make such a comment, and Franklin smiled back, unoffended.

"I'll give it a shot if you'll come to ice hockey and let me educate you about that," said Franklin.

"Deal," agreed Brinkman, happy with the evening. He hoped he'd made a point they recognized by not inviting anyone else.

Brinkman had led the conversation, because he was the host and because he liked telling stories at all gatherings, but he had remained constantly alert and ready to defer if Franklin tried to take over. The American contributed sufficient for politeness but no more, appearing quite content to play a subsidiary role. Ann laughed at all the jokes and anecdotes, the smile almost permanently on her lips. They didn't, however, overstay, excusing themselves before midnight.

Nothing was very distant in the diplomatic enclave and

as they walked back to their apartment, Ann said excitedly, "I can't remember enjoying myself more in a long time."

"It was fun," agreed Franklin.

"Betty Harrison was right."

"What did the font of all social gossip in Moscow decree?"

"That he was the best thing to arrive in a long time."

Franklin unlocked the apartment door, standing back for her to enter. "He's a clever guy."

Caught by something in the tones of her husband's voice, Ann stopped in the passageway. "Don't you like him?"

"Sure I like him. Why ask that?"

"Thought maybe you didn't from the way you spoke."

Franklin shook his head, continuing on into the apartment. "He's all right."

"Wonder why he's not married."

Franklin pulled a face at her question. "How the hell would I know? Guess he doesn't want to be. Maybe he's tried and it didn't work out. Thought maybe Betty Harrison would have known all about it."

Ann had been waiting for the opportunity and decided they were sufficiently relaxed tonight; or, rather, he was. She was already in bed when he emerged from the bathroom. She said, "I went to see the doctor a few days ago."

Franklin stopped, the concern immediate. "What?"

"The doctor. I went to see him."

"I heard that," said Franklin impatiently. "What's wrong?"

"Nothing much. I was having heavy periods so I thought I should talk to him about being on the pill."

Franklin came and sat on her side of the bed, the worry

obvious, and Ann despised herself for the deceit. "It hasn't caused any problems, has it?"

"No," she said, immediately reassuring. "He just thinks I should come off it, that's all."

"Sure," said the American, relieved. "Whatever he says."

"He gave me a very thorough examination: blood pressure, stuff like that," said Ann. "There's really nothing wrong."

Franklin got up, going around to his own side of the bed. "What are you going to do?" he asked, getting in beside her.

"Diaphragm," said Ann cautiously.

"Oh."

"It's just a bit more mechanical, that's all."

"Yes," he agreed in the darkness. "It is, isn't it?"

"I could always use nothing, not bother."

He was silent for a long time. Finally he said, "Does it matter very much to you?"

She turned toward him and said, "Yes, darling. It matters very much. I love you and I want to have your baby."

There was another silence and then Franklin said, "We'll talk about it. Not now, but we'll talk about it."

You don't make babies by talking, thought Ann. But he hadn't said no. It was going to work, she thought excitedly. It was going to work!

Natalia made the move because he hadn't, determinedly, for several nights.

"No," he said.

"What's wrong?"

"Nothing." Coward, he thought. There was never going

to be a simple, easy way: never the *right* time. So why not now?

"Sure?"

"Of course I'm sure." He knew she was looking at him in the darkness but he didn't turn toward her.

"Do you want to talk to me about something?"

"No," said Orlov, running away.

CHAPTER TEN

The American president's response to the supposed Soviet initiative was an example of consummate diplomacy, and consummate diplomacy is impossible without matching, consummate intelligence. Washington delayed replying for two weeks, robbing Serada of the chance of achieving any surge of international momentum. And when that reply came, it was the result of an intensive fortnight of work by both State Department officials at Foggy Bottom and U.S. peace negotiators at Geneva. The U.S. reply was delivered simultaneously to the Soviet Embassy on Washington's Sixteenth Street and to the Geneva conference. The Soviet proposals were displayed point by point and their failings and unacceptability listed against these points.

What followed was even more politically impressive. Before Serada had an opportunity to utilize the anticipated rejection, the American president made a prime-time television appearance, with European hook-up, in which the offer was dealt with more generally—because some of the issues were diplomatically esoteric—but which made it quite clear that the U.S. had no alternative to the stance it took and that despite extensive rephrasing, a lot of the Russian material was old and had already been dismissed from the negotiations with the agreement of both sides.

The politics continued to be impressive. Nowhere was there the slightest criticism or accusation in the president's speech, no apparent attempt to gain any advantage from such obvious Soviet maneuvering. Throughout the American's reply the tone was studiously that of a world statesman, which had precisely the intended effect of diminishing Serada's stature.

And on it went. The news of the Soviet container chartering was leaked—clearly through liaison, Brinkman recognized—through London, with the Lloyds insurance cover being the key, and Ottawa confirmed the wheat deal—further liaison, Brinkman guessed—under supposed pressure from diplomatic correspondents.

From the White House the president declared his sympathy—not outrage—at the Russian move in view of the grain shortages within the country, quoting the publicly announced reshuffling within the Agricultural Ministry as confirmation of an internal difficulty. Humanity overrode differences in ideologies, and for that reason the United States offered to increase its shipments beyond the already contracted amounts to relieve the country's suffering. The fact that common humanity overrode ideologies and differences was repeated here in case anyone had missed the point.

Demolishing completely the Russian leader's ploy, the president said his offer was being formally communicated that day to the Russian leadership and that he looked forward to an early and obvious agreement because what other responsibility did a government have than to help the people it was in office to serve? In anticipation he was arranging special rail transportation from the Midwest storage hoppers so that wheat would be available immediately at ports, reducing to an absolute minimum any delay in shipments once the formal request came from Moscow. *Newsweek* carried a cover story calling him "humanity's man," and public-opinion polls showed his popularity higher than at any time since directly after the election.

Brinkman knew the Central Committee elections were important, and when the announcement came, he devoured it, isolating Orlov among the three newcomers and identifying him certainly as the youngest. The luncheons he had with Franklin—alternating between their respective embassies—became regular weekly affairs, and Brinkman learned at the older and still more experienced man's knee. At first he wondered if Franklin's advice and recommendations weren't too simplistic, but he followed them anyway because he didn't know any alternative. And he acknowledged the American's expertise in their closed society.

Absence—explained or otherwise—was identified by Franklin as a prime clue, which was why Brinkman paid attention to the arrival of a Cuban delegation. The delegation included Raoul Castro, and *Tass*, the official news agency, and *Pravda* had earlier announced that Serada would be meeting the group at the airport. Brinkman did not rely on Soviet television because of the ease with which news coverage could be controlled but instead took the trouble to go out to the airport for the ceremony.

Serada didn't appear.

And because his unexplained absence *was* disguised on the television coverage, Brinkman was able to get the message to London in advance of any speculative news stories, speculation which was heightened by the television manipulation.

Franklin hadn't been at the airport, which gave Brinkman the satisfactory feeling of superiority when the American called seeking confirmation of the Soviet leader's definite absence. The American had an exchange to offer: unusual but interesting late-night arrivals and departures of official Zil cars from the Kremlin, another seemingly innocuous indicator but, according to Franklin, an important one. Brinkman messaged London—rigidly restricting himself to the facts, not offering any opinion—and was glad he did. The following day came the brief official announcement that Lavrenti Serada was being hospitalized for tests for an undisclosed indisposition. No acting deputy was nominated, but at London's request, Brinkman predicted Chebrakin because he calculated the military were important. He accompanied the message with as full a profile as possible on the man.

Two days later Chebrakin emerged as the host at an official reception for the still-visiting Cubans. Franklin's later admission—that was how close they were now—that he'd backed the outsider in Didenko gave Brinkman more satisfaction than the hero-gram from Maxwell. Brinkman conceded it had been a horse race and no one—not them, at least—had been sufficiently on the inside to back the winner with any certainty. But Franklin, the acknowledged pundit, had gone for an outsider, and Brinkman, the tyro, had wagered on the favorite and won. Luck, certainly; but everyone needed luck at the races.

It was for Brinkman a period of exhilaration, not

simply—or even predominately—because he appeared to be so consistently right, but because he felt himself at the center of developments he was able to anticipate. He was a surfer on the highest of the high rollers, able to always perfectly judge the break and catch it just right and ride it into shore, close enough to step off onto the beach of accuracy without getting his feet wet.

The ambassador confirmed the reputation he was establishing in London at the monthly gathering, not offended because Brinkman had usurped his own function as the proper political analyst.

The monthly gathering was an innovation of Sir Oliver Brace, an attempt at democracy where serf could address lord and be sure that all was well upon the estate. It was held at the embassy, the atmosphere glued with embarrassment. Brinkman's successes made it easier; and there had been sufficient offers invoking the friendship of his father anyway to make the encounter smoother for him than it might have been for most.

"Gather we follow similar paths in thinking," offered Brace when everyone had arrived and he had a respite from playing party host.

"I'm sorry, sir?" Brinkman had expected the approach before now, the demand why the earlier offers had not been acknowledged and responded to.

"Get the impression that we're interpreting certain developments in the same way."

That wasn't an impression at all, thought Brinkman. That was the playback from London against his political assessments as compared with the ambassador's. Had Brace got it wrong and gone for Gushkov or Didenko? He said, enjoying the taste of the cliché, "These are interesting times."

"If we get them right."

"If we get them right indeed," agreed Brinkman. This was going to be an easier game than it ever was with Franklin. Despite their now-confirmed friendship, there was always a reserve to the American, a slight holding back. Just as he himself always held back slightly, Brinkman conceded. Lie, he thought. He didn't *slightly* hold back.

"Imagine some changes soon?" pressed the ambassador.

"How do you see the situation?" asked Brinkman, turning the question.

"Like to know whether Serada's illness is medical or political."

"Little doubt about that, is there?"

"That's the problem with trying to interpret events in the Soviet Union," said the ambassador philosophically. "There's always doubt."

Brinkman had already filed his opinion in London so, knowing he wasn't disclosing anything the ambassador might take for his own, he said, "Serada has to be on his way out. And I think Chebrakin will be the successor."

"Chebrakin?" pounced the ambassador, confirming Brinkman's surmise that the man had guessed somebody else.

"But as you said," reminded Brinkman, "there's always doubt."

"Been very impressed with the way you've settled in here," said Brace. "Very impressed indeed. An asset to the embassy. Imagine London thinks so too. Heard from your father lately?"

"Not for some time."

"Give him my regards."

"I will sir," said Brinkman. "And thank you for your words."

"Nothing but the truth," said the ambassador. "Nothing but the truth. And don't forget what I've already told you. Always willing to help."

"I won't forget," assured Brinkman. He didn't then anticipate how quickly the occasion would arise.

"You've lionized him!" said Betty Harrison. The Canadian tried to make it a mock protest, but Ann guessed there was an element of real feeling in what the woman said. Betty coveted the role of grande dame of the diplomatic wives and would imagine it was to her *salon* that Brinkman should pay court.

"We haven't," she said. "He and Eddie just seem to get on well." She felt a bubble of satisfaction at the other's jealousy.

"What about *you*?" asked Betty archly.

"We both went to Cambridge, although not at the same time. Seem to have a few mutual acquaintances though," said Ann.

"That wasn't what I meant."

Ann, who understood fully what the Canadian had meant, laughed dismissively. "I think he is very amusing and great company at a party. But he doesn't attract me in the slightest."

"I don't *believe* you!" said Betty. "Have you seen those hands?"

Ann had. And wondered idly how Brinkman was able to stay so apparently hard-bodied when he didn't take any exercise that she knew of, and she had noticed the boyish way he flicked the dark hair back from his forehead. But only in the way of noticing things about a friend with whom she was frequently in contact. She hadn't lied to Betty. The thought of physical attraction had never arisen.

"He doesn't seem too interested in getting involved with anyone, does he?" asked Ann carelessly.

Betty seized the remark, able to see several meanings in everything. "You don't think he's strange, do you?"

"Strange?" frowned Ann, not immediately understanding.

"You know, strange," prompted Betty.

"You mean gay!" said Ann at last. "No, of course I don't think he's gay." Poor man, she thought; it was like being picked over by a hyena.

"He dropped Sharon Berring like a hot potato," said Betty, warming to her theme.

"He did not drop her like a hot potato," said Ann, conscious that she was in at the beginning of what Betty was rapidly formulating into the week's top story. "He just didn't submit to having the choice made for him."

"How do you know?" demanded Betty at once.

Ann sighed, mildly irritated by the interrogation. "I don't know," she said. "I just guessed. It seems obvious."

Betty stared at her friend with her head cocked artificially in obvious disbelief. "How's Eddie?"

This was getting ridiculous, thought Ann. To openly lose her temper would be a mistake. "Fine," she said. Was that true? Ann wondered, letting her mind slip sideways. He was fine physically, and she knew enough about the government changes to understand that he should be preoccupied, but there had been times recently when she felt he had been closing up against her. Not *recently*, she thought, annoyed at the conscious vagueness. She could date precisely the beginning of his closing up: the moment when he agreed that they should try for a baby. And they weren't doing that as often as she had hoped, although his work could be a reason for his tiredness. And certainly they weren't having any success. Ann knew her attitude

was illogical. You didn't become pregnant just by *wanting*
to become pregnant. But she'd expected something to have
happened by now. Maybe she should go back to the
doctor, to discover if there were a problem.

"Just fine?" said Betty, still showing disbelief.

"Absolutely and utterly fine," replied Ann, controlling
herself. She was glad now that at the beginning, when she
was enjoying the other woman's jealousy, she had not
boasted about the ballet tickets she had gotten to surprise
Brinkman.

That night in bed she said to Franklin, "You know what
I think about Betty Harrison?"

"What?"

"I think she's poisonous. I don't think she spreads
rumors, I think she makes them up."

"What about?"

"Whatever takes her fancy."

"I thought you liked her," he said mildly.

"I do," said Ann. "But I don't think I trust her."

She waited, hopefully, but felt him turn away.

"Good night," he said.

"Good night."

CHAPTER ELEVEN

Very occasionally—so occasionally that it was considered the most sensational good fortune—it was possible to cultivate and maintain a source with some internal knowledge in Moscow. Some intelligence officers forged personal links with dissidents, but it was dangerous because the KGB monitored the dissidents' activities rigidly and sometimes infiltrated provocateurs, so there was always the risk of seizure and some highly publicized diplomatic incident, usually expulsion. The majority of intelligence came from assessment, from closely analyzing official announcements and seeing who was and who was not in official photographs or at official receptions, frequently drawing conclusions from details like who was standing next to whom at those events. Sources for those assessments were usually the approved newspapers or the approved television coverage.

To be able to observe personally was a bonus, which was why Brinkman had gone to the airport for the arrival of the Cuban delegation, and there he had been a long way away, only able to establish Serada's absence. To get anywhere near the Soviet hierarchy practically ranked with managing to establish an internal source. When Brinkman realized his opportunity, he went after it with the unwavering determination with which he had prepared for every examination and every interview and every aptitude test. The care he had taken to establish himself with everyone within the embassy helped. And so, at last, did the offered personal relationship with the ambassador. Independence had to make way for necessary advantage, Brinkman now decided.

The visit of the British parliamentary party was planned to be a big event, including not just the leader of the opposition but the shadow Foreign Secretary and the shadow Trade Secretary and three other MPs who would form part of the Cabinet if they were successful in the next election. The defeat in the last had been extremely narrow, and the forecast for the next gave them a very strong chance, which was undoubtedly a factor in the Russian decision to greet and entertain them at such a high level. There would be two state banquets and a Kremlin reception, with private talks agreed upon.

Despite his determination to get what he wanted, Brinkman went about his bid to be appointed official interpreter as properly as he had always conducted himself within the embassy, making the approach first to the head of Chancery and rehearsing his arguments: his official position as cultural attaché made him ideally suited for the function, and his Russian was unquestionably equal if not superior to the majority of other likely choices. Having started in the right way, Brinkman took the gamble and approached Sir Oliver Brace directly. The attitude of proper career diplomats to intelligence personnel in embassies varies and is frequently ambivalent, intelligence agents are a necessity, like daily bowel movements, but not usually things to be acknowledged. And certainly not to be allowed into any sort of situation that might involve ambassadors in present or future problems.

Brinkman was immediately aware that Brace's face closed as he made the request, the older man's experienced professionalism at once coming to the fore. Brinkman quickly changed the subject, telling Brace of Sir Richard's best wishes and his gratitude at the friendship being shown his son in Moscow—and disclosing Sir Richard's impending promotion to permanent head of the Foreign Office. Brinkman knew Sir Oliver saw a concluding career for himself at the Foreign Office when his Moscow posting finished, a career his father would be in a position to sanction or not. Brinkman said he could understand any hesitation Brace might have in appointing him interpreter—it would have been ridiculous for him not to acknowledge it—but offered a personal as well as professional guarantee that nothing would arise that could cause any embarrassment, a guarantee the ambassador would know to be sincere from the man's knowledge of the Brinkman family. Brace refused to commit himself, but promised to consider the request.

Brinkman endured the most uncertain week he had known since his arrival in Moscow, guessing the discussions would not be confined to the ambassador and head of Chancery but would extend to London as well. He wished the diplomatic cable channels were not separate from his own, another precaution against embarrassment. He actually considered making a direct approach to his father toward the end of the week when he heard nothing, abandoning the idea because he realized the contact would have to be made by telephone, which was not secure, and would unquestionably cause the resentment he had so far managed to avoid.

He got approval on the following Monday.

Brinkman set about preparing himself. He had full biographies and information details on the MPs pouched from London and then requested—and got—a lot of additional material he considered lacking from the first shipment. He extended the preparation beyond learning about the personalities, finding out the purpose of the visit—creating a statesmanlike impression in Britain, now in readiness for the next election and the expected outcome.

Although it wasn't his responsibility, Brinkman involved himself in every aspect of the tour, checking and rechecking accommodations and travel arrangements and sightseeing schedules. Because of his early days' groundwork, he was able to do so without upsetting anyone else in the embassy. In some cases there was actually appreciation: A two-day visit to Leningrad, for instance, had been planned with inadvertent underbooking in hotels and transport, so his fortuitous intrusion was correctly seen to have avoided a mistake for which the embassy could have been criticized.

For Brinkman the importance of the visit began from the moment of arrival. It was Serada's first public appearance since the announcement of his indisposition. Brinkman was less than ten yards away from the man after the party landed, and he moved forward to fulfill his supposed function.

Serada didn't look ill. He was sallow, certainly, and Brinkman could see the man's hands shaking, but he thought the cause of both more external than internal. There were handshakes and traditional hugs and a short ceremonial walk to inspect the waiting guard of honor. Serada's welcoming speech was given in a halting, hesitant voice, the prepared notes appearing very necessary for the man. The response from the British opposition leader, whose name was Birdwood, was robust by comparison, the man alert to the British newsmen and television crews, the speech verging on pomposity. Birdwood actually arrived with a working-class cap but he stopped short of wearing it, carrying it obviously in his hand instead.

The politicians had brought their wives, and on the way into the capital, with Brinkman riding in the same car as Birdwood, it became obvious they saw his role as more than that of a simple translator. Brinkman didn't mind combining the functions of baby-sitter, nursemaid and general factotum; there was nothing wrong with making himself indispensable to a group who might within a couple of years emerge as his country's leaders. Insurance was, after all, what one took out against the unknown.

Because he had immersed himself so fully in everything, the arrival at the Metropole and the baggage collection and room allocations went without a hitch. Brinkman established an immediate advantage in their reliance upon him, able to convince—occasionally almost bully—them into being ready at the times he stipulated at the places he stipulated.

The Kremlin reception the first night was more worthwhile than the airport arrival. Serada headed the Soviet party, but only nominally. Brinkman was certain of it. Conscious of his incredible opportunity—but equally aware of how it could be misused—he tried to clear his mind of any preconceptions and was sure he obtained the necessary

objectivity. Objectively Serada had all the appearance of a
cast-aside man. Once, on the receiving line, Chebrakin
practically thrust him aside and shortly after that intruded
again to make introductions that Serada should, according
to protocol, have made. Brinkman was tight with excitement.
He concentrated upon Serada, searching again for any sign
of definite illness, and then he concentrated upon Chebrakin—whom he knew from Franklin to have disabilities—
and then he concentrated upon the other governmental
figures who had been assembled. He was particularly eager to study the younger ones.

Didenko was a full member of the Politburo, and
Brinkman recognized him instantly from the frequent
photographs. Didenko was a burly man whose red coloring
was heightened by the complete whiteness of his hair. He
moved about the gathering with the sort of confidence
Chebrakin was showing, giving little deference to Serada,
who at times seemed isolated and completely alone. There
had been three newcomers in the most recent Central
Committee elections, and Brinkman's proper purpose enabled him to identify one of them since he was communicat-
ing the introductions. Vladimir Isakov was nervous on his
first public outing at such an elevated level, judged
Brinkman. He was a thin, bespectacled man in an ill-
fitting suit and a collar that gaped. It was more than thirty
minutes after the official greetings were over and Brinkman
was feeling the first stirrings of unease before he identified
the next. Viktor Petrov appeared nervous too, like Isakov,
keeping himself on the periphery of everything, which was
how he missed being named to the British group. He was a
short, inconspicuous man, better dressed than Isakov but
not by much, overawed like the other man at his surroundings. Where was the third? Orlov, he remembered from his

preparation. He found him soon thereafter, the identification easier because Orlov had spent some time in the West, at the United Nations, and when the Central Committee elections had been announced, there had existed more pictures of him than of the others.

Orlov was a marked contrast to the other newcomers. He was tall and deeply tanned—Georgian, recalled Brinkman—and very dark-haired, impeccably tailored compared to the rest, even to the Politburo. He was standing urbanely to one side, smoking a cigarette through a holder and examining everything about him with the same interest that Brinkman was showing. As the Englishman watched, Orlov turned and bent slightly to the man at his left, and Brinkman mentally ran the projector, trying to identify the other's high-cheekboned, narrow face, irritated that the name would not immediately come. Sevin! he remembered at last. Stiffly upright despite his age, the cane more for ornamentation than practical use. One of the original Bolsheviks, recalled Brinkman, a youthful follower of the older Lenin and Trotsky and then of Stalin and then of Khrushchev. And a survivor of them all. There weren't many such men left.

And then Brinkman's memory served him again, and he looked with renewed interest at the old and young Russians in head-bent conversation. Franklin had called Sevin the kingmaker. And the kingmaker was huddled with a complete unknown who had just been brought into the inner circle of Soviet government. Franklin had said something else too: *We might see changes that will take us all by surprise*. The encounter he was witnessing was insufficient by itself, despite the straw-clutching way they had to operate. But it was worth careful note, very careful note indeed.

Serada made a speech of platitudes, and Birdwood made a speech of platitudes, and then Chebrakin, sounding as though he wanted to harden the speculation, made a speech of platitudes, and the shadow Foreign Secretary, a broad-accented Yorkshireman named Moss, rounded everything off in the same way. Brinkman devoted his attention to the translation because that was the job at hand, but full concentration was hardly necessary.

There were a lot of glass-emptying toasts, and the vodka and the champagne were good. By the time the evening ended, Moss was straining back from the edge of drunkenness and two of the wives who had already fallen over the edge, giggling and then laughing uproariously at some secret joke in the car going back to the hotel. One of them stumbled over the curb when they arrived. Nursemaid now, Brinkman supervised the key allocation and personally escorted Birdwood to his rooms, he on one side, the ambassador on the other. Birdwood offered them a nightcap, which they both declined, and within fifteen minutes Brinkman was back in the ambassador's official car, en route to the diplomatic compound.

"God knows how many groups like this I've had to handle throughout the world," said Bruce distantly. "And I've never gone through one without wondering what the British public's reaction would be if they knew how their elected leaders conducted themselves."

The permanent politician's contempt for the passing amateur, thought Brinkman; it could have been his father talking. He said, "I didn't think they were too bad."

"Do you know what those stupid women were laughing at?" demanded the ambassador.

"No," admitted Brinkman.

"Breaking wind," said Brace in disgust. "One broke

wind and the other heard her and they thought it was funny.''

Brinkman smiled too, at the older man's outrage. "At least they didn't fall over at the reception.''

"You did very well, incidentally,'' said the ambassador. "Afraid the demands can become a bit irritating at times.''

"No problem,'' assured Brinkman. "No problem at all.''

And there wasn't one. In the next days Brinkman met every request and every need, from a bath plug where there wasn't one at the Metropole to souvenir shopping at Gum to simultaneous and superbly accurate transcription of everything that passed between Birdwood's party and the Russians they met. On five more occasions he was within touching distance of the Russian leaders and removed from his mind any doubt about Serada's decline. On two occasions Orlov was present. Briefly Brinkman regretted that his translator status did not permit him to get the Russian involved in some sort of discussion.

A scheduled visit to Leningrad turned out to be most useful because of the restrictions of travel imposed upon embassy personnel. They toured the shipyards—for the visiting Englishmen a necessary chore—and actually went into some of the repair sheds to which Brinkman would never normally have gained access. What he saw in the yard and the machine shops enabled him to send a whole separate file to London on the apparent disrepair and backward operating methods in the Soviet engineering works, information which by itself was sufficient to impress Maxwell.

There was no period of Brinkman's life when he could remember working so hard or with such concentration, intent on catching every crumb that fell from the table.

And it did not end, of course, with the conclusion of each day's chaperoning. After settling the British party, he always sat down to compose the day's file. His files were always extremely long and always had to be encoded into a secret, designated cipher, and for over a week Brinkman existed on never more than three hours' sleep a night.

Returning on the final day from the farewells at Sheremetyevo, wondering greedily if he would ever again be able to get as close for so long to the Soviet leaders as he had during the past few days, Brinkman allowed himself to relax for the first time and was engulfed in a physical ache of fatigue. Utterly exhausted, he realized. And worth every moment of it. He knew—confidently, not conceitedly—that in months he had achieved more in Moscow than most other intelligence officers achieved in years. So he'd proved himself again. Proved himself to his father and to those in the department who had carped about favoritism and prayed he was going to fall on his ass. Most important of all—always most important of all—he'd proved himself to himself.

There wasn't much time for immediate rest. The intelligence community in Moscow had discovered from the first day what he was doing, and the approaches began practically before the arriving British aircraft had cleared Soviet air space, the attitudes showing some envy and jealousy but predominantly admiration for being clever enough to get himself into such a position. He was the most open with Franklin, although he held back from disclosing the apparent friendship between Sevin and Orlov, and comparatively helpful to Mark Harrison. The approach from the Canadian coincided with that from the Australians, and Brinkman helped them too. He even offered something to the one-sided French, feeling that he could be generous because he had done so well. And he never knew when he might need to call favors in.

Within a week of the British departure, there was a personal letter of thanks from Birdwood, and Brinkman was picked out by name in the letter of gratitude the opposition leader wrote to the ambassador. Maxwell wrote from London too.

"An outstanding success," the controller called it.

Brinkman wondered how difficult it was going to be to maintain the standard he had set himself.

Ruth drove Paul back from the court, shaken by what she had heard. She didn't trust herself to speak to the boy; she didn't know what to say anyway. He remained silent beside her. She couldn't handle this by herself, she determined, taking the car across Memorial Bridge. She was prepared to do most things—indeed she'd asked for custody during the divorce—but there had to be a cutoff point, and this was it. Even though Eddie was on the other side of the world, Paul was his son as much as hers. In the overly polite immediate aftermath of the divorce, she and Eddie had established a method of communication through Langley in the event of an emergency, and Ruth had always determined never to use it, looking upon it as an admission of failure. Which perhaps was the reason Paul had done what he had. So if she had failed, it was time for Eddie to see if he could do better.

The CIA personnel official was courteous and helpful and tried to commiserate by saying it was the most common problem parents had to face in America today, which didn't help Ruth at all since she wasn't interested in the problems of other parents in America, only in her own.

The official promised to get a message to Franklin overnight, and he did.

"Drugs!" exclaimed Ann when Franklin told her that night in their Moscow apartment.

"Marijuana apparently. And cocaine," said Franklin. "There wasn't a complete rundown, obviously, but it seems to have been going on for quite a long time."

"Oh, darling, I'm sorry," said Ann. "I'm really very sorry."

"Yeah," said Franklin distantly, and she wondered if he were thinking it might not have happened if he hadn't become involved with her.

"What are you going to do?" she asked.

"They've been very good," he said. "Immediate compassionate leave."

"Of course," said Ann. Why hadn't she thought of his going back to Washington? It was the most obvious thing.

"I don't know how long I'll be gone."

"It doesn't matter." She suddenly remembered the coveted tickets to the Bolshoi and realized he would miss the performance. It was too inconsequential to mention, too inconsequential to think about at a time like this. "I wish there were something I could do," she said.

Franklin looked at her, grave-faced. "I was just thinking the same thing."

CHAPTER TWELVE

Franklin changed planes at Amsterdam and arrived at Dulles Airport unshaven and crumpled. He didn't enjoy flying and sleep would have been impossible anyway, so he was jetlagged, his head feeling as though it were stuffed with cotton waste. He went mechanically through the process of renting a car, blinking to concentrate when he reached the Beltway on his way into Washington. Muscovites drove faster than this, often dangerously so, but here there seemed so many more cars.

Franklin had his first reminder of how long he had been out of the country. He guessed there would be many more: like the reason for his being summoned home. He felt easier when he was able to leave the Beltway for the Memorial route. It took him directly by CIA headquarters—openly signposted—and he stared in its direction, unable to see the familiar building through the screen of trees.

He'd make contact, obviously, but not yet. For the moment the career for which he'd made so many sacrifices could be put on the back burner. Franklin halted the slide, recognizing the search for excuses and irritated at himself for the weakness. Getting Paul sorted out was the only consideration. The excuses and the who-and-what-was-to-blame recriminations could wait until later. And his commitment to the Agency would be pretty low on the list anyway.

He approached Washington looking for landmarks, the widening thread of the Potomac and by the bridge the topsy-turvy canoe club he always expected to fall down but that never did, the cathedral beyond, proudly grand, and far away, misted by the heat haze, the most familiar markers of all, the wedding-cake dome of the Capitol and the exclamation mark of the Washington Memorial. He took the Key Bridge exit to get into Rosslyn, conscious at once of the changes. It was really the road system, the huge roundabout directly in front of the bridge leading across into Georgetown, but he had the impression there were more buildings too. There never seemed anything newly built in Moscow.

Ruth was in jeans and a workshirt and without any make-up—actually with a smudge of dust on her nose—when she answered the door to him, frowning when she saw who it was. She looked down at herself in instant embarrassment and said, "I thought you'd call from the airport."

He should have, Franklin realized. "Sorry," he said. "I forgot; wasn't thinking."

They stood momentarily staring at each other, each unsure. Then she stepped back into the house. "Sorry. You'd better come in."

Franklin entered hesitantly, stopping in the hallway. There was another moment of uncertainty between them. Despite the disarrayed hair and dirt on her nose, Franklin thought she was very pretty but it wouldn't be right to tell her so. He'd had two hours to kill at Schipol waiting for the Washington connection and he'd spent it in the bar. He should have looked at the airport shops instead and bought her a gift. The boys too, for Christ's sake! Why the hell hadn't he thought of that?

Ruth broke the moment by going into the living room, and he followed. She said, "I'm glad you're here now though, with the boys off at school. It means we can talk."

"Yes," said Franklin. Everything was extremely neat and tidy, but then Ruth had always been neat and tidy. Ann was always cleaning, but. . . . Franklin closed his mind against the comparison. That wasn't what he was here for. "May I sit down?" he asked, unnecessarily polite.

"Sorry, of course," she said.

They each had an eagerness to apologize, thought Franklin, and as he did so, Ruth said, "Sorry, what about some coffee? It must have been a long flight."

"Coffee would be good." As she started to leave the room, he said, "Can I help?" and wished he hadn't as soon as he spoke.

"No," she said. "I'll do it."

Alone, he looked around the room again. There were fresh flowers in two vases, one on a low table in the middle of the room and a more elaborate display on a stand near the main window. On the mantel was a picture of the two boys that he hadn't seen before. It was stiffly posed, and he guessed it was a school photograph. John *was* wearing braces, he saw, remembering Ann's remark. Ruth returned with the coffee pot on a cloth-covered tray, with the cups and the cream.

"You haven't started taking sugar yet, have you?" she asked, pouring.

"No," he answered. She had a good memory. Then again, they had been married eighteen years.

"Sorry I had to do it," said Ruth, apologizing still. "Call you back, I mean. It seemed the only thing to do." Now that the immediate shock of the police interviews and the court appearance was passing, she was unsure of whether she shouldn't have tried to handle it herself.

"Don't be silly," said Franklin at once. "Of course you should have called me back. How bad is it?"

She shrugged helplessly and said, "I don't know, not really. He closed right up after the initial shock. Frightened, I guess."

"What happened?" prompted Franklin gently. "Tell me what happened from the beginning."

Ruth hesitated, arranging the story in her mind, and Franklin saw that while she was in the kitchen, she'd cleaned the smudge off her nose. She said simply, "He got caught trying to rob a pharmacy. He and three others, all from the same class. After pills, they said later. Any sort of pills, it didn't matter. Cocaine too, if it was there. They didn't know whether it was carried or not, but they were trying to find it. Intended to set themselves up—"

"Set themselves up?" queried Franklin.

"As dealers, in the school."

"Jesus!" said Franklin.

Ruth was more comfortable now, still embarrassed at his finding her in workclothes but better than she had been. After getting the house ready, she had wanted to shower and change and be prepared, absolutely, before he arrived. She dismissed his obvious tiredness as the effect of the flight; he didn't seem to have changed much. Not at all, in fact. Had it really been two years since their last meeting? It didn't seem that long. She went on, "Like I said, they were shocked at being arrested by the police. . . ." She smiled, for no reason, and continued. "The cop didn't know what he was confronting, apparently. He actually had his gun out and was threatening to shoot."

"And if they'd run, he probably would have," Franklin commented, sick at the thought.

"Anyway," said Ruth, "that was when it all came out, when they were scared. Seems they had been doing a lot of stealing, stuff from stores that they could sell to get money."

"All for drugs?"

Ruth nodded at the question. "Marijuana," she said. "Seems he's been smoking it for a long time. Now that I've gone back through it, checked it out with the teachers, it seems the reason for the poor grades. Pills too. And there's been some cocaine, although I don't think a lot."

"What the hell sort of school is this?" asked Franklin, needing to be angry at something.

Ruth, who had had longer to recover, said calmly, "Your average American school, no worse and no better than any other. The problem is so bad that the school runs a drug program and has a full-time counselor. He's a nice guy. Erickson. He wants to meet you."

"Sure," said Franklin automatically, not yet wanting to move on. "You said Paul's been smoking for a long time?"

"One of the court orders was urinalysis. He had a high count. I had our own doctor check him out too. There was some irritation of the nasal membrane because of the cocaine—or maybe the filth they cut it with before selling it, but not a lot.'' She stopped and then, disclosing her abrupt new education, said, ''You have to do it for years, apparently, for it to cause real damage. Then it can actually rot your nose away.''

''They were going to set themselves up as dealers?'' persisted Franklin, wanting to understand everything.

Ruth swallowed, arriving at the worst part. ''Paul told the police he'd decided it was dumb to go on as they were. That dealing was where the money was.''

''*Paul* decided.''

Ruth nodded. ''He was the leader, Eddie. Actually set it up. Checked out the pharmacy for the busy and slack times. . . .'' Ruth stopped, lower lip trapped between her teeth, trying to keep herself from crying. Of all the resolutions, this was the strongest, the one she'd repeated and repeated to herself, not wanting him to know how lost she felt. The threat of tears passed, although her voice was still unsteady. She said, ''He'd even planned the getaway, checked the times of the trains on the Metro and worked it out that they could make a connection and be halfway across Washington before the police had time to get there.''

''Holy shit!'' said Franklin, disgusted. ''What's happened since?''

''There was the initial juvenile court appearance and the remand for tests and reports. There's a court-appointed counselor who wants to see you also, a man called Kemp. And Erickson, from the school.''

''What does Paul say about it all?''

''Nothing,'' said Ruth. ''Everything I've told you I got from the police.''

''Didn't you ask him?'' shouted Franklin, immediately

regretting it, holding up his hands as though he were physically trying to pull back the anger in his voice. "Sorry," he said hurriedly. "I'm really very sorry."

Ruth's face had tightened at the eruption, but now it relaxed. There was another resolution, almost as important as not crying, that involved not losing her temper or making any accusations. Maybe it was a fantasy, but it was a nice fantasy to hope that Eddie's return might involve more than the immediate problem. "Of course I asked him," she said. "Not at first, not that first night. I couldn't bring myself to say anything to him. But when I did, he wouldn't talk about it. Just said it was something that had happened."

"Not even sorry?"

"Not even sorry."

"Christ, what a mess," said Franklin. He smiled sadly at her. "I'm sorry, Ruth. Sorry that you had to handle it by yourself, I mean." Apologies after apologies after apologies, he thought.

"Now I don't have to, not any longer, do I?" she said, the gratitude obvious. "Now you're back. Thanks for coming."

"Was it likely I wouldn't?"

"I don't know," she said. "It might have been difficult. There might have been something important happening."

There was something important happening in Moscow, thought Franklin. It pleased him to realize that it had never occurred to him to consider the leadership uncertainty and the part he was supposed to have in analyzing it as a greater priority than returning here. "At the moment I don't think there's anything more important than this," he said. Aware of her quick, hopeful smile, he added, "Don't worry. Everything is going to work out okay."

"I hope so," she said. In so many ways, she thought.

Franklin rubbed his hand over his unshaven face, making a scratching sound. "I need to get cleaned up," he said. "I came straight from the airport."

"You know where the bathroom is," she said.

"You sure that's okay?"

"What do you mean?"

"I didn't want to make any awkward situations. I was thinking of the Marriott down by the bridge." Franklin was trying to be considerate but didn't think he was succeeding very well.

Don't lose your temper, thought Ruth; whatever you do, don't lose your temper and let him see how upset you are. She said, "Wouldn't that be kind of unnecessary?"

"You sure it won't be awkward?"

"I would have thought it was rather essential, considering why you came all the way back," she said, coming as near as she intended to criticism. "There's plenty of room, you know that."

"Thanks," he said.

"You hardly have to thank me, Eddie."

"Thanks anyway," he insisted.

"How's Ann?" asked Ruth, this part rehearsed.

"Fine," said Franklin. "You still friendly with. . . ." His voice trailed at his inability to remember the name.

"Charlie," supplied Ruth. "Charlie Rogers." She paused, wondering whether to make the point. Deciding to, she said, "That's what it is. Friendship."

"Oh," said Franklin. Conscious of the difficulty between them, he said, "You're looking good, Ruth."

"Thanks," she said. "You too."

"Apart from this—if there can be anything apart from this—how have you been keeping?"

"Okay."

"How was Thanksgiving with your folks?"

"Paul acted up," she said. "Now I probably know why. We stayed over for a few days and he wouldn't have been able to get anything."

"Jesus!" said Franklin again, exasperated. There was going to be one conversation between them, however hard they tried. "Everything is going to work out okay," he said, another repetition. "You'll see."

"I wish I could be sure," said Ruth. For a moment her control slipped and before she could stop herself, she added, "I wish I could be sure of so many things."

Ann decided that the problem was Franklin's personal one. She was only peripherally involved, and it was certainly none of Brinkman's business, friendly though they were. She said simply that Franklin had returned to Washington for a sudden family reason.

"Hope everything's all right," he said. The excuse was unlikely, Brinkman decided. It was obviously a recall to Langley for something involving the leadership changes. But what? It would have to be something pretty dramatic to take the American all the way back to Washington. He was surprised, in passing, that they hadn't evolved a better excuse, abrupt though the departure had obviously been.

"I'm sure it will be," she said. "But it's meant an upset."

"What?"

Ann smiled, pleased with her secret. "I know it's your birthday, and I got tickets for the new Bolshoi production. I had planned it as a surprise for the three of us to go."

"What a nice thought," said Brinkman.

"Now Eddie won't be able to make it, of course," she

said. "But there's no point in wasting all the tickets, is there?"

"None at all," agreed Brinkman. "We'll make a party out of it."

Ann wondered what Betty Harrison's reaction would be when she found out. It would be better if she didn't.

CHAPTER THIRTEEN

Franklin showered and shaved and changed but still felt cotton-headed. Ruth suggested he try to sleep but he decided against it, not imagining it would be possible despite the aching tiredness. She had prepared meatloaf, knowing it was one of his favorites, and he tried to eat it, appreciating her effort, but that wasn't easy either because he was full of events and airline food. They each tried to overcompensate, urgently beginning conversations—sometimes in competition with one another—and stumbling either into conversational cul-de-sacs or just as abrupt stops, each urging the other to lead. The only positive talk was over how they would proceed when the boys came home, after Ruth confessed she hadn't warned them of their father's return for fear that Paul might run rather than face the confrontation. Like so much else—everything else—Franklin found it difficult to conceive that his son might try to run away from him.

After the difficult meal, Franklin called each of the counselors to arrange the required appointments, putting himself at their convenience and thanking both for the help and consideration they had already shown. Still at the telephone, he hesitated about calling Langley and then decided against it. Instead, with time to occupy and not wanting to crowd Ruth by his presence, he strolled into the bedroom that the boys shared, gazing around, trying to remember it. Very little seemed the same. He supposed it had to be more than two years, nearer three, since he'd been here, actually in the house. It was bound to have changed. Everything was neat like the rest of the house and, like the rest of the house, he guessed that was Ruth's doing, not the boys'. There were a couple of pennants against the wall, and on another an advertising poster for a rock group he'd never heard of. Near the bed he decided was John's because there was a ratty, dirtied-by-love fur dog on the pillow guarding whatever secrets were beneath, were what appeared to be some perfectly assembled model kits. Beside Paul's bed was a baseball bat and a catcher's mitt. The mitt seemed new, and Franklin wondered if that was how the boy had spent the twenty dollars he'd sent for his birthday.

On the bureau between the two beds there was a picture of both boys, with Ruth smiling in between. His photograph was framed on the wall, his face squinting into the sunlight from the open terrace of the Continental Hotel in Saigon, his first overseas posting when he was still young and the American involvement in Vietnam was comparatively new, and no one had realized what sort of war it was going to turn out to be. How was this war going to turn out? he wondered.

Franklin turned at the sound behind him. Ruth had changed. She wore a severe, businesslike suit, the sort of suit to wear to interviews or special meetings—which he supposed this was—and she was carefully made up, not overly so but properly, as though she had taken care over that too.

"They'll be home soon," she said. "Jane Collins has the car pool today. She lives just opposite."

"Yes," he said.

"I'm scared, Eddie."

"So am I," he confessed.

They walked, unspeaking, back into the main room and he said, "They'll see the car I rented."

"It won't mean anything."

"No, I suppose not."

"Can I get you something. Coffee or a drink?"

"No, thanks." There was a silence and then Franklin said, "Do you really think he might have done that, run rather than face me?"

"I don't know, not really," admitted Ruth. "I just spend my time trying to imagine everything that could happen and then doing things to prevent it."

Poor Ruth, he thought. Poor innocent, trusting, decent Ruth, who'd never deserved anything bad and got hit from every direction.

The telephone rang and she jumped nervously, staring at it as though she were afraid to take the call.

"Do you want me to?" he offered.

"No, it's all right." She darted a look toward Franklin the moment she answered it, as though she were embarrassed. Her replies were curt, just "Yes . . . yes, he's here

. . . no . . . fine . . . thanks." She replaced the receiver and, looking away from Franklin this time, said, "That was Charlie. He's been very good. Calls most days. Wants to do anything he can to help, but I can't think of anything."

"That's good of him," said Franklin, saddened by Ruth's difficulty. Did he have one? No, Franklin thought honestly. He didn't feel any jealousy at Ruth's seeing another guy. How could he? That part of it—whatever that part of it had ever been—was over now.

She was alert to the sound of the car, more accustomed to it than he was, saying, "Here they are" before he properly heard it. She half rose toward the window, then changed her mind and sat down again.

Franklin remembered a lot of noise about their entering the house, slamming doors and dumped satchels and shouts of hello, but it wasn't like that this time. He heard the door just and then they were at the entrance to the room, halted in the doorway by his presence. No one spoke or moved for what was only seconds but seemed much longer, and then John's face opened in an eye-awash smile and he shouted, "Dad! You've come home!"

Franklin was standing, waiting, as the younger boy began running across the room. Behind him, Paul said, "Of course he hasn't, stupid!" and John halted before he reached his father, the smile a look of suspicion now. "You have, haven't you, Dad? You have come home?" he implored.

Franklin felt the emotion lumped in his stomach and intentionally didn't look at Ruth, he wasn't sure it would remain at just that if he did. He said, "I'm home for a while."

John backed away as though physically rejected. "What does a while mean?"

"It means I'm going to stay here for some time but that then I have to go back, to where my job is."

"To where *she* is," said John, utterly hostile now.

"To where my wife is," said Franklin. One of the agreements with Ruth, during the uncomfortable lunch, was that whatever happened and whatever was said, he wouldn't lose his temper.

"Mom's your wife," said John.

"This isn't what I came here to talk about," said Franklin.

"It's what I want to talk about," said the boy.

"Don't talk like that to your father," intruded Ruth, her face flushed.

"Is he your husband?" demanded John.

"You know the answer to that," said Ruth. "Don't be silly. And don't sass your elders."

Undeterred, the smaller boy said, "If he's not your husband, then he's not my father."

"Shut up!" said Franklin, his voice loud. "Shut up and get in here and sit down. Both of you." Damn what they'd decided at lunchtime. Everything was degenerating into a hopeless mess and he had to stop it. When neither moved, he said again, still loud, "I told you to *sit down!*"

Franklin tensed, knowing that both boys were considering whether or not to disobey him and not knowing what to do if they did. John was the first to move, still attempting defiance in a strutting walk, and then Paul. He didn't strut. He slouched forward, shoulders hunched, both hands in his pockets, the attitude one of complete disinterest. Paul's hair was longer than Franklin remembered or liked, practically lank and almost to his shoulders. Franklin knew his shoes would have been cleaned before he left the house that morning because Ruth always cleaned their shoes, but now they were scuffed and dirty, as if Paul had consciously tried to make them so, and his shirt was crumpled, half in and half out of his waistband. He looked scruffy and neglected. John looked better—his shoes had been kept cleaner and there wasn't as much disregard for his clothes, but it wasn't good by a very wide margin. As Franklin watched, he saw John become aware of how his older brother was walking and try to change his strut in mid-stride to conform. They sat down side by side and Franklin supposed that a child psychologist would recommend that he thank them for their cooperation. He didn't.

Ruth said, "Can I get anybody anything, root beer, a. . . ." She stopped too quickly, just as she tried to recover too quickly by finishing with ". . . A soda?"

Paul laughed, a mocking sound. "Pretty close, Mom. Almost said coke, didn't you?"

"Is that funny?" Franklin asked.

Paul turned back to him in open insolence. "Sometimes she's funnier."

Franklin's hand tingled with the urge to slap his face. Instead, he said, "When? When she's in a police station hearing how you planned big, important robberies? When she's in court, hearing how you show what a great guy you are, ripping off nickle-and-dime stores? When she's in a doctor's office with a bottle of your piss on the table in front of her, hearing how it shows that you're part of the crowd, not brave enough to be different, passing around butts with everyone else's spit on them in some shit-smelling bathroom? Is that when she's funny? Is that when she's a laugh a minute, full of wisecracks, unable to believe her luck at having a son like you, someone she can trust and know she can be proud of?"

This wasn't how he'd intended to handle it—not that he'd had any clear idea of how he was going to handle it—but the bravado had gone now and they were paying attention to him, so it would do. "Well?" he said.

Paul looked away, unable to meet his father's eyes. "Just a crack," he said. "Didn't mean anything."

"So tell me what means something," insisted Franklin, not letting him get away. "Tell me why my son—a son I love, despite your not believing it—wants to become a thief and a drug dealer. I want to know, Paul. Tell me."

Paul's head moved with the aimlessness of a cornered animal and his body twitched. "No reason," he said.

"Look at me," ordered Franklin. "Look at me. Stop shuffling like some idiot. And don't say no reason when I want to know why you stole and why you wanted to sell drugs and why you want to take drugs."

"What's it to you?" asked Paul, trying to recover his insolence.

Franklin rubbed one hand against the other to wipe away the urge. "Okay," he said, extending the gesture to put both hands between them, their own physical barrier. "Okay, so because of what happened between your mother and me, you can't believe that I have any more feelings for you. Any more feelings for her, even. So answer me this. If I'd been coming in along the parkway this morning and I'd seen some perfect stranger, someone I'd never seen in my life before, lie himself down in front of my car, what would you have expected me to do?"

John looked sideways at his brother and sniggered, and Paul sniggered too. "Stopped, I guess."

"Stopped," echoed Franklin, glad the boy hadn't suggested swerving, which would have taken a lot of the point away. "I would have stopped to have prevented his getting killed. Don't you think I'm going to try to do something, everything, to stop someone who's not a stranger—someone

I love, despite what you think—from killing himself? And not just for yourself. For your mother. And for a younger brother who admires and respects you so much that he actually tries to walk like you halfway across the room."

John blushed at being caught out. Franklin wondered desperately if he were penetrating any of the barriers.

"Not trying to kill myself," muttered the older boy.

"You've lain down in the road and invited everyone to run over you," insisted Franklin, pleased at the way his impromptu analogy was working. "You're not stupid, Paul. Not really. What you've done is stupid, but you've *known* that it was. Haven't you known that?"

"Suppose so," conceded the boy reluctantly.

"Suppose so," Franklin said relentlessly. "You don't suppose so. You know so." There'd been training courses on interrogation at Langley, long lectures on when to be soft and when to be hard. But hardly in circumstances like these. Was he doing it right?

"Maybe," said Paul.

Franklin realized he wanted to open the door, not smash it into the kid's face. Switching from hard to soft, even softening his voice, he said, "Okay. So why?"

"Everyone else was doing it. Decided to try it." Paul was still reluctant, biting the words out.

"So if anyone else lay down on the parkway, you'd do it too, to see what it was like?"

Beside his brother, John gave a small laugh. Franklin hoped the child was laughing with him and not against him. Just as he hoped the roadway analogy wasn't getting a bit thin.

"Course not," said Paul.

"What's the difference?"

"Lot of difference."

"Feel good when you were stealing? And when you were smoking? Good enough to want to go on doing it until the time when a cop didn't wait to see you were a kid and blew you away? Or was that the next move after you'd set yourself up as a dealer—to get ahold of a Saturday-night Special and become a real hotshot?" Franklin was aware of Ruth turning away toward the window, unable to face the onslaught.

"Didn't think about it."

"What did you think about? Did you think about your mother and breaking her heart? Or me, who loves you? Or John, who looks up to you?" Franklin realized he was risking repetition but he wanted to get more reaction than this out of the kid.

"When did you think about me?" blurted the boy.

It had been a long time coming. "Who are the others, Paul?" he asked.

"Others?"

"Arrested with you."

"Jimmy Cohn," set out the boy, doubtfully. "David Hoover . . . Frank Snaith . . . Billie Carter."

"So tell me about Jimmy Cohn and David Hoover and Frank Snaith and Billie Carter. How many of their parents are divorced?"

"David Hoover's," said Paul at once.

"But not Jimmy Cohn's or Frank Snaith's or Billie Carter's?"

"No."

"So what's their copout?"

"Don't understand," said the boy, who did.

"It won't do, Paul," said Franklin. "Don't try to use what happened between your mother and me as the excuse and expect us and every counselor and social worker to sit

wringing our hands and sympathizing with what a raw deal
you got. Okay, I'm demanding you be honest with me so
I'll be honest with you, as far as honesty need go to *be*
honest. You did get a bad shake. So did your mother. So
did John. And I've never stopped thinking of you. Or your
mother. Or John. Or being aware of what I did and feeling
sorry for the way it happened. But it did happen. There's
nothing any of us can do now to turn the clock back. Life
isn't like that, a place for second chances. Not often
anyhow. And don't try to con me or anyone else by
pretending that this was some half-assed attempt to bring
your mother and me back together, because I'm not buying
that either. You didn't think of anyone else when you stole
and robbed and smoked grass and shoved shit up your
nose. You just thought about yourself. You made yourself
a self-pity blanket and wrapped yourself up in it and
decided there was no one else in the world more important
than Paul Edward Franklin.'' Maybe he shouldn't have
sworn, and maybe he'd gone on too long, but he hoped
some of it was getting through.

Ruth looked back into the room. Eddie was being far
harsher than she had expected, far harsher than she imagined the juvenile officer would want him to be, but a lot of
it needed saying. What had he meant by there not often
being an opportunity for second chances? Would he have
talked about their getting back together if he hadn't obviously thought about it? She stopped herself guiltily. She
and Eddie were not what they were talking about, not
directly anyway.

"You haven't said much, Paul," encouraged his father.

"Nothing to say," replied the boy.

"That's a kid's reply," said Franklin. "You a kid?"

"No," said Paul.

"No what?" pressured Franklin.

Momentarily Paul didn't comprehend. Then he said, "No, sir."

"So when are you going to stop behaving like one? When are you going to start thinking of someone other than yourself?"

The boy made another of his animal-head swings. Or was it something like being punch-drunk? wondered Franklin. He'd hit him hard.

"I've been out of the country for a long time," said Franklin. "Expressions change but I remember the expression to describe people like you, Paul. It was punk. And before that it was jerk. They meant the same, really. They described people who were small-time but thought they were big-time and went around screwing up their own lives and the lives of people all around them. I'm not going to let you do that. To yourself. Or anyone else. We're going to talk it through and we're going to bring out all the problems, imagined or otherwise, and then we're going to solve them, imagined or otherwise. And you're going to grow up and stop thinking you need special favors and special treatment."

Ruth interceded, saying it had gone on long enough and getting the long-ago offered sodas. Franklin stopped. Objectively deciding that to attempt any sort of family meal on the first night would be impossible, Ruth fed the boys first and put them to bed. Franklin stood once more at the bedroom door and watched while she kissed them good night but didn't attempt to himself. He knew Paul would resent it, and John might be confused, and he didn't want either reaction.

She had steaks and he cooked them outside, remembering his promise to Ann, and afterward he and Ruth sat in the living room.

Franklin said, "I'm not sure I did it right."

"I'm not either," she said. She added quickly, "Not that I think you said anything wrong. I just don't know how it should have been done. Who the hell does?"

"He used to be a bright kid, able to express himself," said Franklin, exasperated. He looked at his watch, working out the time difference. It was too late to call Ann now.

"You have to go somewhere?"

"No," he said.

"It's good having you here," she risked. "I agree with everything you said about the divorce not being an excuse or a reason or a cop-out, but I could never have spoken to them the way you did. Women can't kick ass like that: not this woman anyway."

"We just agreed that we're not sure kicking ass was the right way."

Damn, she thought, disappointed at the response. "You haven't said how long you can stay."

"As long as it takes," he said. It was an exaggeration, and he'd better call Langley tomorrow and talk to someone. But he sure as hell wasn't going to run out on them again, not until everything was sorted out. And call Ann too. He hoped she was all right.

Brinkman went back over everything, examining all the clues and indicators. Then he met with Mark Harrison and offered more from his period as an interpreter—glad he'd held something back to bargain with—in the hope of getting from the Canadian a hint of what he had missed or overlooked, what had taken Franklin back to Washington.

And found nothing. He'd been too long ahead of the pack, with the plaintive cries behind him, and decided he didn't like being back there among them, with someone else out in front.

He considered making some kind of social approach to Ann before the planned birthday celebration; not that she would have known anything positive, of course, because that wasn't the way things were done, but there might be a hint or a nuance that would be sufficient to show him where to look. But he decided against it. If she told Franklin—which she undoubtedly would—it would show he was anxious. Using the friendship, in fact. Better to wait. It wasn't long. He'd make it a good celebration though.

CHAPTER FOURTEEN

Franklin was still disoriented by the time changes, and despite the final, head-dropping tiredness as he sat with Ruth, he awoke early, while it was still dark. He'd have to call Ann today. He had to call a lot of people today. Franklin lay quietly, feeling the familiarity of his former home wrapped about him, thinking about the previous day and trying to decide whether he had handled it right. Still unsure about some of the things he'd said to the boy. Maybe thousands of kids stayed straight and all right after their parents divorced, but could he dismiss the argument entirely? No, he thought honestly. He'd tried to take the divorce out of the discussion as much for his own conscience as to get through to Paul. Maybe more. The realization discomfited him, made him feel guilty.

He had given the kid a bad shake. He'd given all of them a bad shake. Ruth worst of all; they were only kids but she'd been able to understand it. He'd behaved like a shit and she'd behaved like a saint. She still was. He had to do more, he determined. Not just now—he was doing all he could now—but later, when this had been settled. She deserved it; the kids deserved it. Conscience again? Sure it was. What else could it be? But proper conscience this time.

Franklin reviewed the day ahead, watching the sky gradually lighten outside and waiting for the sounds of movement elsewhere in the house. When they came, after two hours, he remained where he was, the earlier feeling of familiarity giving way to the awareness that it was no longer his home and that he was a visitor to it, and like a polite visitor, he must wait until the people who really lived there went through their established morning routine and cleared bathrooms before he intruded.

The boys were at the breakfast bar when he emerged, Ruth making pancakes at the stove. She wore a housecoat, but her hair was carefully brushed. The boys were tidy; he saw that Ruth had cleaned their shoes again. The tightness remained between them all, but Franklin thought the atmosphere was slightly less strained than on the previous day. Awake for so long, he had prepared for the encounter. Deciding it was important to create some sort of balance— even if the effort appeared obvious—and not refer constantly to the reason for his being there, he asked if there was a team they supported, and hesitantly, almost unconvincingly, they said the Orioles, and Franklin asked if there was a home game that weekend and would they like to take it in? The acceptance was hesitant, too; they said they didn't know the team's schedule.

John made an effort, asking what Moscow was like. Franklin said it was very different from America and that he had a lot to tell them about it, and why didn't they talk about it over dinner? John nodded eagerly, his excitement at having his father again in the house obvious.

Paul gave no reaction. Why the hell does he behave all the time like some goddamned dummy? thought Franklin irritably.

They were waiting, lunch boxes ready and packed, when the car sounded outside. Ruth kissed them both but Franklin held back, as he had the previous night. Maybe it would be possible to show them his affection before he finally went back, he thought.

He telephoned Langley while Ruth was clearing the boys' breakfast things away and preparing their own meal. He didn't know whether the division chief would already be in; he was glad when Ray Hubble came on the line. It was insecure, so the conversation was necessarily general. Hubble had been the supervisor in Rome when Franklin had been there, and they'd worked together at headquarters before Franklin's London posting, so a friendship of sorts existed between them. Hubble said he was sorry to hear Franklin had a problem, and was there anything he could do? Franklin said that was what he wanted to come in and talk about. Hubble offered that day, but Franklin said tomorrow. He wasn't going to rush his encounters with the counselors. He'd thought about them in the early hours, wanting to get the maximum out of them, so he telephoned both men and suggested a combined rather than separate encounter. Each agreed. Erickson's office was decided upon.

By the time he finished, Ruth had brewed fresh coffee, which was all he wanted. He told her about the altered appointment with the counselors and the reason and asked, in afterthought, if she wanted to come.

"Would it help?" she asked. "I've seen them both several times. But if it would help, of course I'll come."

"Maybe better to go by myself the first time," he agreed. He finished his coffee and said, "I'd like to make another call."

"All local calls are free in Washington," she reminded him, imagining he had forgotten.

"This isn't a local call."

"Oh," she said, realizing. She seemed to spend longer than was necessary with her back to him, getting more coffee, and then she said, "Sure, go ahead."

"Collect calls are difficult in Moscow," he said. "If you'll let me know the cost when the bill comes in, I'll send you a check." Polite visitor, he thought again.

"No problem," said Ruth. She looked down at her housecoat as though surprised to find herself wearing it. "I should get dressed."

Franklin used the kitchen extension. It was a bad connection and he had to shout over the echo on the line. Each agreed they were fine. Ann asked how things were and he said he didn't know, not yet. He didn't know, either, when he would be returning. She told him she was taking Brinkman to the ballet, and he agreed it was a good idea.

"I miss you," she shouted.

"Me too," Franklin yelled back.

"I love you."

"Me too," he yelled again. He supposed Ruth, even in her bedroom, would be able to hear every word and would guess at the gist, but he'd tried. Polite visitor.

Franklin promised to call again, and Ann said she hoped everything would turn out all right. She said once more that she loved him, but Franklin didn't say anything this

time. He finished the call before Ruth came back into
the room.

"Thanks," he said.

"Everything all right?"

"Seems to be. It was a bad line."

"So I gathered. Shall I fix lunch?"

"Thought we might eat out."

Ruth smiled, looking pleased. "Fine."

"Any place you particularly like?"

"You choose," she said hopefully.

"Dominique's used to be good."

She smiled again, glad he'd remembered. Dominique's
had been important to them, the place where they'd cele-
brated birthdays and wedding anniversaries and news of
his promotions and postings. It would be nice to have
another special occasion to celebrate there. "Dominique's
it is," she said.

Franklin was early for his appointment with the counselors, arriving at Erickson's office ahead of the other official.
Both men were similar, and Franklin wondered if it were
the job. They were dressed uncaringly, pants unpressed
and creases concertinaed in the bends of their arms, ties
straying from their collars. Kemp was taller and wore
spectacles, but both were overweight, their stomachs bulg-
ing over their belts. Erickson offered coffee, which Franklin didn't want but took anyway.

"Thanks for seeing me like this," said Franklin. "I
thought it was best."

"Makes our schedules easier anyway," said Kemp.

"So you're busy?" Franklin asked the counselor.

Erickson smiled, an attempt at reassurance. "Believe
me, Mr. Franklin, what you're going through right now
isn't unusual for American parents today."

Franklin recognized the effort but found the man faintly patronizing. Would kids feel the same way? He said, "It's unusual for me. I want to get it sorted out."

"That's what we all want," said Erickson.

"So how do we do it?"

"I wish I knew," admitted the school official. "I've got seventy kids I'm trying to help, and I'd guess there are that many again I don't know about yet."

"And I've stopped bothering to count the number I'm responsible for," said Kemp.

Fuck their problems, thought Franklin; all he cared about were his own. "You're the experts," he said, holding his temper. "If I can't get answers, then I'm looking for advice."

"You live abroad?" asked Erickson.

"Moscow," Franklin told him.

"Have you had a chance to talk to Paul?"

Franklin nodded. "I tried to last night."

"Tried?" picked up Kemp.

"I couldn't get through to him," said Franklin. "Maybe I did, toward the end, but I'm not sure. But he wouldn't talk to me . . . say anything. I asked him why he did it and he just sat there like a dummy!"

"That's usually the way," said Kemp.

Franklin decided the man was definitely irritating. "So you're the experts," he repeated. "So you tell me. Why *do* they do it?"

"I wish I knew that too," said Kemp. "There's never one single reason. Or a way of assembling all the factors into any understandable answer. There's peer pressure, being shamed into it by someone they admire, a bigger guy. There's experimentation. There's boredom. There's the availability of the stuff, all sorts of stuff. It's easier to buy dope on a street corner than it is to buy bread. Supermarkets close; dealers are always there.''

"So why aren't they cleared off the damned streets?''

"They are,'' said Erickson. "And the moment—literally the moment—they go, there are two more to take their places.''

Franklin felt the frustration building up inside him. "Let's talk specifics,'' he tried again. "Let's talk about Paul, and let's talk about me, and let's try to find something we can *do*. I'll take your word about its being a common problem and I'll take your word about all the reasons it can happen, but I want to find a way—will find a way—to stop Paul fucking himself up.'' Franklin hadn't intended to swear but didn't really care whether they were offended or not.

"How did you talk to him last night?'' asked Erickson.

"How?''

"Calmly, trying to understand? Or did you lose your temper?''

The question was justified, after his outburst. "Calmly, as far as I was concerned,'' he said. "I don't think I shouted and I don't think I lost my temper. But I let him know how I felt. I let him know I thought what he had done was stupid and weak and that I thought he'd let everyone down and that I wasn't accepting the fact that my wife and I are divorced as any excuse. That there wasn't an excuse. . . .'' Franklin paused, then said, "And I am trying to understand. I keep asking questions but no one seems able to provide any answers.''

Franklin saw the two men exchange looks and realized they considered he'd handled it wrongly. Erickson asked, "You were aggressive?''

"No,'' said Franklin. "I was direct and straight, the

way I felt a father should be." Except, perhaps, that a father should be at home and not a polite visitor.

"A factor I didn't mention was that sometimes drug-taking is a rebellion against authority," said Kemp in his lecturing voice.

"Rebellions against authority get crushed. That's what law and order mean," said Franklin, impatient at the vapid cliché. "Growing up, becoming an adult. . . ." He stopped, unsure of where his argument was leading him. "Okay," he resumed. "Making the mistakes that growing up means, that's all right. That happens. . . . It happens. That I can understand. Accept even. If he got drunk, I'd understand it. . . ."

"Why?" demanded Erickson quickly.

Franklin blinked. "Kids get drunk. It happens," he said badly.

"Do you know what the worst drug in existence is, Mr. Franklin?" Kemp appeared to regard himself as the spokesman. "Alcohol is the worst drug. It kills more people and causes more lost work days and more lost school days and more accidents than marijuana and cocaine and heroin and pills put together."

"Whose side are you on?" asked Franklin, letting the exasperation show.

"Paul's side," said Kemp. "I'm not on your side, and I'm not on your wife's side, and I'm not on anybody else's side. Just Paul's."

"At last!" said Franklin. "At last someone said something positive."

"We always try to be positive, Mr. Franklin," said Erickson. "I've sat through a hundred meetings like this one, and let me tell you, your reaction is the reaction of practically everyone else. You think we're inconclusive and you think we're weak, and you get impatient but try not to show it because you love your kid and think you might in some way affect how we'll try to help him if you loudmouth us. We're not interested in making our own points, Mr. Franklin, in expressing our opinions and our attitudes, because our opinions and attitudes are middle-aged and already formed, and at the end of every frustrating day we go home to a home where there's a sixpack in the fridge and if it's been a bad, particularly frustrating day, we might even blow the whole sixpack and get drunk, and when we're drunk, we might believe that things aren't really as bad as they are. Which is what taking drugs is all about, Mr. Franklin. Not wanting to know how things are—not dramatic, major, world-shattering things—but the really important things, things that directly affect you and worry you and wake you up in the middle of the night . . . those things. Not wanting to face up to how bad—or how easily solved—those things are.''

Franklin felt the words crash over him like a wave at the very moment of hitting the shore, when it's stronger than any resistance you have and knocks you over, sending you sprawling on the sand looking a fool. They'd had their shot and he'd had his, and they were still at either end of a very long bridge. He said, "You've seen Paul, both of you? Talked to him?"

"Yes," said Kemp.

"So what's his problem? What wakes him up in the middle of the night and seems insoluble?"

"We don't know," said Erickson. "Because he doesn't know. That's the problem. It's the problem with so many of the kids, not just Paul. That's why he sat like a dummy with you last night, and when you asked him why he did it, he said something stupid like he didn't know. Is that what he said, that he didn't know?"

"About that," agreed Franklin. Wanting to air the doubt, he said, "*Could* the divorce, the fact that I'm thousands of miles away and his mother has to cope by herself, could that be it?"

"Maybe," said Kemp unhelpfully. "Or maybe his problem is not being able to hack his school work, or pimples, or how much or how little pubic hair he has, or how some girl is more interested in somebody else."

"I didn't smoke dope or snort coke and hold up stores because I couldn't hack my school work or had pimples or was worried about getting laid!" said Franklin.

"Because that was thirty years ago," said Erickson. "Didn't you drink a beer occasionally?"

Yes, thought Franklin, giddy on the carousel. Determined to achieve something, he started, "My problem . . ." and at once stopped. "Paul's problem," he began again, "is that he lives in Washington and I live in Moscow. I'm here now—*will* be here now—to see him through whatever needs to be done, but then I'll have to go back and I won't be around to follow up on what the court decides and whatever you guys try to do. I know I should be, but I can't be."

"What about visiting?" asked Kemp. "Not just for Paul. I know there's John as well. What are the visitation arrangements?"

"Whatever whenever," said Franklin. "My wife and I remained extremely friendly. But I've been in Moscow for two years and it isn't easy, bringing kids there. . . ." He hesitated. "And if there's one thing I'm certain about, about my kids, it's their resentment of my second wife."

"You haven't seen the kids for two years?" asked Erickson.

Franklin took the rebuke, knowing now—no, knowing as he had for too long—that it was justified. "Eighteen months," he said in desperate qualification. "I came back eighteen months ago to sort some things out." For two days and didn't stay at the house, he remembered.

"Divorce things?" asked Kemp, refusing him an escape.

"Yes," said Franklin, trapped.

"Thirty years ago when I was a kid too," said Kemp, "I think I might have taken a drink—maybe even two—if I hadn't thought I was important enough for my father to bother about for eighteen months at a time."

"How was it?" asked Ruth when Franklin reached Dominique's. He was late and she was already in the small side bar, nursing a whisky sour.

Franklin didn't answer, not at once, still not through with stripping away his own self-protective attitudes, a process that had started at the end of his encounter with the counselors and continued in the cab on his way to the restaurant. "Good," he said self-reflectively. Expanding more forcefully, he went on. "I'm not sure—because nobody's sure about anything—but I think it was good, and I think I've found a way to help Paul."

Now it was Ruth's turn to hesitate. "How?" she asked at last.

"I've been wrong, Ruth," said Franklin, intent upon a complete catharsis. "I abandoned Paul. John too. I have to work out some way to be their father again. Their proper father."

Ruth sipped the whisky, wishing it were stronger. "How?" she managed.

"I don't know," admitted Franklin, still self-absorbed and not fully aware of how intently Ruth was waiting. "Find some way of getting them into Moscow . . . of their liking Ann. And if that isn't possible, then making Ann understand there will be times I have to spend with my kids."

Ruth's drink became really sour, curdling in her stomach and coming back into her throat so that she had to swallow against it. She coughed to clear the sensation. If it helped Paul—please, God, cured Paul—then it was a special occasion, more special than any before. But not special in the way she'd wanted it to be.

Natalia sat awkwardly before him, cowed like a beloved pet who'd always obeyed and done every trick, only to suddenly be brutally beaten for some misdemeanor it didn't understand. "*Why?*" The question came out as a wail.

"I just don't feel anything any more." Orlov was wet with perspiration, forcing himself on, feeling like a man trying to wade a swamp without knowing where the safe ground was, the mud dragging him down deeper and deeper.

"But why?" she said again. "You haven't given a proper reason."

"Apart too long," said Orlov. "Not the same any more." Where were the rehearsed sentences and the balanced arguments, point carefully anticipated against point, everything arranged so there wouldn't be a scene like this?

"It can be the same," she pleaded. "We can learn to love each other again. I *love* you."

"No!" he said. Orlov wished the mud were real and he could be engulfed by it.

"*Please!*"

"No!"

She fell sideways against the edge of the chair, once trying to raise her head for another protest but being swept away by tears before the words would form, staying huddled there with the sobs shuddering through her. This hasn't worked as it should have, thought Orlov. Not at all. Would the rest?

CHAPTER FIFTEEN

It was not a sudden idea. It had been with Ann for some time but she'd refused to acknowledge it. Then she realized how ridiculous she was being and decided there was nothing wrong with it anyway. Jeremy Brinkman was a friend and she was by herself and almost climbing up the wall with boredom and what was wrong with seeing a friend? She'd even discussed it with Eddie. Well, that wasn't strictly true. She'd told Eddie about the Bolshoi and that hadn't happened yet. But there wasn't a lot of difference. Eddie wouldn't see anything wrong with it. How could he? There *wasn't* anything wrong with it. She just wanted to talk to someone else before she started talking to herself. Nothing wrong with that at all. Nothing that any sensible adult could find wrong anyway. Betty Harrison would probably make it into something rivaling *War and Peace*, but sod Betty Harrison.

Brinkman, who was growing increasingly frustrated because everything had gone quiet while he knew—was absolutely convinced—that Franklin was involved in something big, was delighted to get Ann's call. Despite his previous decision not to, he was approaching the point of calling her. He told her dinner sounded like a good idea, and no, he wasn't doing anything, and she had no need to apologize for her cooking, and he'd be there at seven. Which he was, on the dot. With a bottle of wine—French, not Russian—and a gift-wrapped box of Floris soaps that he'd had sent from London in the pouch to thank her for the Bolshoi but had decided to invest earlier. Hopefully.

Ann wasn't, in fact, a particularly good cook and she'd tried too hard, knowing that he was, which made it worse. She hadn't marinated the tough meat sufficiently and she had added the cream to the stroganoff too soon and it was on the point of turning.

"Fabulous!" exclaimed Brinkman. "Next time show me how you do it!"

"Don't be silly," she protested.

"Would I lie?"

"I don't know," she said. "Would you?"

He laughed. "If I had to. But here I don't."

"How often elsewhere?"

"All the time," he parried. She was in a funny mood and he wondered why. "How's Eddie?" he asked. It wasn't too soon; it was an obvious question.

"He called me today," she said, immediately brightening. "But it wasn't a good line. He seems okay."

"How long is he going to be away?" That was an obvious question too.

"He's not sure," she said. "Not yet."

Big, thought Brinkman. Eddie Franklin was onto something *big*. "Wouldn't have thought he'd stay away for too long," coaxed Brinkman.

"The embassy has been very good," she said. "I think he can have as long as he likes."

What the hell did that mean? She'd have been given a cover story, of course. He'd already decided that. Wrong to look for shadows where none existed. "Why didn't you go with him?" he tried.

Ann smiled at him sadly. She was using him, she decided; so he deserved some sort of explanation. "I don't think it would have been a very good idea for the wife of the second marriage to go back and get involved with the wife of the first, do you?"

Brinkman knew about the divorce, of course. They'd made no secret of it during the growing friendship and he'd guessed it anyway because of the obvious age difference. It would have made a very easy cover for Franklin to get back to Langley. He said, "Battlefield, eh?"

"Oh, no," said Ann. "Ruth's super."

Brinkman thought that if the circles got much tighter, he'd disappear up his own ass. "So why didn't you go with him?" he persisted. In an effort to make it seem a casual remark, he picked up the bottle, adding to her wine.

"It wouldn't have been a good idea," she said.

Time to lean forward and time to lean back, he thought. So it was time to lean back. Instead, he said, "Even if Ruth's super, it can't have been easy."

Important things—history-changing events and revelations of secrets that shouldn't be revealed—never have important beginnings. When they are examined impartially later, the trigger is invariably inconsequential, so inconsequential it's difficult—sometimes impossible—to see how something so insignificant caused such a reaction. Brinkman had been pressing, certainly, but it wasn't a considered question; he was filling in, actually, trying to determine another route to the destination he wanted.

"Christ, it hasn't been bloody easy!" erupted Ann, and with that the floodgates abruptly opened and everything poured out. She told him about her first meeting with Franklin in London, when he was attached to the Grosvenor Square Embassy and she had been a junior research assistant at the Foreign Office, just six months down from Cambridge. How she'd liked Ruth and initially actually been amused at Franklin's Texas mannerisms—"all John Wayne and howdy"—and how he'd been, without Ruth, the only friendly face she'd known at another reception, British this time, within a month. How it had been a boring affair she intended to leave early and when he said he was going too, it had seemed a good idea to have another drink at a bar he knew just off Sloane Street, which was on her way home anyway. That's all it had been, a friendly drink, but then he'd called her to suggest lunch and she'd agreed, curious and flattered—but positively not interested even though she found him worldly and comfortable to be with. Funny too. He'd been very funny in those days. The realization came as she talked: He wasn't funny any more, not as he had been then.

Brinkman sat unspeaking and receptive, like a fisherman who'd put himself in precisely the right spot on the running tide, trawling with a net so fine that not even a minnow would get through. He topped her glass again.

Ann talked on. About the guilt of the affair and the decision to be honest and how Ruth had behaved—"super" was a frequent word—and how guilt wasn't easy to get used to, ever. Any more than Moscow was easy to get used to, ever.

Brinkman had known about her irritations because she'd hinted at them before, and he'd assumed they were the sort of irritations that a lot of Western embassy wives had and he hadn't considered them any more important than that—the frustrated anecdotes of the frustrated problems of frustrated people, always exaggerated for no one was willing to concede his disappointment was less than anyone else's. As he listened, however, Brinkman became aware that what Ann was saying wasn't small talk but something causing her genuine unhappiness. He let her purge herself, trying to perceive the catch as it went into the net, not sure he wasn't wasting his time. Well, fishing was a time-wasting exercise anyway. He tried throwing in a lure occasionally, but she didn't bite.

"It's Moscow," she said. "I know it's Moscow. Anywhere else and things wouldn't have been so difficult."

"Doesn't Eddie like it?" asked Brinkman, attempting a brighter bait.

"It's very important for him here. It's his career. He's very good at what he does."

So what's he doing *now*? thought Brinkman. "Maybe it'll be better when he gets back," he said, more direct than he had so far been.

She frowned at him, confused. "Why should it be?"

Tangled in his own line, Brinkman said, "I thought maybe he might have gone back to discuss what happens next."

Ann's frown stayed. "I told you, it's a family thing."

"So you did," said Brinkman. "Wasn't thinking."

"It would be wonderful, though, to know there was another posting," said Ann, retreating into her reverie.

"Where would you like?" asked Brinkman.

"Anywhere but here!" she said, suddenly vehement. "If there were an embassy at the North Pole, I'd happily swap it for here."

Momentarily—but only just—putting aside his personal interest, Brinkman decided that Ann was one very unhappy lady. He was closer to Franklin than to Ann and was surprised that Franklin hadn't mentioned the problem at some time since they didn't always talk shop. Maybe Franklin didn't know. Brinkman thought that unlikely; he was a perceptive guy. "It's not that bad," he soothed.

"Not for a man," she said, still intense. "Not for you. You've got something to do."

Brinkman hadn't thought about it until now, but he conceded that things couldn't be all that good for her, stuck here. Maybe he was lucky, not being married. He said, "You won't be here forever."

"That's what I tell myself every morning when I wake up and every night before I go to sleep."

Was it Moscow? he wondered. Or had she *made* it Moscow, transferring the pain of other things and blaming a difficult city? What other things? He'd never been aware of any strain between her and Eddie, and he'd been with them enough to think he would have noticed if there had been. Had he got it wrong then? Had Eddie genuinely gone back to Washington for something to do with his first wife? What was it she'd said? *I don't think it would have been a very good idea for the wife of the second marriage to get involved with the wife of the first, do you?* Something similar to that. Things like that had happened before. Not all divorces stuck. But she'd said something else. *Ruth's super*. She wouldn't have said that—certainly not in her present mood—if anything like that was happening.

The circle was getting tighter, he thought. "What does Eddie say?" he asked outright.

"He's busy," she said. "It wouldn't be right to bother him."

"You told *me!*" said Brinkman, throwing the inconsistency at her.

Ann looked at him in sudden surprise. "Yes, I did, didn't I?" She actually blushed and Brinkman thought she looked very pretty and very vulnerable. "I'm sorry," she said. "That was unforgivable."

He felt across for her hand and she let him take it. "You're forgiven," he said. "Isn't that what friends are for, to have convenient shoulders?"

"I'm not sure that other friends are supposed to cry so openly on them," she said, still embarrassed.

"It's allowed, for special friends."

"Thanks, for being a special friend," she said.

After the meal, which he praised again, they left the table and drank brandy, sitting in easy chairs. They listened to some Verdi and he promised to let her have the latest Graham Greene novel, which he'd had sent from London and which he'd almost finished. Refusing, absolutely, to give up, he told her to give his regards to Eddie when they next spoke, and she said she would and then stopped, so he failed again. But she'd opened up to him about a lot of other things, Brinkman realized. Maybe he was expecting too much too soon in his impatience. There was the Bolshoi yet. Perhaps he'd get a clue when they went to the Bolshoi.

"It's been a wonderful evening," he said, rising to go. "And it was a super meal. Really."

"You said you lied all the time," she remembered, happier now the confession was over.

"Not to you," he said. He extended his hand in invitation, little finger crooked. Joining in the game, she linked her finger with his in a childlike handshake. "I promise never to lie to you, and if I break that promise, the witches will see that all my teeth fall out."

She laughed at the nonsense of it and said, "Eddie used to say things like that," and then wished she hadn't.

Brinkman disentangled their fingers. "Thanks again."

"You're welcome."

He leaned forward to kiss her good night and she offered her cheek, allowing it.

He hadn't learned a thing—not a thing he'd wanted to learn at least—and the meal had given him indigestion, thought Brinkman on his way home.

It had been a wonderful evening, decided Ann. She didn't feel as uptight or miserable or lonely as she had. And it had been a comforting shoulder to cry on. Jeremy Brinkman was very nice. She liked him.

That night they ate together as a family because Franklin insisted on it. Barriers were bullshit and he was determined to bulldoze them. He thought he'd come close to losing the kids in every meaning of the word. And he thought he'd been lucky, if it were possible to imagine luck emerging from what had happened to Paul, because it had brought him back and made him see what he was doing. Or not doing. It was their barriers that needing bulldozing. And his bullshit. Franklin ignored their silences and their resentment, insisting they help him prepare the barbecue even though he knew they didn't want to and he didn't need them to, deputing John to fan the coals into life and Paul to put in the hickory chips when the time was ready. He hadn't discussed it with Ruth but she understood what was happening and joined in as well, an actress enjoying the play, setting the patio table and bringing Franklin beer, which he drank from the can.

Because John had asked about Moscow in the morning, Franklin had a comfortable subject to talk about. He started telling them about the 1917 revolution and how Moscow hadn't been as immediately important as St. Petersburg. The boys didn't know what his job was but he knew they'd be interested in spies because kids were always interested in spies, and so he told them about Dzerzhinsky, who founded what was now the Soviet intelligence service and whose statue adorned the square in front of their headquarters. He could have lectured about all the others, of course, but he skipped the dull ones in favor of Yagoda, who started as a pharmacist and later turned, using his pharmacist's expertise; and Yezhov, who epitomized a terror the like of which they could never imagine; and Beria, who came within an inch—maybe less than an inch—of seizing power after Stalin's death. He told them about the decay of the Romanovs and of a monk called Rasputin, and how— although a lot of people didn't believe it—he himself believed that a woman called Anna Anderson, who'd died within the last few years, was genuinely Princess Anastasia, who had mysteriously survived the Bolshevik massacre at Ekaterinburg.

And he got them. Franklin worked hard—physically worked hard so he ached—but he got them, and then he said, "You'll like it."

He had been presenting a monologue, so when he stopped, they didn't at first realize it. It was John—more responsive throughout—who reacted quickest. "Like it?" he asked.

"When you come," said Franklin.

"Come . . ." started the younger boy and then jerked to a halt.

The final stripping time, realized Franklin. It was like nakedly exposing himself and he didn't like the idea. But he disliked more the idea of losing the kids. "I wasn't honest yesterday," he admitted. "I used the word but I wasn't honest."

He looked at Ruth. She was sitting quietly, not looking at anyone, both hands cupped around her can of beer. Their drug, thought Franklin.

He said, "I got near to something when I talked about your mother and me not being together any more. What I didn't say—admit—was that only your mother, who's a very special lady, has fully adjusted to it. I hadn't—haven't—and you certainly haven't. But it's mostly my fault. Nearly all my fault. You can't accept that I love you because I haven't given you any reason for believing me. But I do love you. Now I want to say I'm sorry and show you how I feel. Your very special mother and I agreed when we divorced that we should each spend as much time with you as we could. . . ."

Franklin stopped, looking at Paul. If you were naked, then everyone automatically looked at your private parts, so what the hell! He went on. "I accused you last night of copping out. Because you have. You've copped out. But so have I. More than you. I've known—understood—how you feel about Ann, and instead of trying to find a solution for that, I've used the distance of Moscow as an excuse. . . ." He stopped again, Paul and John were important, not his own stupid, fucking pride. He said, "I ran away, Paul. I ran away from you and I ran away from John, just like you tried to run away from whatever it was you didn't want to confront—which was probably the thought of my not wanting you any more, which was never the case but which I can understand your thinking. . . ."

Ruth hadn't moved and the boys were not looking at him either, embarrassed at the admission that Superman couldn't really fly. He said, "I can understand why you hate Ann." Franklin paused, unhappy at the word applied to someone he loved. ". . . Why you dislike her," he resumed. "I want that—am determined—that should stop." He slapped the table to keep their attention. "I've told you tonight about Moscow and I want you to come to see it. See it with me. And that means meeting Ann and understanding what things arc likc—not what you'd like them to be instead—and learning to accept the fact that I have a new wife who won't intrude into your life but would like to be part of it if you'd let her. It means us becoming friends again. I'd like to be your best friend, the person you come to when you have a problem instead of running away from it to some street corner. And it means that I'm going to come out of Moscow whenever I can—with or without Ann, while you're learning to adjust to the fact that she's now my wife—and be with you as often as I can."

Franklin stopped, all the words used up, needing a gulp from the can. He didn't know how it had sounded but it was the best he could do. He said, "As things are—as you know things are, not perhaps as you'd like them to be—let me come back. The track record so far isn't impressive and I'm ashamed of it, but let me start being a proper father again."

The sort of silence developed when there seem to be sounds although really there aren't any. He'd taken control and now he had to exercise it. "Well?" he demanded.

John, predictably, responded first. "Sounds good," he said. Then, hurriedly, "Dad."

There was a further loud silence. "Paul?" prompted Franklin.

The key turned and the dam broke. The boy's tears burst from him and Franklin reached for his hands—to have risen, to have stood to comfort him, would have been wrong, and Franklin was still measuring everything with a slide rule. Paul grasped his hands and Franklin started to cry too, unashamedly, even wanting to if it would help Paul, which was, after all, what he was trying to achieve.

"Please, Dad," said the sobbing child. "Please."

"Sure," soothed Franklin. "Sure."

Ruth was crying too. The reconciliation between Eddie and the boys was the excuse, not the reason.

CHAPTER SIXTEEN

Franklin glanced at the statue of Nathan Hale, the American patriot hanged as a spy by the British during the Revolution, in its imposing setting in front of the CIA headquarters and then, while his ID was being checked at the entrance, at the inscription carved in the marble hallway, "And ye shall know the truth and the truth shall make you free."

Did he know the truth yet? He thought so after the soul-baring with the boys. It seemed to have helped. He knew realistically that it was too early to know, but the signs were good. John had made it very clear the previous night that he wanted to be kissed goodnight, and that morning's breakfast had been like those he remembered, actually with some noise and the boys talking between themselves and then initiating conversation with him and Ruth. Franklin's thoughts stayed with Ruth. He thought it was a breakthrough of sorts and would have imagined she would think so too. Yet she seemed strangely subdued. He supposed it was understandable. She'd gone through a lot more than he had; maybe she knew the apparent signs weren't what he thought they were at all.

The division chief's office was on the fifth floor, high enough at the back that he could see a silver thread of the Potomac just beyond the tree line. If there weren't an Orioles game this weekend, maybe he'd take them out on the river.

Ray Hubble strode across the room to meet him, hand outstretched. There were the predictable assurances of how good each other looked and had London really been that long ago, and then Hubble said, "Sorry to hear about Paul."

"Seems a common problem from what I've been told since I got back."

"Hope everything works out okay."

"I've got to see it does, don't I?" said Franklin. "Appreciate the understanding everyone's shown here."

"No problem," said Hubble. He was a polished man, polished cheeks and polished hair and polished shoes; the sort of man to gleam in the dark. Having given the reassurance, he immediately contradicted it by saying, "When do you think you'll be able to go back?"

"As soon as possible, obviously," said Franklin. "But first I have to make sure everything is settled here. There's still the court appearance and I don't know when that's going to be. I'll have to be certain the boy gets into a remedial program, even if the court doesn't order it. So I can't give positive dates."

Hubble made an upward movement with his head, toward the sixth and seventh floors, where the director and the deputies were quartered, to indicate that the pressure was not his doing. "You know how they are."

"I'll let you know as soon as I know myself," said Franklin.

"Just a bitch of a time to be away, that's all," said Hubble. "Everything is popping over there, and you've confirmed quite a reputation for yourself from it."

"That's good to know," said Franklin. At least his professional life wasn't screwed up, he thought in brief self-pity.

"You'd better believe it," said Hubble enthusiastically. "State was telling the president to behave quite differently over the Geneva offer, but it was our counsel that prevailed. And when everything was examined, the Soviet thing turned out to be a bunch of bullshit, just like you said it was. . . ." Hubble extended his hand, one finger crossed over the other. "That's how the Agency and the president are at the moment. And the director likes it very much indeed. Which makes you a pretty important guy around here, because although he's a funny bastard in some ways, he doesn't deny anyone the credit he's due. Getting it as completely right as we did was your doing and he's letting everyone know it."

Franklin felt satisfaction stir through him. It seemed that his professional life was anything but screwed up. "That's pretty decent of him," he said.

"But he wants everything to stay that way. . . ." Hubble put out a finger-crossed hand again, ". . . him and the president. Which means he's nervous having you off base. Because it's known to be so important, of course, I had to tell him. He said okay, but he's pressing to know just how quick you can get back."

Franklin felt discomfited at the director himself knowing

why he'd had to come back from Moscow. Would it have any effect on his career? The feeling of guilt was immediate. Of course not; and if it did, so what? The Agency could take their job and stuff it. No, that wasn't true. He loved the job—couldn't imagine any other—and relished the ability that he seemed to have to do it. "As soon as possible, just as I said," he reminded his immediate superior.

"How long before Serada's officially dumped?" asked Hubble.

There might have been hints over the last few days, nuances from something in *Pravda* or on *Tass* or the way a proclamation was issued and signed or not signed. "Difficult to say," said Franklin. Aware of how lame that sounded, he went on, "Maybe not yet awhile." That wasn't much better, he knew. And it was an over-assessment as well. He didn't know whether Serada would go tomorrow or next week or next month. He was just trying to reassure them and take the pressure off himself. He wouldn't be pressured, determined Franklin. All right, so he liked the job and he liked the praise, but he wouldn't renege on the promise he'd given to the boys and to Ruth. He wouldn't stay longer than he had to—he'd never intended that in the first place—but he was damned if he'd cut anything short either.

"Bitch of a time to be away," repeated Hubble, who'd seen the weak reassurance for the snow job it was.

"I'm sorry," said Franklin, not quite certain of what he was apologizing for but unable to think of anything else to say.

"It's not just the immediate situation," said Hubble.

"I'm not sure I know what you mean," frowned Franklin.

"You've been in Moscow two years?"

"A little over," agreed Franklin.

Hubble nodded, the minimal correction unnecessary anyway because he had Franklin's personnel file in the desk drawer on his left and knew everything about the man's career. He said, "Normally we'd be thinking of some reassignment now; three years is the term, as you know."

"*Normally*?" queried Franklin, picking out the important word.

"Like I said, Eddie, the director's impressed, impressed as hell. He thinks you've got the handle on Moscow in a period that is going to turn out important. So he says—and the logic is difficult to fault—why put someone else up at bat when you're scoring all the homeruns? If we pull you out, as we would normally do after three years, it means someone else has to go in there cold and learn the tricks. The director thinks—and again the logic is difficult to argue with—that at a time like this we should stay just as we are, ahead of the game."

"You want me to remain in Moscow?" asked Franklin, irritated by all the awkward metaphors.

"Just that," replied Hubble.

"For how long?"

"For as long as it takes," said Hubble expansively. "Then you can go wherever you like, in full glory."

"What does that mean?" asked Franklin.

"It means—and the director has personally asked me to make this clear to you—that if you agree to stay on, then when you finally move, you can call the shots. You choose what you want and you get it. You can have another overseas posting. Or you can come here to Langley. And if you come to Langley, it won't be for the doorman's job. You'll get a division at least. What do you say?"

During all his thoughts and discussions with the boys and with everyone else, Franklin had always calculated, without consciously counting the months or considering it too definitely, that he'd be out of Moscow according to the normal custom, in three years. That was why he'd been so forceful in the talk of their being together more often, because if it had proven difficult to get them into Moscow—or for them to accept Ann—then he knew it would have been only months before he was somewhere else more convenient. Would it be difficult to get them in if he stayed on? He could make it a condition of his agreeing to remain that the Agency—through the State Department—make damned sure they could get in whenever he wanted them to. And impose another condition too: that he be allowed to come out whenever he wanted to be with them.

What about Ann? She said she hated Moscow but he'd always thought that was an exaggeration. So she disliked it. But so did a lot of people at first. Two years was hardly at first, so maybe she hadn't tried hard enough. She'd understand when he explained it; she knew how important the job was to him. And it was a pretty impressive promise, anything he wanted afterward. He could let her choose. That wouldn't be bad, telling her that for her understanding this time she could pick anywhere in the world to go next.

And why should it be such a long time anyway? Serada could be dumped tomorrow and everything nicely tied up before the normal three years were over. And then he'd be holding the basket with all the promises and it wouldn't have cost him anything. Except that he expected whoever succeeded Serada to be a caretaker for a younger man, and it could be two or three years—maybe longer—before that man emerged and was identified. He was sure Ann would understand.

"Well?" urged Hubble, uncomfortable with the long silence.

"I'd like to think about it," hedged Franklin.

"Sure," conceded Hubble. "But not too long, eh?"

"A couple of days," said Franklin carelessly. "Just give me a couple of days."

"That'll be good," said Hubble. Maintaining the earlier pressure, he said, "You might have a clearer idea then of when you can go back as well. And, Eddie?"

"What?"

"You know what we want and you know how much we want it. How much the director wants it. But there's no catch. If you say no, we'll understand. It won't be held against you later."

Crap, thought Franklin. The supposed guarantee had come out exactly as the man had intended, a threat. So much for friendship, he thought. Maybe that was unfair. Franklin was sure the pressure *was* coming from the seventh floor, so Hubble couldn't do much else but watch his own back. If the place were as political as this, maybe Langley wasn't the spot to come back to. Franklin braked the thought. That reflection indicated he had a choice, and he had a choice only if he accepted their offer. He said, "I understand."

"I know a lot of guys who'd sacrifice a lot of things to be in the position you are, Eddie," said Hubble.

"Yes," agreed Franklin. "I suppose you're right."

"A couple of days, eh?"

"A couple of days," promised Franklin, unhappy now at the self-imposed time limit.

It was only when he was driving back down the parkway that Franklin fully realized that if he kept the schedule he had agreed on with Hubble, it would mean making the decision without the opportunity of talking it through properly with Ann. Or talking it through at all, really, because he didn't think it was something he could discuss with her by telephone. Which reminded him. He should call her again. But not yet; not today. He had too much to think about.

As it turned out, he didn't call Moscow for two days. Still undecided, he had talked to Hubble and gotten a reluctant extension on the time limit, citing Paul's impending court appearance as the reason for him to delay. The line to Moscow was better than it had been the first time. He told her he thought things were going better than they had been and that there was a date for the court hearing, and because Ruth was out taking her turn with the car pool, he was able openly to tell Ann he loved and missed her. She asked when he was coming back and he said he didn't know, and she said she was looking forward to the Bolshoi with Brinkman, which he'd forgotten she was going to attend.

In Moscow, Ann thought how limited her news was—nothing bloody well ever happened anyway—and in Washington, Franklin put down the telephone without mentioning Langley's wish to extend his posting in the Soviet capital.

Brinkman arrived promptly, which he invariably did, and insisted upon their drinking the champagne he'd brought because it was his birthday. So she insisted on giving him the present she'd bought for him, an icon she had been assured was a genuine antique. He'd promised to stage the birthday dinner when he'd telephoned earlier, and when she asked where they were going, he said to his apartment because he didn't want anything about the evening to be

spoiled and therefore didn't want to sit for hours in a
Russian restaurant waiting for food he could prepare and
cook better at home. Ann was glad. The Bolshoi was risk
enough; she didn't want to extend that risk by going
somewhere public afterward. There were a limited number
of embassy favorites, and she and Brinkman would have
been seen. She didn't want any stupid stories to begin,
especially when there was no basis for their existence.

"Eddie called," she said as they left her apartment.

"When?" asked Brinkman, at once attentive.

"Day before yesterday."

"How is he?"

"Fine."

"When's he coming back?"

"He still doesn't know."

What the bloody hell was it? thought Brinkman.

CHAPTER SEVENTEEN

The new production was superb. Ann thought she had never heard Tchaikovsky's music sound so wonderful nor seen dancers so weightless and so synchronized. During the intermission there was more champagne, and on their way to the bar they passed an exhibition on the history of the Imperial School, with prints and photographs of legendary figures such as Marius Petipa and Enrico Cecchetti and of principal dancers such as Mathilde Kschessinka and Olga Preobrazhenska and Anna Pavlova and Tamara Karsavina. Ann could identify them without reading the notations and as she talked, she realized she knew more about the ballet than Brinkman. The knowledge excited her. In the cloistered, formalized embassy life, she found she rarely knew anything more than anyone else. She showed off, consciously, and Brinkman let her, isolating another indication of her unhappiness by her throwaway

165

admission that she'd studied the Russian ballet soon after she arrived in Moscow "to fill the days." She chattered on about the Summer Gardens performances in St. Petersburg and the origin of the Moscow School.

Brinkman decided he was enjoying himself. There was still the ulterior motive of finding out what Franklin was doing, just as there had been an ulterior motive in cultivating the friendship in the first place, getting himself next to someone whom Ingram designated the best. But the friendship had moved on from the initial reason. He genuinely *liked* Franklin now, better than he liked Harrison or any other man in the Western enclave. And he liked Ann. He guessed that Betty Harrison and her intimates might think Ann was gauche and he supposed she was, which was her charm. Despite her feelings at being in Moscow, she had about her a freshness, an air of being genuinely interested and wanting to be involved with everything she did and everyone she knew. She held his arm as they strolled through the theater, an unconscious gesture for her, and Brinkman decided he liked the touch. Not only a freshness but a softness, he thought.

The conclusion surpassed the commencement. He stood, matching her enthusiasm and the applause of everyone else, clapping as loudly as anyone for the curtain calls that went on and on. Even when the curtain finally came down, they left the Bolshoi unhurriedly, as though reluctant to sever the moment absolutely by leaving the place.

"Wasn't that exquisite?" said Ann. "I actually feel I'm floating, just like the chorus."

"Why the chorus?" he asked. "Why not the prima ballerina?"

She giggled, pleased with his lightness. "I could never be the lead, only ever the support."

"You can be my prima ballerina." Wasn't he being gauche now?

"I accept," she said.

She still had her arm in his. Immediately outside the Bolshoi they stopped together, not sure of what to do, and she said, "Let's not go home straight away. Let's walk."

"Okay," he said.

They went along Sverdlova, slowed by the crush of people near the metro entrance, but almost inevitably they drifted toward the Kremlin. Ann stared up at the huge illuminated red stars on top of the towers and said, "I've never been able to understand why they've done that."

"It is sort of odd," admitted Brinkman.

"Looks like the biggest circus attraction in the whole world."

"Sometimes a good description," said Brinkman.

"Want to know something?"

Damned right I do, thought Brinkman. "What?"

"Tonight I like Moscow."

"About time."

"*Tonight*, I said," insisted Ann. "Just tonight."

They returned in the direction of the theater, near which his car was parked, as slowly as they had set off on the outing, and Brinkman even drove slowly back to the complex. He had left Chablis on ice because he felt there was a limit to the amount of champagne it was possible to drink, particularly before a meal. He'd arranged cold fish, which was good in the concessionary places, and caviar because, as he kept reminding her, it was his birthday. With the caviar he served vodka, deeply chilled, taking it the Russian way, down in one. She obeyed the instructions and laughed and coughed at the same time, protesting that she would get drunk. While they ate he tried to guide the conversation to Franklin but Ann appeared reluctant to bring her husband into any conversation, insisting instead on talking about the Cambridge they had both known, most of which they had already talked about.

For Ann it was all a part of the evening, still gripped as she was by the beauty of the ballet performance and edging into reverie, wanting to find other, special memories. For Brinkman it was a confirmation of something by now he didn't need confirming. He didn't think either that Ann could help him, even inadvertently. Consummate professional that he was, Franklin wouldn't have allowed her the opportunity of letting anything drop by accident. There was an unexpected feeling that he could now relax and be completely at ease with her, not forever alert for openings. He was finding Ann very comfortable to be with.

After the meal they left the table uncleared and Brinkman played more Tchaikovsky, not *Swan Lake* because that wouldn't have been right, but *The Sleeping Beauty*, which he thought would complement Ann's mood. He sat beside her on the couch, his arm stretched behind her along its back. Ann settled into the crook of his arm as unthinkingly as she had earlier held his arm while walking from the theater.

"This is heavenly," she said, her voice distant. "Heavenly."

Brinkman put his face into her hair and kissed her, very lightly, hardly making contact. "Wake up, Princess," he said.

She didn't react against his gesture. "I don't want to," she said. "I want to go on sleeping for a hundred years. The story says I have to."

"It's a fairy story," he said.

She settled against him more comfortably. "I want to stay in the fairy story."

He kissed her hair again, more positively this time, thinking how clean it smelled. Everything fresh, he thought. He said, "Thank you for tonight; for the icon and for getting the tickets too."

"I've enjoyed it as much as you," she said. "Maybe more."

The side ended. There was a slight distortion on the record arm so that it made a loud sound clicking off. He asked, "Do you want to hear the second half?"

"Yes," she said. "But I don't want to move."

"It'll only take a moment."

Ann had to raise her head for Brinkman to move his arm and when he did, making to stand, they were very close to each other. Briefly they stayed just inches apart, faces unmoving, eyes held.

"I'd better change the record," he said.

"Yes," she agreed.

Brinkman turned the disc over quickly, fumbling so that he almost dropped it, glad that his back was to her and she couldn't see his nervousness. He was reluctant, when the record was in place, to turn back to her. When he did, he saw that her expression hadn't changed. He returned to the couch, holding her eyes, and she had to move again, slightly, to let him sit down where he had before. The settling back against him wasn't as unthinking as it had earlier been, and it wasn't the same either. This time her face was nearer to his, not her hair. "Still a fairy story," she said.

He kissed her, high on the cheek, and she turned her head, bringing her lips up. There was a bird-peck hesitancy about them, each unsure of the other, each nervous and ready to pull back from danger. But the pecking became more fervent and they stopped being nervous. Brinkman twisted around so that she lay back the full length of the couch and he knelt beside her, looking down, kissing not just her lips now but her face and her neck and her throat where her dress was open. He plucked at the buttons, trying to open it farther, and she made a token protest, whispering "no, no" several times, but he didn't desist and she gave up trying to stop him, actually turning for the bra to become unclasped and then whimpering at the delicious pain when his teeth trapped her nipple.

He played for a long while and then she felt his hands move and she made another token protest, as ineffective as the first. He tried to make love to her on the couch but there wasn't room enough, so she rolled off onto him and they made love first on the floor, encumbered by clothes and as nervously as they had started kissing. It didn't work because of their awkwardness and nervousness, and he stood up to go to the bedroom and she said "no" again, and again she did. The second time was much better. She was an experimental lover, more so than he, although he tried to match her, not wanting to be shown the more inexperienced. He thought, anxiously, toward the end that he was going to fail her, but he managed to hold back just long enough and they came together, a mutual explosion. Ann didn't let him move away from her. Instead she held him with an almost desperate tightness, fingers pressed into his back, legs encompassing his.

"What have we done?" she said after a long silence. "What the hell have we done?"

"I don't know," he said.

She relaxed slightly, letting go her hold on him. "It

never happened," she said. "It was all part of the fairy
story."

Could they sustain it, in the claustrophobia of their
lives? "All right," he said. Feeling he should go farther,
Brinkman said, "I'm sorry."

"I suppose I should be too."

"Are you?"

"I don't know. I suppose so, yes. But I don't know, not
really."

"Neither do I," said Brinkman, changing the earlier
automatic apology.

"I wish I *could* sleep for a hundred years."

"With me?" he asked, trying to lift her depression. It
wasn't the end of the world, not yet. A mistake and an
embarrassment, but not the end of the world.

"That's something else I don't know," said Ann. "I
think the answer might be yes."

Franklin tried to anticipate everything, determined against
any oversight. He went to see the parents of the other boys
who had been involved with Paul and found them as
resentful and confused and bewildered as he had felt. *Had*
felt. Franklin left each meeting increasingly convinced that
he'd crossed more bridges with Paul than any of the others
had with their sons. Jim Hoover, who was divorced like
Franklin and had returned like Franklin, was convinced
that the marriage breakup was the only cause and wouldn't
consider any discussion. As well as the other parents,
Franklin saw again the two counselors, knowing that Erickson was submitting a report to the court—and guessing
that maybe Kemp would as well—and wanting the two to
know all about his talks with the boy. Both men seemed
impressed and Franklin was glad; they were supposed to

be experts—more expert than he was at least—and if they approved, maybe it was some sort of indication that he'd gotten it right.

He talked things through with Ruth at every stage, and the day before the court hearing he went over it all again, insisting that she try to find something he'd forgotten while there was still time to catch it. She couldn't.

"I know I've said it before, but thanks for coming back, Eddie. I don't know what I'd have done without you."

"I meant what I said about staying as close as possible to the boys," said Franklin. "I fouled up. Badly."

"We found out in time," said Ruth.

"Let's hope it's in time."

"You were the one who used to reassure me, remember?"

She deserved the honesty, thought Franklin. That was the new, inviolate resolution. "Something's come up," he said.

"Come up?"

Franklin told her about the meeting with Hubble, not everything but enough for her to understand that he was being asked to extend.

"But there's one thing," he said. "One paramount, overriding thing. If I accept, it's going to be only when I'm completely satisfied it'll allow the new situation with Paul and John."

"*Are* you going to accept?" she asked.

"I haven't decided." Invoking the convenient excuse, he said, "I'm not even going to think about it until after the court case." He paused. "What do you think I should do, Ruth?"

"I can talk only as far as the boys are concerned," she said. "And about them I think you should do whatever makes it possible for you to keep your promise. I sincerely believe that if we stand any chance of getting Paul back in line and preventing John from going the same way, the most important thing is not letting them think—suspect even—that you're not going to come through like you've said. But that's where my responsibility ends now, Eddie. Ann's the person you have to talk the rest through with. And then you're the person who has to make the final decision.''

"Yes," said Franklin miserably. "I know."

CHAPTER EIGHTEEN

The surroundings of the Family Court were not the sort
that Franklin had expected and he regretted it. He guessed
the design was based on long experience and that it worked,
but he would have preferred more formality and would
have preferred the presiding judge to have been a man
instead of a woman because he thought a man would have
had a stronger effect on the boys. Frightened them. They
needed frightening, Paul and the others who stood before
the bench now, their hair trimmed and their pants pressed
and their shoes shined, muttering that they understood
what was happening. If they understood it now—which
they undoubtedly did—then they'd understood it when
they'd ripped off stores and planned to rob the pharmacy.

Despite the new accord with Paul and all the promises
and hopes, Franklin was still objective enough to accept
that his son had been a little bastard. The parents had

employed counsel to represent the boys because it was the system, but Franklin knew there wasn't anything lawyers could do. Paul had been a little bastard and should be taught a lesson—frightened of ever doing anything like it again, irrespective of any new relationship that had privately been reached between them.

The parents sat behind the children and the attorneys, all pressed and barbered and polished too, tightly enclosed in angry embarrassment at what they were hearing. The evidence, in fact, was not lengthy and the lawyers' questions were nothing more than a formality, men trying to be seen to earn their fees. The pharmacist and an assistant talked of the suspicious behavior of a group of young children—Paul emerging as the leader. There had been an apparent attempt by one pair to stage a theft in the main part of the shop while two others—Paul one of them— tried to get into the restricted area where the controlled drugs were kept. The pharmacist, who had already called the police, testified that one of the boys—thank God, not Paul this time but David Hoover—pulled a knife, which he dropped in his nervousness.

The patrolman testified that he had entered prepared to shoot but that the children had immediately surrendered. Counsel tried to make something of the surrender, but Franklin wasn't impressed and he didn't think the court was. It was from the patrolman that the evidence came of the previous, undetected shoplifting, which the boys had admitted in statements at the station house. Every child, in separate interviews, had confessed that the purpose was to buy drugs, their taking of which was confirmed by later medical examination. The two drug counselors, Kemp and Erickson, were the witnesses upon whom the lawyers concentrated the most, seeking something in mitigation or excuse, but Franklin didn't think much of that either. He was impressed, however, by the main body of their evidence—not the questioning—and felt privately embarrassed at his impression of them at their first interview. Both talked of the boys individually, attesting unasked their previous good character and apparently genuine remorse now.

"So what do you have to say for yourselves?" The demand from the bench was sharp, unexpected, and Franklin started like the kids in front. The judge's name was Bateson, he remembered. She was gray-haired and rosy-cheeked and motherly. Franklin definitely regretted it hadn't been a man appointed to the case.

"And I don't want any 'sorrys' or 'don't knows' or 'nothings,' " she went on. "I want to know *why* you did what you did. And why I shouldn't send you all away for a long custodial period to protect shopkeepers and people on the streets."

Maybe he'd been wrong, thought Franklin. Again. Maybe she was as effective as a male judge after all.

One of the boys, Jimmy Cohn, tried to mumble something but she cut him short, demanding that he speak up. When he did, it was to say he was sorry. She said, "Of course you are. You're sorry you got caught and that you're in court here today. But you wouldn't be sorry if you hadn't been caught, would you? All you'd be worrying about was getting more drugs to sell and to use." She hesitated, jabbing a finger out. "You!" she said. "You talk to me."

Paul, Franklin saw.

Paul was standing now, shame-faced like the rest. He shifted under the demand, his shoulders humping, and Franklin thought come on! Come on, for God's sake, boy!

"Well?" she persisted.

"Made a mistake," started Paul, trying. "A stupid mistake. I know that now. And I *am* sorry and not for being here today . . . not just for being here today. I'm sorry for what I stole, and I'm sorry I tried to rob the pharmacy."

"What about the marijuana and the cocaine?" demanded the judge relentlessly. "How sorry are you about that?"

"Very," said Paul.

"Why?"

She was good, conceded Franklin, very good.

"Because it's wrong. Dangerous," he said.

"You knew that when you were doing it."

"Everyone was doing it," said Paul. "I knew it was wrong but it didn't seem to hurt anybody, not really *hurt* them. I thought the stories about its being dangerous were exaggerated."

"Do you still think that?"

"Don't know," said Paul.

Franklin wished the boy hadn't fallen back upon the cliché at the end, but the rest hadn't been bad.

Judge Bateson kept on at the other boys, forcing reaction from each of them, and Franklin decided that even though the court didn't have the appearance of an adult court, the youngsters weren't getting off as lightly as he imagined they might. And they hadn't been sentenced yet. As he thought it, she reached it.

"You've been taking drugs," she said. "You've been stealing to buy those drugs and you planned a robbery to set yourselves up as dealers." The judge continued, "Which requires a custodial sentence . . ." and then she stopped again for a moment.

Franklin felt Ruth stiffen at his side. She reached out for

his arm and he covered her hand. A positive attitude wouldn't form in his mind. He'd wanted Paul frightened into not doing it—any of it—again, and he wanted some sort of day-to-day control that he himself couldn't personally provide, but he hadn't actually considered imprisonment, although it had been discussed during his second meeting with the counselors. Would it be imprisonment at Paul's age? Reformatory then. He didn't know if such places were officially called that—nowadays it was something cosmetic like corrective farms—but that's what they were, reformatories. Would a period in a reformatory mean a permanent record, damaging when Paul tried to get a job? And what about his schooling? There couldn't be the natural progression to high school if he were in a reformatory. The questions crowded in and Franklin couldn't answer them. The awareness angered him. The counselors could have told him if he'd had the common sense to ask the questions.

"Do you know what a custodial sentence is? What it would mean?" asked the judge oratorically. The boys looked very scared. "It means going someplace where you're not free any more. Not free to steal or frighten other people or to sell drugs. Someplace where people—other kids and other decent people—can be protected from you. Which I think is necessary."

Franklin felt Ruth's hand tighten on his arm. Farther along the line of parents he heard the sound of another mother—he didn't know who—starting to cry, and in front of him the shoulders of Jimmy Cohn were beginning to heave too.

"But I want to achieve more than that," said Judge Bateson. "I want to protect other people and I want to reform you, and I want to ensure that you make proper, fitting restitution for what you've done so that you'll be reminded of it not just for today but for a long time afterward. I *am* going to sentence you to a custodial sentence. A period of two years each. And upon you, Paul Franklin, the ringleader of the others, there will be an additional period of six months.''

Beside him Franklin felt Ruth begin to shake and he squeezed her hand, trying to comfort her but knowing there was no way he could.

"But I am going to suspend it," announced the judge. "I am going to suspend it—which means that you can continue living with your families and going to your schools. Getting, in fact, a chance that many would argue you don't deserve for the things you have done. But you're not going to get that chance easily. A condition of the suspension is that you each enter a drug-rehabilitation and reeducation program to which you will be directed by your counselors. Another condition is that you will, during the period of your sentence, enter a voluntary assistance program, again directed by your counselors, for people less fortunate than yourselves."

Judge Bateson paused, sipping from the water glass in front of her on the bench. "And understand one thing," she resumed. "*The* most important thing. If at any time during the period of your sentence you fail to meet any of these conditions, or if you involve yourselves again with drugs or get into any sort of trouble whatsoever, you'll return to this court and the custodial sentence *will* go into effect. Plus whatever new sentence is imposed upon you."

It didn't alter his resolve, Franklin realized. His own intentions could be adjusted to coordinate with those of the court. It was a harsh and fitting sentence and could be the making—and saving—of the boy. Providing Paul didn't screw it up.

The last thought was uppermost in his mind as they emerged from the court and Ruth, who hadn't properly assimilated all that was said, asked him, "What does it mean?"

"That he can't make another mistake," said Franklin. "Not one."

Hubble's greeting at Langley was as effusive as before. Maybe even more so, thought Franklin; this time it was Hubble who was seeking concessions. He politely asked about the court hearing but Franklin sensed the other man's impatience to get to the point—his decision over Moscow.

Hubble timed the question for the exact moment at which he could not be suspected of disinterest in Franklin's personal problems and then said, "You said you'd let me know."

"Yes," agreed Franklin.

"So what's it to be?"

Franklin refused to be hurried. He went carefully—actually irritatingly—through the court sentence and conditions and then he listed his own decisions involving Paul. He said he wanted further time in Washington to set everything up with the counselors and that, if he agreed to stay on, he wanted an absolute guarantee that he would be allowed out of the Russian capital whenever and as often as the counselors—and Paul—considered it necessary. He also said that although he knew the State Department had no control or pressure it could bring against the Soviet immigration authorities, he wanted a further absolute guarantee that whenever he wanted the boys to visit him in Moscow it would make sure there was no hitch in the arrangements.

And then, coming finally to Ann, whom circumstances had thrust into the background but who didn't deserve second place, he said that he wouldn't agree to a completely unlimited period, spending the rest of his operational life in Moscow. Even though he knew how important Moscow was, just as he knew there could always be an argument for maintaining someone already established there rather than bringing in someone fresh, there has to be a limit to his extension.

"That's sure a bunch of reservations," said Hubble.

"They're not reservations," argued Franklin. "They're reasonable concessions in exchange for what you're asking me to do."

"If we agree, you'll stay?"

"If you agree to every one in every respect, I'll stay," Franklin spelled out.

"I should discuss this with the director," hedged Hubble.

"Then do so," agreed Franklin. "I told you I want to stay here in Washington for a few more days yet to make final arrangements. There's time enough."

Hubble smiled, shaking his head. "I was told to negotiate and try to reach agreement. So I've negotiated and we've reached an agreement."

Crap, thought Franklin. They'd been prepared to let him have this from the start. He wished he could have thought of something else to add to his advantage. "Every point?" he asked. It had to be set out, without any misunderstandings or caveats.

"Every point," assured Hubble. "Guaranteed."

"Then okay," said Franklin. "I'll stay."

Because he owed it to her—because he owed her far more—Franklin told Ruth, of course, as soon as he got back to the house.

"Yes," she said.

"Is that all? Just yes?"

"What else is there?"

"It won't affect whatever I arranged with Paul," Franklin assured her. "That's positively guaranteed."

"Sure," she said, sounding unconvinced.

"They won't renege on me; I know they won't renege."

"Good."

"You think I made the wrong decision?"

"I didn't say that."

"I don't think you have to."

"My only consideration—my only worry now—is Paul. As long as Paul's all right, nothing else is my business, is it?"

"I just thought you might have had something more to say about it."

"Ann's the person who has to have something more to say about it, not me, don't you think?"

CHAPTER NINETEEN

They had known, of course, that it wouldn't be easy. They'd tried to anticipate the problems in the last few weeks, when Orlov's recall had been confirmed, imagining they already had all the training necessary in avoiding difficulties. After all, their affair had existed for more than a year and that hadn't been easy either; Russians at the United Nations, even at Orlov's rank, suffer severe restrictions and surveillance. But Harriet knew now how ill-equipped they'd been. How ill-equipped at least she had been. She didn't know about Pietr. Which was *the* problem. Not knowing. Naturally they'd considered it, with everything else. There'd been a long conversation about it on one of their last nights, when Orlov had managed to slip away from the Soviet compound and come to the Second Avenue apartment.

Harriet looked around the apartment now, trying to

recapture the evening because memories were important, the things she lived by. They'd eaten there, as they almost always did because to go out was dangerous, and then they'd made love, with the anxiousness of lovers soon to be parted, and then he'd talked about their not being able to make contact—except in the most extreme and dire emergency—and told her not to make monsters out of shadows. Christ, she'd tried hard enough. It hadn't been too bad in the early weeks: months even. There'd been an unreality about the most things—practically a light-headedness when she wasn't working; at work she was never light-headed—but there had been no unreality about the parting and the loneliness and the not knowing. Ironically, the problem of not knowing had started, insidiously, by *knowing*!

Harriet Johnson was unusual—"freak" had been a friendly jibe at Oxford—someone with an outstanding talent for languages. Her Russian was impeccable; she was actually able to be colloquial, and her knowledge extended to tongues within the country—Estonian and Georgian, which she always spoke with Orlov. She was fluent too in Czechoslovakian and Hungarian and German, again with a mastery of some of the internal dialects. The natural outlet of such ability was interpreting, and Harriet was outstandingly able at that, within three years of her joining the UN already at senior-supervisor grade. And as a senior, her supervision of translator readings, alert for variations in usage or new technical terms, was as essential as speaking the languages. And so she read whatever she could from the countries whose tongues she was called upon to interpret. Predominantly she read Russian since it was one of the official languages of the Assembly—not only the yawningly boring communiqués and the officially issued booklets, but daily *Izvestia* and *Pravda*. Which was where she read about Orlov's election.

That possibility had never entered any of their conversations. They had expected his United Nations posting—and the unquestionable successes he'd achieved there—to be adequately rewarded, but they'd never speculated beyond a deputy role within the Foreign Ministry. And now he'd been elevated way beyond that. Harriet—who was conscientious—read far more than the controlled Soviet newspapers; she scoured English as well as American publications also. So she'd seen the speculation about Serada and the Politburo jostling and knew from her own interpretation of Soviet politics that there was definitely a power struggle going on. A power struggle into which her beloved, adored Pietr had unexpectedly been thrust.

So what difference did it make? He loved her. She was sure he loved her. But he wasn't in New York any more. He was in Moscow at the very center of things, and his election could only mean that he'd been picked out to go even higher. And he was an ambitious man, although he denied it. Harriet had never been able to convince herself that if everything worked out as they planned, the greatest agony for Orlov would not be that he had abandoned his country and Natalia, but that he had abandoned his ambitions. Would it be as easy for him to choose now as he'd said it was months ago? Months ago he hadn't realized the opportunities with which he would be presented. Or seen Natalia. Harriet believed his argument for going back—loved him the more for it—but didn't the fact that he'd insisted on returning to officially divorce and distance himself from the woman to spare her any retribution mean that he still loved her? Or felt strongly for her at least.

Harriet had taken the apartment specifically for its convenience to the United Nations. A tightly coiffeured, tightly suited career woman, she emerged promptly at ten, as she did every morning when she was on day duty, and began walking down the avenue, another habit. Was she prepared to give everything up? she asked herself. They'd tried to imagine that as they'd tried to imagine the parting, but were either of them prepared for an existence as official criminals, hiding under assumed names and supposedly guarded by strangers? She was, decided Harriet. She knew it wouldn't be anything like she had thought; being apart wasn't anything like she had thought, but she was prepared to go through with it, no matter how bad it became. She turned at Forty-second Street. But was Pietr? If only she *knew*!

Harriet reached the top of the incline, where she was able to see the green-glassed skyscraper of the United Nations jutting upward from beside the East River. What about the plans they'd made to establish contact, giggling at the theatricality of everything and not really sure it would work? Only in the most extreme and dire emergency, she remembered. This wasn't an extreme and dire emergency. This was simply Harriet Johnson, not having properly prepared herself and now making monsters out of shadows.

Harriet showed her identification at the security check and walked into the familiar building. If only, she thought, things didn't seem so damned difficult.

Which was precisely the reflection of Pietr Orlov, sixty-five hundred miles away in Moscow. Natalia appeared resigned to the divorce—reluctantly agreeable even—and the guilt was lessening, but everything else was becoming a nightmare. Every week, every day, he was being drawn deeper and deeper into the inner workings of the government.

Realistically Orlov knew it would make his acceptance easier in the West when he chose the moment, but his reputation in the United Nations would have been sufficient for that. More painfully he recognized what it would mean to Yuri Sevin when that moment came. It was becoming accepted by others now that Sevin regarded the grooming and eventual election of his protégé as his final achievement, the triumphant swan song of one of the last of the true Bolsheviks. And Yuri Sevin was a true Bolshevik, reflected Orlov, another guilt growing. The man had embraced the Revolution, believing in the true philosophy of Marx and Trotsky and Lenin—and then watched Lenin and Stalin and Khrushchev and Brezhnev and Andropov enact the philosophy practiced by the czars, the right of the select elite to rule.

Orlov knew without conceit that Sevin saw him as someone who might, after far too long, initiate a change. Since his return he and Sevin had had innumerable discussions, sweeping debates and arguments deep into many nights. Sevin, a pragmatic realist after so many years of disappointments, didn't expect that change to be anything but initiated and for others to follow. But Orlov knew that a major river eventually changes course because of the first small erosion of the existing banks.

Already Sevin's influence had maneuvered him onto two committees, one the prestigious, and reputation-making, central planning body. And already—always—there was the preparation, the rehearsal and the advice, the influential members identified, the fading ones pointed out, the recommended stances to take and the positions to avoid. Orlov felt like a puppet, his arms and legs and head tethered so that he jerked and twisted when someone else pulled the strings. He had to cut those strings soon. He had to cut them and escape before everything engulfed him.

There had been a committee meeting in the morning, where he had recited his lines and backed those he should have backed, and in the afternoon he tried to concentrate on a policy paper on the agricultural difficulties that were going to bring down Serada. Orlov knew it was the most pressing difficulty of the moment, and while whole committees of agronomists and experts were trying to evolve fresh approaches, his appointment should have gone to someone more senior and more experienced. Sevin again, he thought.

His contact with the man had become predictable summonses most evenings, about which he was ambivalent; while the situation enmeshed him deeper and deeper in things of which he wanted no knowledge, it created reasons to delay his return to the tense unnaturalness of life with Natalia.

The expected call came that evening, and Orlov made his accustomed way through the corridors to the old man's office, recognized now by the secretaries and attendants. They'd gossip, Orlov knew; had already done so.

Sevin greeted him with a self-satisfied smile. "The decision has been made," he proclaimed.

"When?" asked Orlov.

"This afternoon."

"Is there to be an announcement?"

Sevin nodded. "Within the week. It will state that Serada has been replaced, to be succeeded by Chebrakin."

Orlov frowned. "What about ill health?"

"No," said Sevin. "Just that."

"Publicly disgraced, like Khrushchev," remembered Orlov.

"He doesn't deserve anything more," said Sevin. Impatiently he brought his hands together in a tiny clapping gesture. "But Serada and his fate aren't important, not any more. What's important is you and the next two or three years."

"Yes," said Orlov.

"How's the agricultural policy-shaping?"

"It's going to take a long time," hedged Orlov. "This time it has to be right."

"Exactly!" said Sevin, like someone seizing the truth. "It has to be right and it has to be *seen* to be right. It's going to be the first step for you, Pietr."

But not in the direction I want to walk, thought Orlov.

Orlov had done nothing about finding another place to live, accepting the difficulty that it created between himself and Natalia. Although the whole purpose of returning was to spare her later, he did not want to draw any attention to himself, and trying to get separate accommodation would have created curiosity. The guards and attendants and secretaries by whom he was now surrounded had other functions than to make his life easier, Orlov knew.

He and Natalia had settled into a formal existence, like acquaintances temporarily beneath the same roof but knowing it would be for only a limited period. They were considerate to each other in the way of acquaintances, neither irritated nor pleased by anything the other did.

But they were very conscious of one another. Immediately Orlov entered the apartment, late because the discussion with Sevin had turned into a detailed examination of the agricultural options, Orlov was aware of a difference in Natalia's demeanor.

"I've been waiting," she said. "Waiting to see if you would change your mind. I still love you, you know."

"No," said Orlov tightly. "I haven't changed my mind."

"Then to go on like this is pointless, isn't it? We might as well get the divorce."

"Yes," he agreed. He'd imagined feeling relief at the agreement, pleasure in fact at what it meant for himself and Harriet. Instead he felt a deep sadness.

"Will you make the arrangements?"

"Yes," said Orlov. He looked around the apartment. "You'll have this, of course."

"Thank you."

"It shouldn't be difficult," he told her.

"Accepting it but not understanding why is going to be difficult," she said.

CHAPTER TWENTY

The letter from her mother was as sterile as all the others, about as fascinating as a report of a meeting of the Mothers' Union. In fact, her mother's appointment as the secretary of the Union was the highlight of the letter. Ann guessed that her mother would have written the Mother's Union report first and put more effort into it. Her father sent his usual regards. What would he have sent if he knew what she had done? Maybe he wouldn't have been surprised. He'd called her a whore when he learned of her involvement with Franklin. Other words too. Slut was one. She hadn't felt like a whore or a slut then. She'd felt like someone who'd fallen in love with a married man—despite trying not to—and wanted the understanding she felt she deserved but which they had been unable to provide.

Had she proven herself to be a whore and a slut now? She didn't feel like either, any more than she had the first time. She felt ashamed and she wished it hadn't happened, but it had and so she had to face it. Face what, exactly? All right, she'd cheated. She'd had too much to drink, and it had been a beautiful, wonderful evening, and she'd let go emotions she should have kept in rein. That didn't make her a whore. Or a slut. It made her a stupid woman who should have known better—about all of it—but who hadn't. A stupid woman who'd made a mistake. Surely the important thing—the adult thing—was recognizing it for what it was. A mistake. And nothing else.

But was it nothing else? Ann tried to analyze it dispassionately, which was ridiculous since passion was what it was all about. Now it was important to get it all in the proper perspective. What had happened with Jeremy Brinkman hadn't in any way affected her love for her husband. The opposite, in fact. It made her realize just how much she *did* love him. No danger then. No reason for making a bitterly regretted mistake into anything more important than it was.

What about Jeremy though? Of course she didn't love him. How could she? He was charming and made her laugh the way Eddie used to, and he was unquestionably more socially able than Eddie, and if she were to be honest, in bed he was. . . . Ann jarred to a stop. Of course she didn't love him, she thought again. You didn't fall in love after sleeping with someone once. There had to be other feelings, the feelings she had for Eddie and certainly not for Jeremy. Christ, why couldn't she have stayed inside the fairy story? Fairy stories always had nice endings, with everyone living happily ever after. She'd shared the fairy story with the wrong man, she thought, coming out of the fantasy.

How was it for Eddie in Washington? The boy's trouble would have drawn him and Ruth together; things like that always did. But together as what? Adjusted, accepting former husband and wife; friends, in fact? Or a couple who realized that they had made a mistake. Mistakes, after all, weren't difficult to make. That wasn't fair, Ann recognized. She was creating a scenario like a cheap television soap opera and imagining situations she had no reason to believe in simply to assuage her own feelings.

She jumped at the sound of the telephone, staring at it as though she were frightened and not answering for several moments.

"I was just going to ring off. I didn't think you were in."

Ann felt a thrill of excitement at Brinkman's voice. Was that what it was about? she wondered. Had she done it for excitement, for just a moment in which to lift herself from the unexciting awfulness of Moscow? A slut's attitude, she thought. She said, "Hello."

"How are you?"

"Okay."

"Sure?"

"Sure."

"What are you doing?"

"Nothing much. Nothing at all, in fact. Just sitting here, thinking."

"What about?"

"I would have thought that was obvious."

"Sorry," he said. "Stupid question."

"What are you doing?" This wasn't the right sort of conversation, Ann thought. This was the inconsequential, almost intimate, talk of two people who didn't recognize they'd made any mistake at all.

"Nothing much," he said. "Just sitting and thinking."

"Oh."

"Sorry I phoned?"

Ann recognized the chance. It had happened because they'd allowed things to drift, and things that were allowed to drift ended up on the rocks. This was the moment to talk about it—why not, it *had* happened and they were adults, not children—and label it for what it was and try, as best they could, to forget it had ever happened. She said, "No, I'm not sorry you phoned."

"Have you eaten?"

"I'm not hungry." What a hell of a resistance, she thought.

"If this were Cambridge, we could go out for a drink," he said. "Remember the wine bar opposite Kings?"

"Very well," said Ann. A million years and a million happenings ago.

"I got a new shipment of books today," he said. "There's an Anthony Burgess and a couple I haven't read by Paul Scott. And Updike's latest."

"Maybe I could borrow something when you've finished?"

"I can't read them all at once."

Were they adults? This was kids' stuff, first-kiss-and-fumble stuff, she thought. "Why not come on over?" she suggested.

"You sure?"

No, she thought. She wasn't sure about anything except perhaps that she was out of her mind. "Why not?"

He must have been waiting for her invitation because he arrived within fifteen minutes, with no indication of any hurried preparation. He'd made an effort at the pretense though, bringing a book. Updike, she saw. She would have preferred Burgess. "Thanks," she said.

"That's all right."

They stood facing each other in the short corridor leading into the living room. He went to kiss her but abruptly she evaded, presenting only her cheek. He hesitated and then finished, his lips briefly touching her. She backed away and then turned, going into the room. "I started without you," she said, indicating the glass. It was vodka, and already her glass was half empty. She'd had a sudden need for courage.

"The same," he said.

He sat on the couch, one very much like that in his apartment. Ann began heading toward a chair and then decided that was ridiculous and sat down beside him.

"What were the thoughts?" he asked.

"I don't understand."

"When I phoned, you said you'd just been sitting here thinking."

"And you agreed it was a stupid question."

"Sorry?"

"Of course I'm sorry! Aren't you?"

"I don't think so."

"You haven't as much to be sorry about."

"I don't think I would be even if I had."

"That's stupid too," she said. "It's also the most appalling syntax I've ever heard."

He put his arm along the back of the couch, the way he had before, but this time he played his finger through a coil of her hair.

"Don't," she said, but she pulled away only fractionally. Determinedly she added, "It was a mistake."

"Was it?"

"Of course it was," she said. "Please don't be so difficult."

"I'm not trying to be difficult."

"Well, you are. It was a mistake and I think we should regard it as such."

"Okay," he said.

"Just that? Okay?"

"What else do you expect me to say?"

"That you're sorry."

"I said I didn't think I was. Maybe it was my bad syntax."

"It's not a joke!"

"I'm not joking."

"Do you realize what we've done?"

"Is it a capital offense?"

"Yes," she came back at once. "In some countries it is."

"Only if you get caught."

"We should recognize it as the mistake it was," Ann set out again, positively. "Recognize it and then try to forget about it."

"Now you're being stupid."

"Why?"

"We're not going to be able to forget about it, are we?"

"We're going to have to," she insisted.

"Put our heads in the sand and wait until it goes away?"

"Stop treating it as a joke; as if it weren't important!"

He teased her hair again and this time she didn't pull away. "Jokes are forgotten," he said. "You're the one making it important."

"Wasn't it, to you?"

"Yes," he said.

It was like wandering in a desert, thought Ann desperately; they'd lost direction and were coming back upon themselves. "What are we going to do?" she asked pleadingly.

Instead of replying, Brinkman put his hand behind her head and drew her to him. There wasn't the fumbling of the first time. They kissed and then Brinkman stood, pulling her up, not wanting the clumsiness of the couch. The thought of making love to somebody else in Eddie's own bed halted her momentarily at the point of entering the bedroom and then she went on, recognizing the hesitation as hypocrisy. If she was going to do it, did where matter? The betrayal was just as great.

Their lovemaking was better than before because they were a little more used to each other and Brinkman didn't feel as inadequate as he had then. When he finally stopped, exhausted, he said, "You're the most incredible woman I've ever known."

"Don't you think I'm a whore?"

"What!"

"A whore."

"Of course I don't think you're a whore."

"What then?"

Brinkman thought a long time before replying, wanting to get it right. "I think you're very lonely. I think you're very unhappy. I think you're looking for something you haven't got; maybe can't have. I think you are very beautiful. And I think you are a fantastic lover."

The remark about wanting something she couldn't have didn't refer to a baby, thought Ann; there was no way he could have known her feelings on that. Unless Eddie had told him, and she didn't think that was likely. "What about you?" she asked.

"I think we should stop trying to follow Freud and analyzing everything," he said.

"So it's a casual fuck?"

"No," replied Brinkman, "it isn't a casual fuck. And it isn't *Romeo and Juliet* either. What's wrong with you?"

"Thanks," she said. "For being honest."

"Wasn't that what you were insisting upon?"

"Oh, Christ," she said hopelessly. "I don't know what I want."

The telephone sounded from the other room, startling them. Ann hesitated and then got up, walking naked from the room, conscious that he was watching her. She had to raise her voice and so Brinkman knew who it was, and because he could hear her side of the conversation, he knew too what it was about before she came back into the bedroom.

"It was Eddie," she said unnecessarily. "He's coming home."

Whore, she thought. Whore and slut.

Orlov felt relief in initiating the divorce. From the casual, almost dismissive attitude of the officials it was obviously not going to be difficult, and at last he seemed to be doing something positive, making the moves he'd come back to Moscow to make. Now that the divorce was underway—promised quickly—there were other moves to make. His new party status, with so many people in constant attendance, was going to make everything more difficult than he had anticipated. He'd needed an embassy reception as a cover for the approach . . . so maybe the status had a balancing advantage after all. When, he wondered, was the next function at the American Embassy? And how easy would it be for him to attend? It didn't matter. Whatever the difficulties, he'd overcome them. He wished he were able to let Harriet know.

CHAPTER TWENTY-ONE

In the end Franklin had been reluctant to leave Washington. He thought he had allowed himself enough time but then decided he hadn't. The day before his departure, after he'd confirmed his return reservation to Moscow, he fleetingly considered asking Hubble for a further extension. But only fleetingly. He'd won his concessions and he intended to invoke them—every one of them—if and when it pleased him. And there wasn't anything left undone; it was just that he enjoyed Washington.

The sessions with the counselors had taken all day because he wouldn't be conveniently on the end of a telephone like the other parents. The counselors arranged interviews for him at the rehabilitation center and he went there with Paul; they ran through the schedule and Franklin was impressed. With Erickson, Franklin saw the school principal to satisfy himself that there was no need for the boy's school grades to suffer, and he left convinced that they wouldn't. He didn't know what social work the boy would be required to do; that had to be coordinated into the drug program and school, but Franklin had sufficient confidence now in both Erickson and Kemp—and in their knowing how he felt—to leave that to them. He was confident too that by the time Paul finished with school work and the drug program and whatever social-work requirements were imposed, the kid would be so bushed he wouldn't be able to get into trouble if he wanted to.

He involved himself with the boys to the exclusion of everything else, taking in an Orioles game, boating on the Potomac, going to movies and eating at McDonald's, setting himself up in competition the following night, grilling the hamburgers over their own barbecue and being declared the winner. Ruth passed on the Orioles game but joined in with everything else they did.

He kept the last night to themselves, but the night before that he met Charlie Rogers. He thought Ruth might want him to and there was no reason why he shouldn't, after all. Franklin guessed Rogers was about five years younger than he was, maybe even younger, an open-faced, easily smiling man. Franklin liked him. There was the understandable uncertainty at first, which Franklin worked hard to dispel, the smiles and the laughs just a little too anxious. Rogers had served in Vietnam—although later than Franklin—which gave them something in common. Rogers talked about the airport—he worked in the control tower at National—but didn't ask what Franklin did in Moscow, so Franklin guessed that Ruth had told him. So what the hell? The usual explanation—"working for the government" —was so well understood in Washington that it was like wearing a sign on your forehead; a sign like the one at Langley.

It was as difficult for the boys to relax as it was for Rogers but Franklin insisted that they all eat together—cooking out again because it was less formal—feeling it important that Paul and John saw there was no tension. After the kids went to bed, while Ruth was still with them, Rogers said he hoped Franklin didn't consider he was presumptuous but with Franklin away so much, he was willing to do anything and everything he could to help Paul. Franklin said he appreciated the offer but he thought he'd seen everyone and done everything necessary.

When Rogers got up to leave, Franklin remained discreetly in the living room, letting Ruth see him off, and when she came back, he said Charlie was a terrific guy and Ruth said she thought so too.

Ruth and the boys came with him out to Dulles, which had seemed a good idea at the house. Franklin wasn't so sure when they got to the airport. He bought them Coke in the cocktail bar, from which they could see something of the aircraft, and forced the conversation. He told Paul to keep out of trouble now, you hear, and Paul said he would. He told them that as soon as he returned he'd establish his schedule then and liaise with the school principal and the counselors and the drug program organizers about a Moscow trip, and when they went down the concourse to look at the shops, Franklin made Ruth promise, needlessly, that she'd get in touch with him the moment she didn't think things were going right.

At the actual moment of departure, when the final calls were being made for the flight, Franklin decided he'd swept away any barriers between them by the way Paul and John clung to him as though they were physically trying to hold him back, John's tears wet against his cheek and Paul trying hard not to break up too. He kissed Ruth as well, and she held him tighter than Franklin had expected, saying "Thanks again" and seeming to have the same difficulty as Paul.

After he'd had his drink and refused the earphones for the in-flight movie, Franklin put the seat back and considered the visit. Good, he decided. Better, upon analysis, than he could have expected. He'd done everything he could, and the court had done everything it could, and he was sure the counselors and everyone else were going to do everything they could. And most important of all—no, not *most* important, equally important—he'd come to know his sons again. .

A lot achieved, but still not all. Getting Ann together with the boys wouldn't be a problem, providing the kids didn't make it one. And he thought he'd crossed sufficient bridges on this trip to make that unlikely. Persuading her to understand the extension in Moscow might be more difficult. He'd have to explain it carefully, setting out all the advantages. And when the time came, he decided, he'd take a Washington posting. Ann would still have a say—he'd determined that already—but he'd make it very clear what he wanted.

Franklin slept better on the return trip than on the outward journey. He changed again at Amsterdam, and remembering the omission of the last time, he bought Ann perfume and a diminutive gold cross and chain in the duty-free shop. Still with time to spare before the Moscow connection, he bought her a watch too, inexpensive but quite stylish, which she could interchange with the one she already had and throw away without any qualms when it went wrong.

It was late afternoon before Franklin got into Sheremet-yevo, feeling tired. His customary dislike of flying, he decided. He called Ann from the airport and frowned at her unusual quietness, guessing the reason and apologizing for being away so long. She said it was all right and that she was looking forward to his getting home.

The apartment looked as nice as it always did and Ann looked as beautiful as she always did. She kissed him anxiously and held him tightly, and Franklin thought maybe he'd misconstrued the telephone conversation. She'd gone to the trouble of welcome-home champagne and after they opened it, he made a little performance of giving her the gifts. He would have expected her to show more enthusiasm than she did, but he was apprehensive of making the announcement now that the moment had come and decided against reading too much into small things.

Ann had wondered what her feeling would be. Now, at the actual moment of confrontation, she realized it was embarrassment. Deep, numbing embarrassment. Did whores feel embarrassed? Or was it something they got used to with practice? It made it difficult for her to react properly to the gifts—which actually increased the feeling—but she tried, dabbing on the perfume and turning to let him put the necklace around her throat, and replacing her existing watch with the new one, assuring him it was lovely.

She was naturally—and sincerely—interested, so she asked him about Paul, but there was a personal reason too; she wanted him to talk rather than her having to respond to a lot of questions about what she had been doing. It took him a long time to tell her and she was grateful. Franklin went into every detail and confessed the new awareness of his own failings and how he believed they had contributed to what had happened. When he set out the promises and the resolutions to stay closer to the boys and to have them here in Moscow, she took his hand—her reluctance until now had been her own embarrassment, not any hesitation at physical contact—and said she'd do everything she could to make it work, as he'd always known she would.

"I went to Langley a couple of times," he said at last.

"I thought you would."

"Talked about a lot of things."

"Like what?" she asked, suddenly even more attentive.

"They've asked me to stay on."

"They've what?" The question was asked quietly, the voice neutral, as though she thought she'd misheard.

"Stay on after the normal three years," said Franklin. He knew he hadn't done it right and so he hurried on, enumerating the concessions, wanting her to see how much to their advantage it would be.

"You mean you've already agreed?" The outrage was there now, the anger rising.

"They wanted a decision on the spot."

"Without even discussing it with me? Asking me how I felt?"

"That wasn't possible; you know that."

"And you know how I feel about this place! How I hate and loathe it."

"Because you haven't given it a chance."

"I've given it two years!" she shouted. "Two years that have been like a damn prison sentence."

"What's the matter with you?" Franklin hadn't anticipated this sort of tirade.

Ann was angry—furious—but mixed up in the emotion was her own guilt and embarrassment and feeling of being a whore. Being able to shout at him as though everything were his fault slightly lessened it all. Only very slightly.

"What sort of question is that?" she asked, in more control. "You know damned well how I hate it here. How I've always hated it. How I've counting off the days and the weeks and the months like a prison sentence, and hardly been able to wait until the time was up and we could be released. . . . " She laughed, a jeering sound. "That was actually the first word that came into my head, believe me," she said. "Released."

Franklin sat silent under the onslaught. He *had* misunderstood. He'd had some idea of her unhappiness but had not guessed that it was as bad as this. Not the obvious bulging-eyed, nostril-flared fury. Or had he? Hadn't he known it all along and chosen to ignore or minimize it? Wasn't it another cop-out as it had been with the boys, a refusal to let anything interfere with what he, Eddie Franklin, ultimately wanted to happen?

"It might not be any longer than three years," he said weakly. "You know the uncertainty that exists here. That's *why* they want me to stay. If the leadership is settled, we'd hold the aces and the kings. . . ." Abandoning his private resolution, he said, "And you get to choose. Wherever you want, we'll go."

"Christ!" said Ann, striding around the room. "I can't believe it! I just can't believe it! What if everything *isn't* settled? We could be stuck here for years!"

"No," said Franklin. "I made that clear. It's not an open ticket."

She stopped abruptly in front of him, staring down. "Okay," she said. "So how long? How long if it's not an open ticket?"

"Not more than another three years," promised Franklin, the first figure that came into his head.

"Three years!" echoed Ann, the outrage returning. "You

mean you expect me to stay here for another three lousy years?''

"No," said Franklin, his temper finally giving way. "I don't expect you to stay here for another three lousy years. If Moscow and your dislike of it—okay, your hatred of it—is the biggest thing in your life, I don't expect you to stay.''

His reaction quieted her at once, the thrust striking the rawest and most exposed nerve. She felt her face burn red and hoped Franklin would believe it was in anger. "You telling me to get out?" she demanded.

"No," he answered. "And you know I'm not. I love you and I don't want you to go. It's for you to decide whether you love me enough to stay.''

He sat motionless, waiting. For several moments she stared down at him, and then she burst into tears.

Brinkman responded at once to Franklin's invitation, knowing of course that the American wanted an update on anything that had happened while he'd been away and hoping he might get a lead to what Franklin had been doing by the man's questions. They met at the American Embassy, at their usual table in the cafeteria. Brinkman felt the briefest spurt of embarrassment at the moment of shaking hands, but almost at once it disappeared. Private life was private life, and this was business and quite separate. If that made him a bastard—if cuckolding Franklin made him a bastard—then okay, he was a bastard. Successful men often were.

There was the customary shadow-boxing, the inconsequential small talk, and then Franklin said, ''May be staying here longer than I planned.'' He was realist enough to know he wouldn't get anything unless he gave.

"What?" said Brinkman.

"Been asked to extend. Feeling is that the current leadership uncertainty makes this an important place to be."

Bollocks, thought Brinkman. They'd discussed the leadership a dozen times. Franklin's disclosure about extending meant he *was* onto something, but he was bloody sure it wasn't something as unfocused as leadership interpretation. They'd interpreted that already, both of them. Was his suspicion correct? Did Franklin have a source, buried deep? "For how long?"

"No specified time."

How would Ann react to that? Brinkman suddenly wondered. Private, he thought, quickly shutting the door. Deciding he wouldn't get anything by direct questioning, he thought of offering something that had occurred— professionally—while the American had been away. Chebrakin, he said, had appeared publicly ahead of Serada in a photograph of the Central Committee—which confirmed what they already guessed—and there had been increasing criticism in *Pravda* of food shortages, which was a rare admission but an indication that someone was soon to be blamed for them.

"Not much news then," commented Franklin.

"Not really," conceded Brinkman. "Still not the slightest indication of what's happening beyond Chebrakin."

"That's the kicker," said Franklin. "That's what everybody wants to know."

And Franklin did know, decided Brinkman. Somehow— he didn't know how—Franklin had a lead on what the other moves were and that's why he'd been recalled to Washington. But that wouldn't have been enough to recall him. That could have been covered in a normal cable. Something about the leadership but important enough for him to go back to Washington personally to discuss it. But *what*? What in the name of Christ was it?

"Thanks, incidentally, for looking after Ann while I was away," said Franklin.

Brinkman met the American's gaze across the table. "I enjoyed doing it," he said easily.

Two days later the official announcement was made of Serada's removal from the Politburo and leadership of the Soviet Union. Anatoli Chebrakin was named successor.

Things were moving, decided Brinkman: moving away from him.

CHAPTER TWENTY-TWO

Ann telephoned Brinkman at the embassy, which she hadn't done before, and he was momentarily irritated because it blurred the divisions he'd created in his mind. And then he accepted the fact that divisions were an infantile effort on his part to ease his conscience. There couldn't be any divide.

"I must see you," she announced.

"That's not going to be easy any more, is it?"

"Do you know what's happened?"

"Yes," said Brinkman. "And we shouldn't be talking on an open line."

"Damn an open line!"

"I'll try to think of something."

"I want to see you *now*! We had the most terrible row."

People who had terrible rows sometimes said things they

didn't mean to say. . . . It was still only eleven o'clock. "No chance of Eddie coming home to lunch?"

"He never does. He'd phone if he decided to."

"I'll drop by."

"Thank you, darling. There isn't anybody else."

As Brinkman drove back to the compound, he decided that his initial reaction to her call had been the right one. Now that Franklin was back in Moscow, it wasn't going to be easy to see Ann any more. It would be actual madness. Did he want to anyway? Although he'd disguised it better than she, Brinkman had been as bewildered and confused as Ann by what had happened after the Bolshoi and made the same resolutions about forgetting mistakes. So why had it been he who made the first approach afterward? He'd told her it wasn't a casual fuck and that it wasn't *Romeo and Juliet* either. So okay, what was it? A personal involvement hadn't featured in his plans for Moscow. True, he'd imagined affairs, pleasant conclusions to pleasant evenings—which was how this had started, he remembered—but he hadn't wanted a telephone-at-work, see-me-at-once situation. And not with the wife of a man at the American Embassy doing the same job as he was. So what was he doing driving across Moscow for a lunch-time assignation? It wasn't an assignation, he thought in immediate correction. And there *was* a purpose—what if Franklin had inadvertently revealed something to Ann during their argument? Which was an excuse for what? Brinkman couldn't decide, and Brinkman didn't like being unable to decide anything, certainly not anything about himself.

There was no hesitation any more. As soon as she let him into the apartment, Ann clung to him and kissed him, and Brinkman held her and kissed her back, realizing he was even more undecided than ever.

"When did he tell you?" she asked.

"We had lunch at the embassy."

"Can you believe it?"

"Professionally, yes," said Brinkman. He was trying to be fair as well as guide the conversation.

"But he *knew* how I felt!"

"It's a very important time here just now," said Brinkman, still steering.

"That's all I bloody well hear! I couldn't give a damn about how important situations are here at the moment. I came here willingly because I knew how much it mattered to Eddie's career, and I've endured it for the same reason. To be with him I've been virtually cut off by my family, and I abandoned all my friends, and until now I've tried not to complain too much. . . ." Ann held up her hand, a physical correction. "I let him know, clearly enough. But I tried not to go on about it like some spoiled brat. And all right, I know that's how I might sound now to you and to him. But we could have discussed it! Didn't I deserve that at least?"

Brinkman supposed she did. Who had let whom down? She appeared to have excised what had happened between them while Franklin was away. Maybe he wasn't the only one to try to create divisions. "It wouldn't have been easy, talking on the telephone from Washington, would it?"

"Why not? What's all this crap about open lines and secure lines? We wouldn't have been talking about anything secret. We'd have been talking about our future. And why was it so important to get a decision there and then? Why couldn't he have come back here to Moscow so we could have talked it through?"

No reason at all, conceded Brinkman. Except that wasn't how these things were done. He wouldn't be able to make her understand. It was time to try to get the conversation back on course again. He asked, "How long is the extension?"

She snorted. "He says no longer than three years but I don't believe him. Or that it could be sooner; maybe that we'd be able to keep to the original schedule if the leadership thing is sorted out."

Where the hell was a lead he could understand and follow? He said, "So you could be getting upset about nothing?"

"Nothing?"

"Chebrakin has been declared the new leader," he said.

She smiled up at him, in sudden hope. "So it is sorted out?"

"What does Eddie say?" he asked, directly and hopefully.

"We haven't talked about it. We haven't talked about anything much since he came back," she confessed.

Seeing a lead, Brinkman said, "Knowing—as he does now—how you feel, I would have thought he would have said something if everything had been solved by Chebrakin's election."

"So would I," she agreed.

Come on! thought Brinkman. He said, "Hasn't he?"

"No," she retorted shortly.

So his conjecture in the embassy cafeteria had been right. Something was sufficiently important beyond Chebrakin to send Franklin back to Washington and likely to keep him here longer than his scheduled posting, as much as three years longer. Ann hadn't believed that limit, remembered Brinkman. Maybe longer then. It had been worth the risk, coming here today.

Greedily Brinkman said, "So it was a bad row?"

"Terrible!" she answered. "The worst ever."

"What did he say?" asked Brinkman.

Ann looked away. "That if I didn't like it, I could leave."

Not just important enough to go back to Washington for, but important enough to consider sacrificing his marriage for. Jesus! thought Brinkman. Trying for still more, he said, "People say things they don't mean during arguments."

Ann came to him once more and knowing her need, he reached out and held her. "Oh, darling," she said, "I'm so unsure of everything."

So am I, thought Brinkman. So am I.

Until now Orlov's deception of the old man had been unavoidable: Sevin led and Orlov had no alternative but to follow. Today the deception was going to have to become calculated and deliberate. Orlov had wanted to avoid it. He'd tried to think of every other way but there was none he could attempt without arousing curiosity. He entered Sevin's suite with the approach carefully prepared. There was the usual discussion on the agricultural project, and then when the conversation began to flag, Orlov said, "There's something I think you should know."

Sevin smiled at him, waiting.

"Natalia and I have decided to divorce," announced Orlov.

"I'm very sorry," said Sevin. "It's always a tragedy when these things happen."

Orlov knew that Sevin, a widower now, had been married for forty years. He said, "I thought you should know. Our friendship seems well recognized now and I didn't want to cause you any embarrassment." Orlov had no religion but he knew the books. Judas, he thought.

Sevin made an impatient, dismissive movement. "Divorce is one of the few things that don't cause problems."

"I just thought you should know," repeated Orlov. Coming to the moment of actual deceit, he said, "I realize how important it is for things to be seen to be proper by those who matter."

Sevin smiled again, taking the bait. "It is astonishing," he said, "how puerile things like positioning at conference tables in photographs are considered to matter by men who make decisions that can affect the entire world."

Orlov hesitated before the final move and then said, "Who will be attending the reception at the American Embassy?"

"It's important," said the old man. "First outing since Chebrakin's accession. Naturally Chebrakin doesn't plan to attend himself. Didenko is definitely going. I've been proposed but I think I'll decline. Zenin will go. Okulov too. There'll be others of course."

Orlov hadn't expected the advantage. Didenko was one of the men about whom there had already been speculation in the West before Chebrakin's appointment. He said, "There'll be a lot of concentration upon Didenko. There were forecasts that he had a better chance than Chebrakin this time."

Sevin frowned. "That's a good point," he said. "An extremely good point."

Delicately, not wanting the line to break, Orlov asked, "Would it matter?"

"Positioning at tables and in photographs and at public functions are important." The old man stopped for a moment's further reflection, and then he said, "I think you should go."

"Me?" exclaimed Orlov as though the proposal surprised him.

"The first outing since Chebrakin's accession," repeated Sevin. "It might seem premature, but sides will be taken— contenders considered or dismissed as unimportant—as early as now. And, Pietr?"

"Yes?"

"Don't make it obvious, but try to remain as close as possible to Didenko himself. Let's get the idea established now among the uncommitted on the Central Committee, and even within the Politburo, that there's an equality in stature between you."

What was he doing to this man, wondered Orlov, agonized. Despising himself, he said, "If you think it's important."

"Yes," insisted Sevin. "I think it's important."

CHAPTER TWENTY-THREE

They had not met together on any public occasion since Franklin's return from Washington, and Brinkman was glad. The telephone calls from Ann—he never called her because he could never know when Franklin would be at home—were quite frequent. Brinkman knew that Ann was glad too; neither was sure of how they would handle the moment. It had to happen, of course—and this evening it would. Brinkman was grateful it was going to be a large reception, crowded with people and distractions so that any awkwardness wouldn't be obvious.

Brinkman had to arrive earlier than he would have liked because it was an official affair, with protocol to be observed. He didn't see Franklin or Ann immediately. The first face he recognized was that of Wilcox, the British Head of Chancery. After a strained conversation about cricket, Brinkman moved on to the buffet table, although he was not hungry. He hadn't expected the number of people who were there. He'd been determined to attend because the guest list included at least eight members of the inner Soviet government, and if they accepted, he would observe them in close proximity, as during the visit of the British delegation, and watch them on parade for the first time after Chebrakin's election. He hadn't anticipated so many others would be as interested.

He heard a shout and smiled at the approach of the Harrisons. He'd returned their hospitality and accepted it again, without the enforced accompaniment of Sharon Berring the second time, and there'd been occasional encounters at official functions like this, but it hadn't yet become a positive friendship.

"Stranger!" accused Betty Harrison.

"Busy," said Brinkman. It was true after a fashion, he supposed. He and Ann had played games about Betty's reaction had she known. Playing one now, he said to her, "What's all the news?"

"Is there ever any news in Moscow?"

"If there is, you always know about it, Betty."

She gave a mew of feigned offense but Brinkman knew she was pleased at the acknowledgment. "I do hear that the wife of a certain someone at the Australian Embassy is becoming well known to the Moscow authorities for her liking of the local brew."

"Drinking is Australia's national sport," said Brinkman. To Harrison, Brinkman asked, "How are things in the wheat fields?"

The Canadian grinned. "Things seem to have gone quiet, don't they?"

"Tonight might be interesting," said Brinkman.

"I sometimes think you people would be better off reading tea leaves in cups," said Betty.

Harrison frowned, and Brinkman was surprised she had said it, innocuous though it was. Betty smiled over Brinkman's shoulder. "More strangers," she said, beckoning.

Brinkman turned. The Franklins were walking up to them. Because of the level of the reception—ambassadorial rank—dress was formal, and Franklin was wearing black tie. It was the first time Brinkman had seen the American in a dinner suit. He thought the man looked ill at ease. And he thought Ann looked stunning. She wore a black evening dress, one shoulder bared, with a single diamond clip the only jewelry apart from earrings. She had her hair up in a chignon, a style she hadn't adopted before. She smiled at them all, appearing quite controlled, and said "Hi."

"Hello," said Brinkman, relieved she wasn't finding it difficult. He searched for his own feelings and was surprised by them. He was jealous. He resented the proprietorial way Franklin cupped his wife's elbow and the man's closeness to her and everyone's acceptance that Ann belonged to him. Brinkman stopped, astonished at himself. What possible, conceivable, justifiable right did he have to feel jealous? Did he love her? He didn't know, not any more than he knew if Ann loved him. It was a word they avoided, just as they were avoiding actually looking at each other now.

Jealousy wasn't love; it was the coveting of something belonging to someone else. Did Ann belong to Franklin any more? It was another thing they avoided, but he thought he knew the answer. Franklin had offered her the way out—although Brinkman had no way of telling if the man had been serious—and Ann hadn't taken it. There wasn't a single furtive telephone call without some reference to how much she was going to hate staying on after the scheduled time. And there could be only one obvious inference from that.

Ann was talking animatedly to Betty, using the woman as he himself had tried to use her earlier, and Franklin was discussing something with Harrison. As a waiter passed, Brinkman said to Ann, "Can I get you a drink?" aware the moment he spoke that he was being overly solicitous and that Franklin was turning toward the waiter anyway. Committed, Brinkman said hurriedly, "Both of you," and Betty saved the moment by saying, "Always the perfect gentleman." Brinkman handed glasses to both of them, wondering if the flush he felt burning his face were obvious.

"I was just saying to Ann that we haven't seen nearly enough of each other."

"No, we haven't," agreed Brinkman, happy to be taken over by Betty.

"Things have been a bit disorganized, with Eddie being away," said Ann.

Soon, thought Brinkman, Betty Harrison was going to realize how steadfastly he and Ann were looking at her to avoid looking at each other.

"Well, he's back now," said Betty, taking over her role as social leader. "Let's make a definite date. Here! Now!"

"Not sure what I'm going to be doing in the next few weeks," said Brinkman too quickly. He certainly didn't think he could sustain an enclosed evening with only six or eight people present.

"Nonsense," rejected Betty. "Whatever is there to do in Moscow?"

"We'll talk on the telephone," said Brinkman, still retreating.

"Tomorrow," persisted the woman. "I'll fix things up with Ann and then we'll make contact with you." She turned brightly to the other men and said, "I'm fixing up a party."

Her husband, resigned, said, "Fine," and Franklin said, "That'll be swell."

It was becoming ridiculous, and if they didn't do something soon—right now—it would be obvious. To Ann he said, "There are more people here than I thought there would be," the only thing he could think of.

She looked at him finally, the rigid set of her face the single indication of difficulty. "You haven't been before," she said. "There usually are."

She risked a smile, quickly on and off. What the hell was there to talk about? he wondered. Taking the chance that his voice wouldn't carry in the hubbub, he said, "You look fabulous."

She blushed slightly and said, "Thank you."

"The Russians are late," said Harrison from his right. Brinkman turned away from Ann, snatching at the interruption.

"Maybe they're planning to make a big entrance," said Franklin.

"I would have thought they were assured that anyway," said Brinkman. He had to escape. He'd stayed with them long enough; his departure wouldn't look out of place. To the group generally he said, "I think I'll mingle," and moved away as he spoke so there couldn't be any delaying discussion with Betty about any damned dinner party. He couldn't think of an excuse, but he'd find one before she called tomorrow. He'd behaved like an idiot, Brinkman acknowledged. A stumbling, first-time out idiot. Betty Harrison was an irritating, constantly tittle-tattling nuisance, and she'd become that way by seeing what went on about her. Even so, he was less worried about Betty Harrison than he was about Franklin. The American was the acknowledged leader of the pack, and he'd become that way by seeing what went on around him too.

Brinkman tacked himself onto the edge of the group surrounding the British ambassador and was allowed to get away with the presumption because of Sir Oliver Brace's awareness of who his father was. He endured Wilcox and more cricket and then managed to buffer himself with the trade counselor who had helped him initiate the wheat success. Street, remembered Brinkman, with some difficulty. Street was a vague, wispy-haired man with a habit of letting his sentences drift away as though he had suddenly lost conviction of the views he had first started to express. Brinkman small-talked, only half-concentrating, alert for the Russian arrival and alert too for any movement that might bring him close again to the Franklins.

He'd been close enough for one night.

There was the briefest dip in the level of sound when the Russians arrived, as though everyone had stopped talking at the same time to draw breath. The ambassador's group was near the main entrance and Brinkman had the opportunity of studying the Russians all together, while they were being greeted by the American ambassador and senior officials, before they had time to disperse.

Vasili Didenko led, the acknowledged leader, the redfaced, forceful man Brinkman remembered from the British parliamentary visit. The man marched rather than walked, and from the brief grimaces among the people to whom he was introduced, he appeared to have a hard handshake. Like

a projector throwing up holiday stills against a screen,
Brinkman ran through his mind the images of all the
people who had been pictured and identified during the
recent elections.

He got Leonid Zenin first, a frail, uncertain-looking
man. Then Okulov, whose first name he couldn't remember,
which annoyed him. Okulov was more assured than Zenin,
looking around him with an arrogance almost matching
Didenko's. Brinkman knew that Yevgeni Aistov had been
most recently attached to the Agricultural Ministry, so his
appearance clearly indicated he had survived any purge
and should therefore be recognized as an emerging strongman.
He had a full file for Maxwell in the morning, thought
Brinkman confidently. He blinked at the last man in the
line, immediately recognizing him from the parliamentary
trip. Pietr Orlov was as imposing as he'd appeared then,
the impeccable tailoring that Brinkman had admired obvious again here. He was the last in the Soviet party, just
coming to the end of the official receiving line. Maybe a
fuller file than he had imagined, thought Brinkman.

Orlov's identification during the British visit had been
important because he was one of the youngest members
ever. But there had been two other young members—
Vladimir Isakov and Viktor Petrov, remembered Brinkman.
They weren't here. So why was Orlov? Why, with dozens
of other more senior figures available for an important
foreign embassy reception? Why a man so newly promoted
that he probably didn't yet know the names of all the
people with whom he was now daily sitting at meetings?

As Brinkman watched, the Russians formed themselves
into a group. Orlov was next to Didenko, a marked contrast to the red-faced Russian. Across the room Brinkman
saw Franklin gazing at the Russians too and wondered if

he had realized the significance of Orlov's presence. He remembered telling the Americans of the presence of all three newcomers at the English function. But unless Franklin had studied the photographs as intently as he had, and then backed up that study by being able to personally see the man, he might miss it. Doubtful, because Franklin was so good. Brinkman had always regarded himself in competition with the man, but he realized the competition was far greater now. It had always been silly to imagine divisions were possible anyway.

What other meaning could Orlov's appearance have than that he was much more important than the other two newly elected? And much more important than some who were there ahead of him. He watched intently, seeking any deference toward Orlov from the others in the party and trying to establish Didenko's attitude toward the man. He couldn't tell. There were some photographs being taken, and Brinkman realized miserably that they would help Franklin; the American would now find it easy to identify everyone in the group. Shit, he thought. After the photographs, Didenko remained talking to the American ambassador but the other Russians moved away, joining Sir Oliver in a loosely knit group, all socially ill at ease. Except for Orlov. The immaculate Russian edged away from all of them, engaging in almost immediate conversation. Irritably Brinkman saw that Henri Baton, the French resident, was part of the group.

Brinkman carried on a desultory conversation with the sentence-lapsing Street, using the man as a cover, trying to watch all the Russians at once. Other people had joined the fixed Soviet group and Didenko was moving toward them, so Brinkman decided to stay where he was. Orlov had continued on, apparently toward the Canadians. Didenko joined the other Soviets, nodding cursorily. Everyone politely stopped talking while the Russian and Sir Oliver made their exchanges. It was meaningless—cocktail party regulations—but Brinkman noted sourly that Didenko spoke good enough English not to need an interpreter. He had hoped it might have been necessary. With his own excellent Russian it might have been possible to pick up a tidbit between what was actually said and what was actually translated. Didenko left the group. Brinkman went too. He had regretted not being able to talk to Orlov during the parliamentary visit; he meant to make up for it now.

Easing himself through the crowd, Brinkman saw that Orlov was already in conversation with Franklin and the two appeared momentarily alone. He thrust on with more determination.

Had he not been concentrating so entirely, he would not have seen it. The two were against the wall at a point where an ornate curtain swept out in a flamboyant drape, obscuring them completely on two sides from everyone else in the room. Orlov had his back to the *salon*, restricting the view from the main body of the guests so that the only clear visibility was directly parallel with the wall—the direction from which Brinkman was approaching. Franklin's expression of surprise would have been too brief for anyone but Brinkman, as close and as intent as he was. And he saw the exchange, the briefest brushing of hands.

Brinkman was *sure* it had been an exchange. And with that conviction, all the others came tumbling in. He knew now what was important enough for Franklin to be recalled to Washington. He knew what was important enough for Franklin to regard his marriage as dispensable. He knew now why Franklin had extended, and knew too that he would go on extending, and why Ann had better reconcile herself to a lifetime in Moscow if she wanted to stay married to him. And he knew who Franklin's source was.

There was not the slightest sign of either being disconcerted by his arrival, the smooth professional diplomat and the smooth professional intelligence officer.

"I don't believe you've met the cultural attaché at the British Embassy, Mr. Jeremy Brinkman?"

"No," said Orlov. "I don't believe I've had the pleasure."

The envy surged through Brinkman, a physical sensation that actually made him feel weak so that his legs trembled briefly. He wanted Orlov! And if he couldn't have him, then neither would Franklin.

"You're late," challenged Ruth.

"I've just left the program, for God's sake!"

"Don't be truculent with me, Paul. Or evasive. You leave the program at five. Even if you don't pick up the five-ten metro, there's another at five-twenty. Mr. Erickson allowed for that. From the metro station it's a ten-minute walk. You're an hour late."

"He timed the whole journey?"

"Yes, Paul, he did. And it seems a good idea that he did, doesn't it?"

The boy stubbed his toe into the carpet, lower lip caught between his teeth.

"So okay," demanded his mother. "Where were you?"

"Got talking to some guys."

"What guys?"

"Just guys."

"What guys?" she repeated.

"Just guys," said Paul again, determinedly.

"It's not yet a month," said Ruth. "Not yet a month since you stood in court and heard what would happen if you did it again."

"I haven't done anything again!"

"So what were you doing?"

"Just talking. That's all. Just talking. Honest."

"I can't expect you to be honest any more, can I?"

"That's up to you."

"No, it's not up to me. It's up to you. That's been made perfectly clear by everyone; it's all up to you."

Paul had made a groove in the carpet and was worrying it into a wider gap, spreading the pile apart.

"Stop that!" shouted Ruth. "And stop being such a stupid little fool!"

"Just talking," insisted the boy.

"I'm going to call Mr. Erickson. And Mr. Kemp. And the program director. I'm going to tell them what happened and let them decide what to do."

"Give me a break, Mom!"

"That's exactly what I am trying to give you," said Ruth.

CHAPTER TWENTY-FOUR

Franklin left the apartment early the following morning—earlier than he ever had. He didn't care if Ann imagined in it some continuation of the coldness that had existed between them since his return from Washington. He didn't care about anything except reaching the secure-doored isolation of his office at the embassy. He needed the absolute solitude, without the slightest distraction or interruption, to assimilate what had happened at the reception the previous night. Just five words—words he had been convinced at first that he had misheard—which must have showed because Orlov had repeated them. "I would like to meet." And the paper slipped into his hand, the paper he had now spread before him on his desk. He stared down at it, willing the neat, sterile letters to tell him more.

"Kuntsevo. Fili Park. 1900. June 11." Today. Pietr Orlov, recently returned Plenipotentiary Ambassador for the U.S.S.R. at the United Nations, recently elected and youngest member of the central governing body, wanted to meet him at seven o'clock tonight at the last pier for the Moscow riverboats, where the vessels change for the trip farther north.

There were standard lectures about provocateur entrapment—not just for people like him but for all diplomatic staff—before any Moscow posting. But they weren't about anything like this. The entrapments were crude affairs by KGB groundmen. They didn't involve people like Pietr Orlov. It *had* to be genuine. Genuine what? That was an impossible speculation. He could absorb all the available file material and imagine half a dozen possibilities and still be a million miles from guessing right. He'd have to go. Unthinkable, of course, that he wouldn't, once he'd considered everything. He'd have to go to the pier and remain as inconspicuous as possible and let Orlov set the pace. If the Russian showed then, whatever it was, he would be involved in the most spectacular moment in his career.

He should tell Langley. It was common sense—apart from inviolate instructions—that he shouldn't try to climb a greasy pole like this without at least attempting to establish some form of safety net. Not that there was much they'd be able to do if it were a setup, inconceivable though that might be. But he was reluctant to contact Washington. It was so little and so inconclusive. Shaking up the beehive without knowing where the honey was. He postponed it, poring over the files. So little, he thought again. Married, no children, comparatively rapid rise through the diplomatic channel, culminating in the most recent election. Flat and empty, a *Who's Who* entry, except that a *Who's Who* entry gave hobbies and pastimes, and what he had in front of him didn't even provide that.

He had to contact Langley about other things that had happened last night, Franklin knew, coming back to his uncertainty. Aistov's appearance was important, after the crop disaster. The sort of thing he would have considered very important indeed, before Orlov. He wrote the message and encoded it and then sat where he was instead of taking it to the cipher room. This was stupid. No matter what the uproar when he shook the hive, he had to tell them. Not to do so for fear of making himself look a fool would be abandoning his expertise as an intelligence officer, and he prided himself on that expertise above all else.

An hour later he had the Orlov message transmitted and then sat waiting. The response came within another hour, which, considering the procedural channels at Langley, was practically at the speed of light. He responded patiently that he couldn't amplify because he had included everything in his first message. They asked for interpretation; he wrote that that was impossible, glad he'd thought it through before the request came. Langley said a special desk was being established inside the twenty-four-hour Watch Room and that he was to communicate immediately after the meeting took place. If it occurred. Langley ordered him to take all possible care and to avoid anything that might lead to an incident embarrassing the United States. Then, as an apparent afterthought, Hubble personally signed a message wishing him luck.

The two-way exchanges meant that he missed lunch, but Franklin was too excited to eat anyway. He telephoned Ann to say he would be home late, probably very late, and that she wasn't to wait up for him. She'd been in bed that morning when he'd left, so he asked her how she was and she said okay, and how was he, and he said okay, anxious to get off the telephone. She appeared to sense it and ended the conversation.

Franklin realized he would be behaving like an amateur if he didn't carry out a reconnaissance. He knew entrapments weren't set up instantly. They took planning. If he made a practice run early, he would be able to identify any preparation.

He made the complete trip, from start to finish, boarding at the pier in front of Kiev Station and staying out on deck near a bend in the rail, which meant he only had two directions in which to look for any surveillance. He'd taken more than the usual precautions on his way from the embassy to the river and didn't think he was being followed, but he could have been mistaken. The boat was full of tourists. Franklin decided that if it were to be a genuine meet, Orlov had chosen his protection well. He gazed at the upthrust colonnades and obelisks commemorating the Battle of Borodino as they passed under the Borodinsky Bridge, deciding it was the most attractive of the river crossing points; the buildings were too tall near the Kalininsky Bridge. He turned away, gazing instead across at the Krasnaya Presnya Park, using the movement to check everyone around him. He explored the long stretch of the river before the twist under the railway bridge to continue the search, and by the time they neared his destination, Franklin was sure he was clean. The factories along the last section were uniform and depressing, but Fili Park looked attractive.

Franklin let himself be carried off the ferry by the pressure of the people all around, detaching himself gradually at the end of the pier and staring about. Farther along he could see the larger boats waiting to take the vacationers north to the beaches at Plyazh. This was a junction, people and boats going in both directions, a pushing and shoving melée of a place. Good for an ambush as well as for an unobserved meeting. Franklin wandered with apparent aimlessness, in fact intent upon everything surrounding him. It was chaotic, but with the proper sort of chaos; there was no artifice, no people put on stage to play their part in a performance in which he was going to become a lead player.

There were refreshment stalls and snack bars, under cover and in open air. Franklin chose one in the open, where he could see without obstruction. Hungry at last, he ordered sausage and beer, eating unhurriedly, with time to kill. Around him Russians worked hard in their determination to relax, and Franklin thought that at this level it was difficult to understand why the Russians and the Americans each believed the other wanted to annihilate them. Okay, the fashions and the accents and the amusements were different—very different—but Franklin could see a similarity between this and Coney Island. Or the pier from which he'd taken the kids boating during his trip home. He wondered how Paul was shaping up under the program. Franklin had averaged a letter a week since he got back and hoped that whatever was going to happen tonight would not affect the regularity he'd established. He'd been lectured by both Kemp and Erickson on how essential it was for kids to have stability, for things to not suddenly start and just as suddenly end.

Franklin took another beer—just killing time—and left the stall with some still to spare before seven o'clock. Everything seemed to be normal, he determined, when he got back to Kuntsevo. He was *sure* of it. Where? he wondered, looking around. As well-chosen as it was, the pierhead was still a big area. It was ridiculous, his attempt-

ing to find Orlov, Franklin realized. Orlov would have to
find him. Near the ticket office there was a bench and
Franklin sat down on it, waiting. Back at Langley, station
staff would be bitching at having their nights screwed up
because some half-assed bigshot in Moscow imagined he
was onto something hot, he reflected. He wondered if his
wait and their hurried creation would all be a waste of
time.

No, realized Franklin.

Orlov came inquiringly through the crowd from the
just-arrived riverboat, staring first toward the refreshment
stalls and then, when he looked back, seeing the American.
There was no recognition. Orlov did not approach at once
but moved to his left, as though unsure in which direction
to continue, having left the first stage of his journey. A
signal, or caution? wondered Franklin. Orlov had dressed
down from his usual elegance, which showed thought, but
even in the sports jacket and slacks, he was noticeable
among the other travelers. The approach remained casual.
The man's control was good; if the approach were genuine,
he would be under enormous tension.

Orlov sat down on the bench, not directly beside the
American but with space between them. "Thank you for
coming," he said. He spoke looking out toward the river.

"Did you imagine I wouldn't?"

"I didn't know. I wasn't certain."

"You approached me," reminded Franklin. He still had
to be extremely careful.

"I want to go back," blurted Orlov.

"Back?"

"To America."

"You mean you want to defect, Mr. Orlov?" Franklin

spoke looking out toward the river too, hoping he was disguising his reaction as well as the Russian had covered his emotions at the moment of approach. He hadn't been wrong back at the embassy, he thought. Underestimating, in fact. This would be doubly the most spectacular moment of his career.

Orlov didn't respond at once, appearing unwilling to confirm the word. "I do not consider myself a traitor to my country," he said.

"The Soviet Union will consider you one."

Orlov was silent again for several moments and then he said, "I will be asked to cooperate? Provide information?"

Like you wouldn't believe, thought Franklin. He said, "If you want the United States government to assist you and provide you with protection, which will be necessary, it would expect cooperation in return."

"How much?" demanded Orlov.

Now it was Franklin's turn to hesitate. He'd never handled a defection before, but there were enough records. Usually, in their eagerness to escape, defectors fell over themselves to show what a good catch they'd be. Frequently they boasted an ability to provide information they didn't have. He said, "You can't expect me to know that."

"Considerable?" persisted Orlov.

"You are a man of substantial experience and prestige," hedged Franklin. "I would imagine my government would be extremely interested in having the benefit of that experience."

"I am not a traitor," repeated Orlov.

"My country would not consider you one," said Franklin. Liar, he thought. Defectors were always feted and rewarded and usually looked after and always—deep down—despised as well.

''Will it be possible?''

''Of course,'' said Franklin at once. More than doubly spectacular, in fact. If he got Orlov out, his own position in Moscow would be untenable. Which meant that he could leave—more important, that Ann could leave—right away. The coup Orlov's defection would mean for Langley would ensure that all the promises they'd made him would stand. He and Ann out before they were due and anything they chose, he thought.

''When? It must be soon,'' said Orlov.

Soon? Franklin chanced a sideways look and saw that the Russian was sweating. He was sweating too, he realized. ''I will have to contact Washington, of course. Let them know what has happened. I will make all the arrangements.''

''Good,'' said Orlov, the relief obvious. ''But soon.''

''I need to know more, Mr. Orlov.''

''More?''

''Why do you want to defect?''

Again the word caused the Russian difficulty. He said, ''It is a personal thing.''

What the hell did that mean? thought Franklin. He said, ''I'm afraid that if we're going to work together as closely as will be necessary to get you out of the country, there can't be anything personal.''

''I don't want her put under any pressure.''

Her? Surely Orlov wasn't thinking of abandoning everything for a woman! Would he for Ann? He'd abandoned his first marriage and two kids, he realized. He'd told her she could leave if she didn't like the idea of backing him in Moscow. Except that he hadn't meant it and had been terrified she might call his bluff. Franklin looked quickly at the Russian again. The man was supposed to be married, he remembered from the file.

"Who?" he said.

"There is someone in New York," said Orlov awkwardly.

"She'll need to be contacted," said Franklin. "Protected even."

"Not yet," insisted Orlov. "I don't want her alarmed until everything is settled and confirmed."

Could he give such an agreement? Langley was going to go ape-shit over this, and he couldn't predict what promises they'd keep. He asked, "Is that a condition?"

"Yes," said Orlov at once.

"Do you have any others?" asked the American, avoiding the commitment.

The question seemed to surprise Orlov. "Just to be taken safely out," he said.

Despite what Orlov had achieved and the echelon he'd reached, Franklin thought, he was almost naive. The records were full of defectors demanding millions of dollars, houses with three-car garages and every car a Cadillac. "We'll need to know the name of the person in New York," said Franklin.

"She will not be pressured?" insisted Orlov

"I will let my people know fully how you feel," said Franklin. It was the best he could do.

"I'll want their assurance before I will consider going any farther."

Naive or not, he was a pretty good negotiator. "Of course," accepted Franklin. "I'll need a name."

"Johnson," said Orlov shortly. "Harriet Johnson. She is a senior translator at the United Nations."

Just like a child's jigsaw, thought Franklin, where the pieces are so big they're obvious. "I will contact Washington tonight. But there will be the need for us to meet again, obviously."

"Of course," said Orlov. "Where?"

Franklin looked around and then said, "Public places are good. But not here again." Remembering the trip up-river, he asked, "Do you know the Krasnaya Park?"

"Of course."

"There is a statue near the central walkway. An archer. There."

"When?"

"It isn't possible now to fix times. So we'll make floating arrangements."

"Floating arrangements?"

"Which is best, day or evening?"

"Day," replied Orlov at once. It had been difficult tonight to avoid the meeting with Sevin.

"Noon then, every Friday. This week it is only two days away, by which time I'll have a full reaction from Washington."

"Everything will be arranged quickly?"

"As quickly as possible," said Franklin.

"It isn't easy," said Orlov.

"No."

"I'm very frightened."

"Everything will be all right," promised Franklin.

"I will be accused of being a traitor, won't I?"

Franklin was unsure of the response the man wanted. Orlov wasn't a fool, he thought. He said, "Yes, you will be labeled a traitor."

Momentarily Orlov's head went forward onto his chest. He said, his voice muffled, "I won't betray my country. I will talk to your people because I know I must give something, but I won't betray my country, not completely."

He would, thought Franklin. He might set out not intending to—have assurances that it wasn't expected—but the debriefings would go on and on, chipping and prodding, until Orlov had been picked clean like a skeleton after the vultures. "I understand," said Franklin.

"Noon, at Krasnaya," confirmed Orlov.

"And let neither of us panic if for any reason it's impossible. It won't be for me, I can assure you. But it might be for you. If you can't make it, I'll be there again the same time the following Friday. That's what floating arrangement means."

"I'm not sure I could wait that long," said Orlov.

"Don't take any chances," warned Franklin. "If you panic, everything could be destroyed."

"I won't panic," promised Orlov.

"It's important," stressed Franklin.

"It's a strange feeling," said Orlov. "Frightening, like I said. I can't imagine how my life is going to change, not really."

I know just how mine is going to change, thought Franklin.

At Langley, reaction was as frantic as Franklin had expected it to be. It took a long time to make the exchanges because they used the highest security ciphers, and during a lull in transmission Franklin telephoned Ann to remind her not to wait up, and she said she wouldn't. Langley cabled him to promise anything Orlov required and to assure the man of their complete and utter protection. Halfway through the exchanges the cables started to be signed by the director himself, congratulations first, then demands for clarification on points Franklin felt he had already made clear. One of the last messages was the demand that he return personally to Washington, which

Franklin agreed to do as long as it was after the Friday meeting with Orlov.

It was late, almost four in the morning, before Franklin eased himself as carefully as possible beside Ann into a bed that Brinkman had vacated five hours before.

Brinkman was still awake in another part of the complex. Ann hadn't known anything—he hadn't expected her to—but Franklin's earlier-than-ever departure and later-than-ever return meant that something very important was happening. He'd requested a lot of material from London and knew that it would arrive during the day in the diplomatic pouch because he'd made it highest priority. But he didn't really know what he was looking for. Like trying to find the right road in a thick fog, he thought. Brinkman hated the feeling of helplessness.

Pravda named Orlov as one of the Russians who attended the American Embassy reception and because it was a quiet day for foreign news, *The New York Times* carried a small picture from which she was able to identify him, unsmiling and erect alongside Didenko. Harriet read both reports several times and then stared at the picture, wanting it to tell her something. They'd agreed, during their innocent, grossly incomplete planning, that because she was in New York, the approach, when he made it, would have to be to the Americans. So this had to be it! It had to mean that all her doubts and uncertainties had been stupid and that Pietr was coming, as he'd always promised he would.

Harriet felt ashamed now at not trusting him. Immediately a contradiction came into her mind, the first small cloud that preludes a storm. The picture could also mean that he was being groomed for greater promotion; he was, after all, directly next to Didenko. And that he might be finding the choice difficult. No, she thought positively. It didn't mean that at all. It meant he was coming, as she'd always known he would.

"Hurry," she whispered aloud. "Please hurry, my darling."

CHAPTER TWENTY-FIVE

Wednesday—the day they met—ran into Thursday, until there were only twenty-four hours before Franklin's scheduled meeting with Orlov, but the pressure from Washington was unremitting. The same questions were asked a dozen different ways and Franklin gave the same answers. They offered to send backup, which he refused because of the difficulty in obtaining accreditation and visas and sensibly arguing that the sudden applications might arouse the curiosity they certainly didn't want. They said they would maintain the emergency desk in the Watch Room, and although Franklin couldn't see any purpose in it, he didn't bother to argue, because it couldn't cause him any inconvenience and it kept them busy, which was what all the repeated cables were about, after all. Franklin was instructed, first by Hubble and then by the director, to make a booking on the late Friday plane. He pointed out that there was no guarantee that Orlov would make the meeting; he was told that reservations could always be canceled.

Franklin hated the tension that had existed between himself and Ann since his return from Washington, and the temptation to tell her something—anything—about how it all might be put right was very strong. But he resisted it. Just. He made the reservation and realized he should tell her that at least, but he held back from doing so. If he told her he was going back to America and then canceled because Orlov didn't or couldn't make contact, she'd only be further confused.

But Orlov did make the meeting. Franklin arrived early for the same sort of reconnaissance as before, for the same reasons as before, but it was still before noon when he saw the Russian picking his way along a side pathway toward the statue of the archer. Orlov had made another effort to dress unobtrusively, Franklin saw. This time Orlov chose the bench, and Franklin waited a long time, a few minutes past the appointed hour, before moving to join the Russian, wanting to be completely sure he was alone.

"Is everything arranged?" asked Orlov at once, anxiously.

"I have had very long discussions with Washington," said Franklin, thinking of what an understatement that was. "I have been told to pass on to you the guaranteed understanding that you will be welcome in my country and that we will do everything possible to get you there safely."

It sounded formal, as though he were reading from a prepared speech. And not quite the sort of assurance he'd wanted to give anyway. Trying to improve it, he said, "I am flying to America tonight to make all the arrangements."

Orlov nodded his head. "That is good," he said. "So it will be soon."

"When I return, I will have everything settled at the

American end. All that will have to be planned is your actual exit.''

Beside him Orlov sighed in audible relief. ''It will be so good when it is all over.''

It's only just starting, thought Franklin, momentarily sad for the man. He said, ''I won't be in Washington long but I can't be definite. We'll maintain this as a method of contact.''

''I understand,'' said Orlov. He looked at the American and asked, ''Harriet is not to be involved?''

''I've made that quite clear,'' said Franklin. They'd probably avoid direct contact, but he was damned sure she'd already be under the tightest sort of surveillance. Like establishing emergency desks, it was something active that Langley could do.

''I want her to know, but not yet,'' said Orlov.

''It's going to be a very unsettled time,'' warned Franklin. ''You'll have to be careful.''

Orlov smiled, a resigned expression. ''I've been unsettled for a long time,'' he said. ''And I've been careful.''

''We'll get you out as soon as possible,'' said Franklin. He'd be able to make the evening connection; it would be tight, but he could make it.

''You might need this,'' said Orlov. ''Not yet, but later. It's Harriet's direct extension at the United Nations.''

''Thank you,'' said Franklin, accepting the slip of paper. Naive, he thought again. By now the Agency would know more about the woman than she knew herself. He wondered what she looked like.

''And thank you,'' said the Russian, ''for everything you're doing.''

It is as much for me as it is for you, thought Franklin; maybe even more.

He returned directly to the embassy to alert Langley that everything had gone as they'd hoped and that he was on his way back, telephoning Ann to say that something had come up and that he was making another trip to America. He talked over her surprise, emptily promising to explain when he got there. What *could* he tell her? thought Franklin during the drive to the apartment. Nothing. Officially he had to worsen the already strained relationship between them, use the easy excuse of his family again and make the amends and explanations later.

Ann was red-faced when he entered the apartment, the anger obvious. "You've only just come back!" she said, picking up the telephone conversation.

"I know. I didn't expect it," said Franklin.

"But what is it?"

"Paul again," he said. "Something about the sentence."

"Or is it Ruth?" demanded Ann.

Franklin was at his desk, taking out from his pockets things he didn't need on the journey. He stopped, turning to her, face creased with puzzlement. "What?"

"I said, is it Ruth? Is that why you're hurrying back?"

Idiotic though her fears were, Franklin realized he should have taken more care with the story. Despite his hurry, he calmly walked back to her and put both hands on her shoulders, looking directly at her. "That is stupid and you know it," he said quietly. "I told you how things were between Ruth and me. I told you about the guy she's with and how I liked him. And if you look at it sensibly, you'd realize that if I were going back to try and make up to Ruth—which I'm definitely not—I wouldn't do it like this, with panicked, last-minute flights. I've never lied to you and I've never cheated on you. We've had a row and it's gone on for a long time—too long—but if I'd thought our problems were as big as you seem to think they are, I would have talked them through with you. I didn't run away from anything before, when I fell in love with you, and I wouldn't run away now.''

Her color deepened and her lips trembled. ''What is it with Paul?''

''I won't know until I get back.'' From her distress it was obvious she still wasn't completely sure. ''It won't be as long this time as it was before,'' he said.

''How can you be sure if you don't know what the problem is?''

In his concern for her, he was being careless. ''I just don't think it will be,'' he said. He owed her more, Franklin thought; just something more. He took her shoulders again. ''I know it's been difficult for you, darling,'' he said. ''More difficult than I thought it was. But everything is going to work out okay, you'll see. It isn't going to work out as badly as you were frightened it would.''

''I don't understand,'' she said. Her lips had stopped trembling now and the color was going.

''You won't, not yet. Trust me.''

''When?''

''Just trust me.''

''You mean we won't be staying in Moscow after all?'' The hope was obvious in her face.

''It's vital that I catch a plane and I'm already late,'' said Franklin, knowing he'd let the conversation go on too long already. ''Just believe me. Everything is going to work out fine.''

Franklin ran to pack, using it as an excuse to break away from her, conscious of her standing in the doorway, watching him. Thank God she didn't try to continue the discussion.

"I love you," he said, brushing her cheek with a kiss on the way to the door.

"I love you too," she said.

Brinkman knew he loved Ann. Just as he knew that his jealousy had been love and not covetousness. But despite his readiness now to jump whenever she telephoned, he would still have avoided going to the apartment if she hadn't disclosed Franklin's flight to Washington.

Not that he would have achieved anything by remaining at the embassy. For eight hours he'd bent over his desk, searching through the material that had been sent from London, trying to find a clue and reluctantly coming to the conclusion that none existed. Maxwell had been very thorough, conceded Brinkman. Not only had he sent the London file, but all the material that was available from Orlov's period in New York. It still didn't amount to much. Maybe a hundred sheets that by now he knew by heart and twenty photographs of Orlov at the United Nations, mostly standard glass-in-hand reception stuff and a few of him in the chamber, taking part in debates.

So he'd failed, and Franklin was succeeding even further, thought Brinkman as he entered the apartment block. Why the sudden Washington recall for the second time in just over a month? This wasn't a competition any more, he decided; he was practically out of the race.

He was immediately aware of Ann's reserve as he entered the apartment, a holding back when he went to kiss her. "What is it?"

"Nothing."

"I know there's something. Another row?"

"Not really."

"What then?"

"He said he loved me," she said distantly. "He hasn't said that for a long time, but he said it tonight as he left."

"Oh," said Brinkman emptily. Franklin was winning in everything, he thought, ignoring the illogicality of it. "What happened?"

Ann shrugged. "Everything was so rushed," she said. "He called from the embassy to say he had to go back on the night plane, threw some things into a bag and dashed off."

"But stopped long enough to say that he loved you."

"Don't," she said. "Please don't."

"*I* love you," said Brinkman. It was the first time, the commitment he'd held back from giving.

"Don't," she said again, desperately.

"I told you once before we couldn't ignore it," said Brinkman.

"You weren't talking about love then."

"I am now. Why don't you?"

"I don't want to."

"Ostriches in the sand," he said, another reminder.

"I'm so confused," said Ann. "Completely confused."

"Do you love me?" demanded Brinkman.

"I don't know."

"Do you love me?" he insisted.

"Yes, I suppose so."

"What about Eddie?"

"That's it!" she said pleadingly. "I love him too."

"You can't love two people at the same time."

"Who says?" she demanded. "Where are the rules that say you can't love two people?"

"You're going to have to make a choice."

"I don't want to," she said. "I'm frightened."

Should he tell her what he'd already concluded, that

Orlov was Franklin's source and that Franklin would stay in Moscow until hell froze over? He wasn't so certain of that, not any more. There was definitely a link, but he wasn't sure he'd interpreted it correctly. "Why has Eddie gone back so unexpectedly?"

"He said it was something to do with Paul."

"There wasn't this panic last time."

"No," she said heavily. "I know."

Conscious of the tone, Brinkman asked, "What do you think it is?"

"I told him I thought it was Ruth."

"What about Ruth?" he asked, momentarily not understanding.

"Wouldn't the affair with Paul have brought them together again?"

"There still wouldn't have been this panic."

"That's what he said."

"What *did* he say?"

"Not much," said Ann. "Burst in, like I've already told you. Emptied his pockets on the desk . . ." she gestured over his shoulder. "Packed a case and went off to the airport."

"But told you he loved you."

"There was a kind of a row," Ann confessed. "When I said I thought he was going back to see Ruth. He said I was stupid and that everything was going to work out. That things wouldn't be as bad as I thought they were going to be."

Brinkman tried to curb any reaction and knew he had succeeded because Ann appeared lost in thought. "What did he mean by that—that things wouldn't be as bad as you thought they were going to be?"

"He wouldn't say. I even asked if it meant we wouldn't have to stay here in Moscow, but he wouldn't say."

Brinkman looked over her shoulder. The desk top was still jumbled, which was unusual in their apartment. With accustomed familiarity, he said, "Do you want a drink?"

"Not really."

Neither did Brinkman, but the drinks tray was next to the desk. He made the pretense of examining the selection, lifting and putting down bottles, looking back to see if she were paying any particular attention. She wasn't. He poured scotch and put the glass down not on the tray but alongside, on the desk, jostling the items that lay there. He turned back to her, his body screening what he was doing, spreading the things further so that it would take only one look. "You sure?" he asked.

"Maybe a whisky then."

He turned back, glad of the extra few seconds, looking not at the drinks but sideways at the desk. The official government passes that they all carried for use within Moscow, and some small change Franklin had clearly felt he wouldn't need. And a single sheet of paper, half hidden by a car parking permit. Brinkman shifted the permit, making as though to pick up his own glass. There was only a single printed line. UNXT 481.

Brinkman carried the drinks back and said "Cheers," and she smiled back at him, a sad expression.

"How long is he going to be away?"

"He didn't know. Not as long as last time, he said."

"At least that'll make some things easier."

She smiled, sad again. "Not tonight, darling."

"Why not?"

"I just don't want to."

"I see."

"Don't, darling!"

"How do you expect me to feel?"

"How do you expect *me* to feel? I'm the one who has to choose eventually."

Did Franklin's remark mean he *was* getting out of Moscow on time? Or even quicker? If it did, it would mean that Ann would go with him. Unless she chose. "Okay," he said. "Not tonight."

"Thank you," she said.

"How about tomorrow night?"

"We'll see." Aware of his wince, she said, "We'll talk tomorrow. We'll try to make it tomorrow night."

Brinkman went angrily from the Franklins' apartment. His first inclination was to go home but then he changed his mind, driving back to the embassy and shutting himself again in his office, gazing down at the picture of Orlov. He *wasn't* going to lose! he determined. *Wouldn't* lose. He smiled suddenly, looking down at the uppermost photograph. It couldn't be as easy as that? As simple? But why not? He'd spent hours trying to evolve convoluted scenarios when it could all be childishly, ridiculously simple. He prefaced the lengthy cable to Maxwell with the assurance that he would not be making the request unless he considered what he was asking for to be absolutely essential. And absolutely urgent. Before he encoded it, he looked down, deciding the queries looked like a rather complicated crossword clue. Which, he supposed, was exactly what they were.

Ruth was embarrassed, seeking reassurance now. "So I overreacted then?"

"No, Mrs. Franklin," said Kemp at once. "Okay, so this time it seems that Paul was telling the truth. The urinalysis is clear and the other boys we finally located said all they did was talk. I don't know why he didn't tell you himself who they were; three were from the same program. They just hung around outside for a while. The point is that he *could* have been doing something stupid. And the most important point is that he knows now how you'd react if he were. It's taught him a lesson.''

"It's not going to be easy, is it?'' asked Ruth wearily.

"I never thought it would be, Mrs. Franklin,'' said the counselor.

CHAPTER TWENTY-SIX

Hubble came to the airport to meet him. They bypassed customs formalities and were in the limousine within fifteen minutes of Franklin's emergence from the aircraft. With the dividing partition raised to separate them from the driver and his escort, Hubble said, "You've done it, Eddie. The jackpot. Every bell is ringing."

Franklin was suffering his customary travel fatigue and found Hubble's enthusiasm irritating. He wondered if the man talked like that all the time. He said, "We have to get him across first."

"We're not going to let this one go, buddy. Believe me, we're not."

Franklin looked out at the Beltway, remembering last time. He'd have to call Ruth when he had the opportunity. He'd remembered to buy a gift in Amsterdam, the same sort of perfume he'd bought Ann. He'd had difficulty

259

deciding about the boys and copied himself again, buying them both watches, the heavy, calibrated sort that divers wear. They'd be surprised to have him home again so soon. He asked, "What's been set up here?"

"Everything," assured Hubble. "All the details can wait until we get to Langley, but believe me, there isn't anything that hasn't been thought of . . ." The man paused and Franklin waited for the announcement. "Guess who's going to chair this afternoon's meeting?"

It was obvious but Franklin gave Hubble the moment he wanted. "Who?"

"The director himself!"

The announcement should have had some sort of band accompaniment. "Jackpot, like you said."

Despite its being an official Agency car with a recognizable division chief as a passenger, they still had to go through the security procedures. Once inside the main building, Hubble took over the role as guide. When they entered the elevator, he pressed the button for the seventh floor and Franklin guessed the director had been advised of their arrival. Franklin was crumpled and stubble-chinned and wished he'd had the opportunity to clean up first.

The director's office was a lavish suite, personally designed by Allen Dulles but never occupied by him because he was fired as director over the Bay of Pigs disaster. He hoped this wasn't a disaster, thought Franklin, entering behind Hubble.

Rupert Perelmen was a tall, dome-headed man wearing rimless glasses and a suit almost as crumpled as Franklin's. He looked precisely the academic he had been until his appointment by a president who decided that the Agency needed a political scientist as its head. He stood as they entered, coming forward with his hand outstretched to greet Franklin and guide him to a chair. When Perelmen returned to his own seat, he beamed donnishly and said, "Well done, very well done."

Franklin thought it sounded like he'd gotten good marks in an examination, which perhaps he had. He was aware of the continued sense of fevered enthusiasm. He said, "There's a long way to go yet, sir."

"I know, I know," said Perelmen, "but I'm confident. We've already made a lot of contingency plans. Now I'd like you to run through it for me, right from the start."

They'd already had it in at least four variations, thought Franklin, but obediently he recounted Orlov's approach at the reception, their first meeting and then the previous evening's encounter in the Krasnaya Gardens.

"No demands at all?" intruded Hubble.

"Only about the woman," said Franklin. "What about her?"

The director raised his hand reassuringly. "Exactly what he wanted. No approach whatsoever."

"She's on a lead, of course," elaborated Hubble. "Round-the-clock watch. Cover on everything she does. She doesn't know how safe she is."

"He doesn't want her to know," reminded Franklin.

"They're not amateurs!" said Hubble as though imagining criticism.

"Would Orlov run if he found out?" asked Perelmen.

"I don't know," admitted Franklin. "I don't know why it's something he's so adamant about."

"When does he want her involved?" asked Hubble.

"He hasn't made that clear, not properly. He just talked about when everything is arranged. Maybe when we actually have him on the move. My guess is that he's frightened something will happen to her before they get together."

"It wouldn't if she were under our protection," said Perelmen.

"I'll make the point," promised Franklin.

"You imagine he doesn't want to talk to us, not completely?"

"I don't imagine," replied Franklin. "I know."

"Let's not worry about that now," dismissed Perelmen. "Let's get him here first. Everything else will unfold naturally enough."

Poor bastard, thought Franklin. He said, "We haven't discussed at all how to get him out. It'll have to be during some kind of overseas visit."

"Can he fix that?"

"He has the authority to," said Franklin. "I didn't raise the question until I had the chance to talk to you here; wanted to know the countries in which we were best placed."

"Europe, obviously," said Perelmen. "Anywhere really, although England and Germany would be best. We've a lot of secure airbases in Germany. If it has to be anywhere in eastern Europe, then okay, but it'll be more difficult. Too many things can go wrong in trying a border crossing like that."

Franklin knew Perelmen had met the traditional opposition within the Agency from professionals irritated at having an amateur put in control over them. The man seemed to have adjusted very well. Franklin asked, "How much warning would you need?"

"We've expanded the emergency desk in the Watch Room," said the director. "We've established a complete contingency unit specifically for Orlov's crossing. I've already moved twenty men into Europe. Germany. Like I said, that's where we're best placed if there's a choice.

Every sort of necessary transportation too. We'll need only a couple of hours.''

"If we can make it an overseas visit, we'll have days,'' said Franklin. He hesitated and then asked, "What if we can't fix something that will officially get him across the border?''

"Then it's Action Man stuff,'' said Hubble. "And you'll really be earning your salary. The favorite would be to try for the Finnish border and cross there.''

Christ, Hubble irritated him, thought Franklin. Action Man! He said, "It won't be easy, crossing into Finland. Unless we can get on an airplane in some way, it'll take two days to get there, maybe more. And at the first hint that Orlov has made a run for it, they'll seal that country like a drum.''

"I'd risk a crossing to come in to get you,'' disclosed Perelmen. "Not to Moscow of course. As far into Karelia as we could get.''

"That would require a pickup coordinate. I couldn't give any guarantee to make it on time.''

"Then we'd keep crossing until you did,'' said Hubble. "We'll ship homing devices and the sort of radios you'll need. That's part of the contingency.''

Franklin hoped to God there would be some other way. He asked, "What about here?''

"Everything's set,'' assured the director. "We've got three safe houses, two in Maryland, one in Virginia. We'll use all of course, but he can make his choice. Tell him that after we've talked things out, he'll be given a completely new identity . . . social security, bank account, stuff like that. And a government pension that we can negotiate when he gets here.''

After we've talked things out, reflected Franklin. He

wondered if it would be as obvious to Orlov as it was to him that the promised pension depended on how much he was prepared to "talk things out." If they debriefed the Russian as extensively as he guessed they would, Orlov would be a white-haired old man of pensionable age. "I'll set it out," promised Franklin.

"And a house of course," added Perelmen in afterthought.

"How long do you want me to stay? There's no scheduled contact for another week, even if he's able to make that."

"This is just a preliminary meeting," said Perelmen. "Chance for me to express my personal thanks. Tomorrow I want you to go through everything with the leaders of the group we've assembled, see whether you can think of anything else."

"Sure," said Franklin. It meant the weekend at least with the kids. And Ruth.

"And, Eddie?"

Christian name terms? "Yes, sir."

"I was impressed before," reminded the director. "Everything said then stands now. Doubly so."

"Did I or did I not say jackpot!" chortled Hubble as they walked along the corridor outside the director's office.

Hubble was the sort of talking doll you won at the fair, thought Franklin.

It was a race again, Brinkman exulted. And now that he knew what the medal was, he was going to win it. It was still interpretation of course, but then everything in Moscow was interpretation. He gazed down, tired-eyed, at the second batch of material he'd requested from London, comparing it with the first. He *knew* he was right. What's more, he knew how he could prove it right. It meant expecting Maxwell and maybe someone higher bending the rules, but when they realized the prize, he expected them to do it. He sent the request and waited for the predictable query, assuring Maxwell that it was essential he return personally to London. He kept the name for the second message, but had he not already established the sort of reputation he had, Brinkman doubted permission would have been given.

"Going away?" Ann asked.

"Just a quick trip."

"Where?"

"London."

She closed her eyes in envy. Opening them again, she queried, "How long?"

"Not more than a few days. Quick, as I said." Franklin had more than a head start, so everything was going to have to be quick.

"I'll miss you," she said.

"Will you?"

"You know I will."

"It'll give you time to think," he said.

"About what?"

"I want you to make the choice, darling. I want you to choose between Eddie and me. I'm saying I want to marry you."

"No!" she said.

"Yes," said Brinkman. "While we're both away, it'll give you time to make up your mind." Brinkman didn't want to win just part of it; he wanted to win it all.

"Why didn't you call from Moscow?" asked Ruth.

"There wasn't time. Everything was too quick."

"It's good to see you again."

"And you."

"The boys will be glad."

"So okay. How's Paul making out?"

Ruth told him about the scare and how she'd reacted, and Franklin's reaction was the same as the counselors, which relieved her. She, Kemp, and the school principal were keeping a close eye on Paul's grades, and they hadn't dropped. As part of the program, she'd joined a parents' group. There was a meeting the following night.

"I'll come too," promised Franklin.

She hesitated. "Charlie said he'd come."

"Can't we all go?"

Ruth hesitated further. "Won't it look a bit odd?"

"If you don't want me. . . ."

"Oh, no!" she stopped him. "Maybe I'll ask Charlie not to bother."

"We shouldn't use him as a stopgap, should we?"

"I'll talk to him about it," she said.

The greeting from the boys this time was very different. John ran at Franklin and threw himself into his father's arms, and although he didn't run, Paul allowed himself to be picked up as well. Franklin had to put them down quickly because together they were heavy. He gave them their gifts and both boys strapped them on, their delight obvious.

"Is this really what divers wear, Dad?" asked John.

"All the time," assured Franklin.

"It's terrific to have you home," said Paul.

"It's terrific to be home," said Franklin.

CHAPTER TWENTY-SEVEN

Brinkman was disappointed—actually, worried—that Maxwell didn't appear to share his conviction. The division chief's office was in the inner quadrangle, far away from any traffic. It was possible to hear the ticking of the antique clock on the mantel, and even Maxwell's heavy breathing as he looked down at the evidence Brinkman had placed before him.

"It's very circumstantial," judged Maxwell.

"No," said Brinkman, risking the impertinence of coming around to Maxwell's side of the desk to argue his case. "Orlov has returned within months from the United Nations in New York. . . ." He isolated three of the pictures showing Orlov at UN receptions. "At the United States Embassy I positively saw Orlov make an approach to the CIA resident, Edward Franklin. I'm quite definite about it. Franklin has made two visits to Washington. He's there now, and this time it was a panicked recall. On his desk was this." Brinkman paused again, producing a piece of paper upon which he'd written UNXT 481. "You know from the checks that I asked you to make that extension 481 at the United Nations is a direct line to a woman named Harriet Johnson, a British-born senior translator. . . ."

There was another break while Brinkman selected three photographs of Harriet that had been sent with the second batch of material. "Harriet Johnson," he said, unnecessarily dramatic. One was a posed, full-faced picture taken for her official accreditation. The second had obviously been taken at a UN party, and a third was of her at the point of leaving the skyscraper building. Brinkman made another grouping, placing the pictures of the girl by herself against two of Orlov, both taken at UN receptions. "Pietr Orlov," went on Brinkman, still dramatic. He moved his finger to someone in the immediate background in both pictures. "Harriet Johnson," he said.

"I don't dispute it's the woman," said Maxwell. "So Harriet Johnson attended UN functions and was photographed with a senior Soviet official. Russian is her predominant language; we know that from the files."

"What is the private extension of a senior Soviet translator doing on the desk of a CIA resident in Moscow?" asked Brinkman.

"How *did* you get that?"

Brinkman hesitated. "I'm a friend," he said. "I went to the apartment the night Franklin left. Within an hour or two."

"He left something like that on the desk in his apartment?"

Brinkman paused again, remembering Ann's account of

the row. Remembering the part of it she recalled best. *He said he loved me.* Brinkman said, "There was a lot of rush. Some personal confusion too, I think."

"There must have been," said Maxwell. He looked back to the display before him. "So what is it in your opinion?"

"I don't know, not definitely," conceded Brinkman. "At the moment I think it's a defection."

Maxwell frowned. "Someone of Orlov's rank!"

"Which was why I judged it important enough to come back here personally," said Brinkman. Maxwell was moving, he guessed. Very slightly, but moving.

Maxwell lit a cigarette and coughed. "So what do you want to do about it?" he asked, direct.

"Make him come to us instead," replied Brinkman, just as direct.

A smile, vaguely patronizing touched Maxwell's mouth. "Just like that?"

"No, not just like that," said Brinkman, irritated at his superior. "I think I could make it happen."

"How?"

Brinkman told him, setting out the plan he had carefully formulated, intent upon Maxwell's facial reaction. There was none. When he finished, Maxwell, who had served at the embassy in Washington before his promotion, said, "Do you know the American expression, 'dirty pool'?"

"No."

"Loosely translated, it means shitting on someone from a great height. What you're planning is dirty pool."

"I'm suggesting we get Orlov for ourselves!"

"I know what you're suggesting," said Maxwell. "But why? There's liaison between us and Washington. We'll get what Orlov has to say in time. If they get him across, it's a coup, but if they make a mistake, it's an international incident. What's wrong with letting America take the risk?''

Chair-bound bloody bureaucrat interested only in lunches at the club and whether or not his pension was cost-of-living linked, thought Brinkman. As forcefully as he dared, he said, ''We *won't* get what Orlov has to say. We'll get what Washington condescends to let us have. Sanitized and packaged like processed cheese. And about as tasteless. And I agree, in time: their time. Which will be years from now, when any usefulness will have gone. Why must we wait around all the time, cap in hand, grateful for American handouts? What's wrong with their coming to us for a change?''

Instead of answering, Maxwell persisted, ''What about the risk?''

Damn the man, thought Brinkman. He *wouldn't* be blocked. He said, ''My father says repeatedly that knowing when to take risks in diplomacy—intelligent risks—is a finer part of the art.''

Maxwell stubbed out his cigarette, the force with which he did it his only reaction to the threat. ''You'd be appallingly exposed,'' he said. ''In New York and in Moscow.''

''I know the difficulties,'' assured Brinkman.

''What if you're wrong about Orlov and the girl?'' asked Maxwell.

''Then I'll realize that in New York, where I'll do nothing more harmful than make a fool of myself, and any danger in Moscow won't exist any more,'' said Brinkman, the argument prepared.

''Be careful,'' said Maxwell predictably. ''Be very careful.''

Brinkman went directly from his meeting with Maxwell to the airport. He was anxious to close the gap between himself and Franklin as quickly as possible. Maxwell would take out insurance, he knew. He didn't know what kind or how, but the bloody man would evolve something to get himself as far back from the spray as possible if everything hit the fan. Maybe he wouldn't let the threat involving his father remain as empty as he intended it. There was an afternoon flight from London and he was intent on sleeping.

The necessity of booking into a hotel was an irritating delay, but he was at the United Nations building by eight in the evening. The Assembly was in session, so Harriet Johnson was working split shifts. According to the information he'd already had assembled, that meant she had another two hours to go. From the public gallery he tried to detect her in the translation booths but the glass was smoked and he was far away. He listened to a debate about Third World starvation, knowing the speeches would not alleviate that starvation in the slightest and reflecting on what a useless world forum it was.

He left the chamber, with an hour to spare, to find, among other things, the door from which she would emerge into the corridor. There was a lot of movement in the passageway, which offered him concealment but made it more difficult to find those he supposed would already be watching. He guessed at a man in a fawn seersucker suit but wasn't sure about another in a blue sports jacket. Brinkman bought a periodical from a bookstand and managed to get a seat on a bench near a wall support that furthered his concealment. If he were mistaken about the fawn seersucker and the sports jacket—if she were not under some sort of protective surveillance—it could mean that he was completely wrong, he realized. If she were still here at all. The uncertainties irritated him, nibbling away at his absolute conviction. Harriet Johnson was the essential key—the only key—for everything to work out as he wanted it to. If they already had her in some safe house somewhere, then everything changed. To dirtier pool than even Maxwell suspected.

But they didn't have her. Harriet Johnson emerged from the translation area at ten past ten, a crisply suited, crisply mannered woman whom he recognized immediately from the photographs. She paused to speak to an attendant and then set off toward the elevator that would take her from the building.

Brinkman made no effort to follow at once, waiting to see what would happen. He was wrong about the fawn seersucker but right about the sports jacket. There was also a man in a brown suit and a woman, which he should have anticipated but hadn't. Brinkman allowed them to get expertly in position, the man in the brown suit actually preceding Harriet into the elevator to guarantee cover at all times.

Brinkman slotted himself comfortably behind the others, admiring their professionalism. Halfway along the corridor, brown suit allowed himself to be overtaken and the woman took his place. Had he not been trained—and positively expecting it—Brinkman didn't think he would have isolated the surveillance. He didn't try for the same elevator— knowing they would register faces in such an enclosed area—but caught one sufficiently quickly to reach ground level before she went through the revolving door.

Brinkman followed the followers at an easy pace. Did she have a car or would she take a taxi? Neither, he saw, surprised. Harriet Johnson walked through the waiting vehicles and across the forecourt, passing almost directly beneath the statue of a man supposedly beating a sword into a ploughshare. It had been presented to the United Nations

by the Soviet Union. She went to the left, to the break
with the FDR Drive, where it was easier to cross, and
Brinkman realized, further surprised, that she intended to
walk the four blocks to where she lived. Harriet Johnson
must be a very assured woman to walk four blocks in
Manhattan after ten o'clock at night, he reflected. With that
reflection came another. The attacker wouldn't know what
hit him if he attempted to mug her. She wasn't entirely
uncaring. Having crossed the difficult Drive outside the
United Nations, she backtracked to get to Second Avenue,
walking along the broad, well-lit Forty-second Street.
Brinkman didn't turn immediately right, as she did; instead
he continued across to the west side of the avenue, keeping
parallel but about ten yards behind.

The American surveillance was practically choreographed,
he thought admiringly. They obviously hadn't been sure of
how she would travel, so there were several vehicles, three
at least that he identified. Although they didn't need them,
the Americans still utilized them, and cleverly too, never
keeping their people in the street around Harriet for more
than one block but stopping and changing with the car
occupants. They even bothered with people ahead of him,
walking parallel to her as he was.

Harriet Johnson's apartment was on Second Avenue at
Forty-sixth Street, a modern, obviously new building. From
across the avenue Brinkman watched, able to see through
the expansive, clear glass as the woman went in, smiled at
the doorman, collected her mail and then disappeared
toward what had to be the elevators.

To get himself off the street, Brinkman went into a bar
on the opposite corner. There was a row of tables arranged
directly beneath the window looking out toward the apartment building, and he took his drink there, standing with

his glass held lightly between both hands, gazing out. Six-sixty-seven, he knew, was the apartment. It was easy enough to count up, but it was impossible to tell which of the lighted windows belonged to the woman.

Why didn't the CIA have her under overt protection, if not away from the UN completely? It was obvious from the homeward journey that she didn't have any idea of her surveillors. It didn't make sense. There were cars lining either side of Forty-sixth, but they were too far away and it was too dark for him to see how many were occupied. There would be observers in several, he knew.

Would they have managed to get an apartment within the building? An obvious move if they intended to continue the cover they seemed to be employing now. And putting their own people in as building staff. And installing a monitor on her telephone. Brinkman stopped mentally turning the pages of the manual. Franklin was barely forty-eight hours ahead of him—if the panicked return had been the beginning. He flicked the pages back for another look. The street cover was in place because he'd seen it, but that took little preparation. There hadn't been enough time to get themselves an apartment. Or to install themselves as building staff. What about the telephone? he wondered, looking to the bar's public booth, at the end by the rest rooms. It would have been quick, but not impossible. Too uncertain to take the risk though. He looked back across the intersection toward the apartment building. Hundreds of people lived there, he thought. Hundreds they might try to identify, one by one, if they considered the operation important enough and if they had the time. But they wouldn't have had the time yet.

The decision made, Brinkman left the bar and purpose

fully crossed the avenue like someone approaching his own home. He thrust through the doors, nodding to the doorman but not slowing his momentum until he reached the desk, and there he maintained the demeanor of confidence that would have confused anyone watching from outside.

"This the house phone?" he asked the desk clerk, lifting the white receiver.

"Yes, sir," replied the man.

The woman answered on the second ring.

"I need to see you," said Brinkman without introduction. "It's about Pietr."

There was silence from the other end of the line. Then, "Give me the desk clerk."

Brinkman handed the man the receiver. He smiled, putting it almost at once back into the cradle. "She says you're to go up."

The surveillance had been confirmation that he was right, decided Brinkman, going toward the elevators. Harriet Johnson's reaction doubly confirmed it.

The contingency planning was far more extensive than Franklin had envisaged. Overnight the director had decided to send a Special Forces group on standby to one of the German bases, from which they could get to the Finnish border in hours if there had to be an incursion. Five unmarked CIA helicopters—large-capacity Chinooks—had also been sent in, flying with a Boeing 727, also unmarked, which would be the transport for Orlov's eventual Atlantic crossing to the United States, however he got out.

Franklin addressed the assembled group leaders, feeling self-conscious, baton in hand, identifying Orlov in the hugely enlarged photographs. There was renewed pressure from Hubble to provide backup within the Soviet capital, and Franklin conceded that an effort should be made if the crossover appeared to be taking longer than they expected, which would enable the application for entry permission to be processed routinely. With the number of American diplomats permitted in Moscow strictly limited by the Russians, it meant the director would have to persuade the State Department to surrender some of its allocation, and Franklin wondered how successful Perelmen would be.

He left Langley in good time for the parents' meeting at the drug program. Franklin couldn't see that the gathering achieved much apart from showing the kids they had support—which was, he supposed, the benefit intended in the first place—and afterward they went to the Mexican café in the Georgetown mall. Ruth had told Charlie Rogers not to come, and Franklin wished she hadn't. Both the boys had worn their watches and kept looking at them with the pride of new ownership.

"Can we really come to Moscow, Dad?" asked John.

"That's the deal."

"When?" queried Paul.

Franklin remembered the counselors' warning about breaking promises and thought about how occupied he would be by what was going to happen in Moscow. He said, "We'll plan it once summer vacation's begun. And we have to work around Paul's program, of course. I'll fix it with the counselors."

The vacation was very close. So much could have changed in a few weeks, he thought.

"How often do you think you'll be able to get back like this?" asked Ruth.

"I don't know," admitted Franklin. It would be wrong to make any false promises.

"Will I see a spy in Moscow?" demanded John, who did not know what his father did.

"Maybe," said Franklin.

CHAPTER TWENTY-EIGHT

By the time Brinkman reached the apartment, Harriet had realized her stupidity. She kept the door on its chain, staring out at him, at his face and how he was dressed, keeping most of herself hidden by the door itself.

"What do you want?" she asked.

"I told you, it's about Pietr."

"I don't know what you're talking about," she said, pitifully too late.

"Why did you let me up then?"

"I misunderstood," she said, even more pitifully.

"I *know*, Harriet," said Brinkman. "Let me in so we can talk."

"Who are you?"

Brinkman took out his accreditation and identification designating him a cultural attaché at the British Embassy, passing it through the gap to her. She hesitated and then took it, reading not just the English but the Russian as well. She was very careful, digesting it all. She handed it back to him, her throat working.

"What do you want?" she repeated.

"Not like this," said Brinkman, sure of himself. "Not out here in the corridor."

There was a further hesitation and then she slipped the chain, opening the door. Brinkman nodded his thanks and went in. It was a comparatively small apartment, one main room with a bedroom alcove, an open kitchen area and a door he presumed led to the bathroom. It was in a corner of the building so there were windows on two sides, but it was not high enough for the view to be truly impressive. She'd obviously been preparing a meal. There was a table near the window half laid and there were cooking sounds coming from the kitchen.

"Well?" she asked.

"Hadn't you better turn off the things on the stove?" said Brinkman. "We have a lot to talk about."

"Stop being so damned condescending and tell me what it is you have to say!" she said in a sudden burst of anger.

He was sure—absolutely convinced—that he was right, but at the moment of challenge Brinkman hesitated. Just one miscalculation and he would be doing what he'd told Maxwell in London. Making a fool of himself. Trying to allow himself the widest margin possible, he said, "We know all about you and Pietr Orlov. We know what happened here, and we know what he's trying to do in Moscow. And we want to help."

Harriet had been holding herself stiff, defensively, but suddenly she sagged as the tension of the past months went from her. She actually put out her hand, reaching to a chair back for support.

From her photographs and from seeing her at the United Nations, Brinkman had thought her quite a tall woman, but now she didn't appear to be. She'd taken off the jacket of her suit, showing the white blouse, ruffled and laced at the neck. Her face was drained now but Brinkman guessed she would never have a lot of color. The paleness was accentuated by her hair, which was deeply black. She wore it pulled back, as Ann had the night at the embassy when Orlov had made his approach.

"The stove," he reminded. "You'd better turn off the stove."

Harriet straightened, trying for her earlier control, appeared to consider what he said and then went to the kitchen. As she came back, she smiled and said, "I'm sorry for behaving like I did. We thought we knew what it was going to be like, but we didn't. I didn't at least. These last months have been hell. I don't feel like I've been alive at all. I've felt outside of myself, watching a person called Harriet Johnson go through the motions of everyday life but not really being part of it."

Brinkman smiled, trying for the sympathy. "It'll all be over soon," he said. He hadn't won yet; he hadn't even drawn level. But he was narrowing the gap every minute.

"I thought he was going to go to the Americans," admitted Harriet.

Brinkman knew there was no way to disguise it, to make it pleasant. It had to be brutal and she had to hate him. Just as Orlov would hate him. It was something he had already accepted. He said, "He did."

Harriet's smile flickered uncertainly, like a faulty light, and then went out. She lowered herself into the chair against which she had earlier leaned for support and said, shaking her head, "I'm sorry. I don't understand."

"Pietr did go to the Americans. Last week, at an embassy reception."

"I saw the photograph . . ." started Harriet and then stopped. "But your documentation. . . ."

"Is British," he finished for her.

"What's happening?" she asked. "Please tell me what's happening."

"Pietr has gone to the Americans to defect. They'll be making plans to bring him across. I know they've withdrawn someone from their embassy in Moscow," said Brinkman. "But we don't want Pietr to go to America. We want him to defect to Britain."

Harriet looked up at him warily, with the beginning of suspicion. "You're not working with them? You're not cooperating with the Americans?"

"No," said Brinkman. "And we don't want Pietr to continue doing so. Or you, if any approach is made."

Harriet's head jerked up, her face flushed. "Get out!" she ordered. "Get out of my apartment. You tricked your way in here. Get out!"

Brinkman made no attempt to move. "We'll match every offer the Americans will make," he promised. "You and Pietr will be completely protected. There'll be accommodation and whatever money you want for as long as you want. In time you'll be set up with new identities . . . new everything. . . ."

"Why?" she asked, unable to sustain anger, the plea coming back into her voice. *"Why?"*

"I've already told you," said Brinkman. *"We* want Pietr."

"No," she said, shaking her head more determinedly this time. "No. Not until I've had a chance to talk it over with Pietr. I won't do anything until I know what he wants.''

"That can't happen," said Brinkman. "It isn't possible."

"Why not?" she demanded defiantly.

"Because if Pietr doesn't come to us, he's not going anywhere. You're never going to see him again."

"What?"

"You heard what I said."

"No," she said again, holding her hands together before her as though she were praying. "No. I don't believe it. I don't believe any of this. I don't know what you want or what you're doing, but it's some sort of trick.''

"It isn't a trick, Harriet," said Brinkman evenly. "This is the way—the only way—that you'll ever get Pietr out of Moscow. Our way."

She leaned forward, determined to concentrate. "Tell me what you mean," she said. "Tell me exactly what you mean."

One of the highest hurdles of them all, thought Brinkman. "You've a way to contact Pietr?" he asked.

Her uncertainty lasted just a moment too long. "No," she replied.

"I don't believe you."

"Pietr said it would be dangerous; too dangerous. That I had to trust him."

"Pity," observed Brinkman.

"Why?"

"Like I said, if we can't have him, no one's going to."

"How can you stop it?"

Brinkman laughed at the innocence of her question. "By ensuring that the Soviet authorities discover what's happening before Pietr has a chance to get out."

"*What?*"

"You haven't listened to me," remonstrated Brinkman. "I've already told you—several times—that if he doesn't come to the British, he isn't going anywhere."

"You wouldn't!"

"You prepared to take that chance?" asked Brinkman. "Please don't. Because I would."

"Bastard!"

"Yes," agreed Brinkman, his voice conversational.

"But . . . but . . . I just can't believe you. I just can't believe that anyone would think. . . ." Her voice trailed off as her mind blocked, refusing the words to express her disgust.

"I would," said Brinkman. "Really I would. Now, what's the way of contacting Pietr?"

Harriet started to cry and Brinkman sat back, letting her. She seemed suddenly aware of his calmly being there, watching her, and brought herself to a snuffling halt. She blew her nose and scrubbed her hands across her eyes. "Bastard," she replied, broken-voiced.

Brinkman let her have the last moment of defiance. "The system," he said. "What's the system?"

She blew her nose a second time, composing herself. "Pietr knew he was going back to a favored position . . ." she began haltingly. "I don't think he anticipated what happened—he never said so and I know he would have— but he knew there would be privileges. He was allowed some here. One was books. He was allowed to keep a charge account here, through the bookshop. And to let it stay open when he went back to Moscow. If there was an emergency, but only the most extreme emergency, I was to order a book—it didn't matter what, because if he hadn't ordered it himself, he'd know it was from me—and go through it picking out letters in the third chapter that spelled out what I wanted to say. Under the letters I had to put a tiny pinprick. When the book reached him, he'd search the third chapter and pick out the message.''

It would have remained undiscovered for about three minutes in a well-equipped forensic laboratory, thought Brinkman. But it wasn't bad. "How could you get the marked book to him?''

"It had to be one with several copies in the bookshop there,'' she said. "Having made my message, I then had to go back and switch. Take an unmarked one for myself—for which I'd have a purchase ticket anyway—and personally hand the marked copy to the desk clerk and tell her it was to be charged to Pietr Orlov's account.''

"Send him a book tomorrow,'' ordered Brinkman. He wished there was something more guaranteed.

"Saying what?''

It was a good question. He hadn't worked it out. For safety, it had to be kept to the minimum. Just a meeting then. Knowing it was from Harriet, Orlov would make the meeting. And if the KGB intercepted it, they'd keep it too. As Maxwell had said, the risk would be appalling. "Have you paper and a pen?'' he asked.

While she fetched the materials, Brinkman tried to think of a meeting place. Somewhere public, with as many people around as possible. Someplace where Orlov could explainably be if he were seen. Himself, too. He smiled when it came to him. Appropriate too. The Bolshoi was one of his favorite places, after all. When Harriet returned, he printed out the name in block capitals, then paused. The place. What about the date and time? A date was impossible because he didn't know how long it would take the book to reach the Russian. *Every Tuesday*, he wrote.

Then, *seven-thirty, north entrance*. Anything else? He looked up at her and asked, "Only in an emergency?"

"That was the arrangement," she said. "I've never used it."

Brinkman added. *Urgent*. Orlov would come if he got it, he decided. It was still uncertain; too uncertain. "There was no other way?" he asked.

"No," she said.

What about Harriet? thought Brinkman. Was there any need to move her out of New York? Not really. Orlov was the one who mattered. If they got him, arrangements for a reunion could be made anywhere, any time. For her to disappear suddenly would only alarm the CIA and cause unnecessary ripples. What if the Agency changed the operation and made a direct approach? And she told them? A gamble, Brinkman recognized. He said, "You want to see Pietr again?"

"That's a ridiculous question."

"Then do what I've told you and we'll get him out and he'll be with you for good. But try anything else . . . adding something extra to the message, for instance, or imagining some protection if you make a direct approach to the Americans, and I guarantee—I absolutely guarantee—that you'll never see him again."

Brinkman didn't enjoy the bullying even though it was necessary. In front of him the woman's lips quivered briefly but she managed to hold back from actually breaking down.

"What happens when he gets out?" she asked.

"We'll put you together," said Brinkman. "I've promised you that."

"I meant about Pietr. Do you imagine he'll cooperate

with you—and that's why you're doing all this, I know, in the hope that he'll cooperate—after what you've done?''

Brinkman smiled sympathetically. "Of course he will," he said.

"Don't be a bloody fool!"

"Don't you be a bloody fool, Harriet. The houses in which you'll live for the rest of your lives, and the money you'll have, and the protection you'll have, will all depend on the degree of cooperation Pietr provides. You should know what the Russians are like. How long do you think he'd survive—you'd survive—if your whereabouts became known and there was no protection?''

Harriet looked at him, eyes wide with a combination of astonishment and horror. "You are," she said as though she still couldn't believe it, "you are an absolute fucking bastard."

"Don't let me have to prove just how much of one," said Brinkman.

The strain was showing and he knew it. Orlov became further unsettled, discourteous to secretaries and chauffeurs—which he'd never been before—and unnecessarily critical of assistants and aides, blaming them for his own oversights and mistakes.

Habits had grown within habits for his regular meetings with Sevin. Determined that the agricultural policy paper should firmly establish Orlov's ascendancy, Sevin now had Orlov bringing draft pages to their nightly encounters for the old man to criticize and improve until he was entirely satisfied with them.

Orlov was conscious of tension as soon as he entered Sevin's office. The old man remained at his desk, which he normally left for the more comfortable conference area near the window. As he approached, Orlov saw the last ten pages he had presented spread out in front of the other man, heavily annotated with margin notes and corrections.

"What is it, Pietr?"

"I don't understand the question."

"The document began so well. Clear and concise, honestly confronting the stupidity of the system in insisting on norms from antiquated methods and machinery, without a sensible decision to suffer for two years while everything is reequipped and more land given over to private, peasant cultivation. We've talked it through, night after night. . . ." Sevin gestured disparagingly to the sheets before him. "This is terrible, Pietr. Your arguments ramble and are inconclusive. In at least three instances your figures are wrong. What is supposed to be a treatise that will revolutionize Soviet agriculture is lapsing into the sort of polemic we've suffered from the last fifty years."

"I'm sorry," Orlov apologized.

"So am I," said Sevin. "Deeply sorry. This isn't going to establish a reputation for you. It's going to destroy one."

"I'll rework it."

"Don't rework it," advised Sevin. "Scrap it and start again. Which is what we have to do with our agriculture."

"All right," agreed Orlov.

"So what is it?" prompted the old man again. "Is there a problem?"

Orlov searched desperately for an excuse, hating himself for it when it came. "The divorce," he said. "It's amicable to a degree. But it's always upsetting. You said so yourself."

Sevin nodded and smiled, a mystery solved. "I also said that these things happen, Pietr. The marriage is over. So put it behind you and start concentrating again upon the important thing. And the important thing is your future."

"I know," said Orlov. "That's what I'm thinking of now. My future."

CHAPTER TWENTY-NINE

Ann's affair with Jeremy Brinkman had created claustro-phobia within claustrophobia; she hadn't felt able to breath or think or move. So he'd been right. His absence had given her time to think. Without Jeremy and without Eddie, the tight feeling had gone. She'd been able to examine things—everything—calmly and clearly. She thought. She did love both of them. If that wasn't usual, then it wasn't usual, but for her it was possible. And real love—not merely dependence on Eddie and illicit excitement with Jeremy. So it came down to whom she loved better. Which it always had, she supposed.

She'd been wrong—so very wrong—in treating Eddie as she had. He should have discussed staying on—she *did* deserve that—but she'd been unjustified in raging as she had. Remorse for what else was happening. And she de-served to feel remorseful. He was kind and gentle and he did love her. And she believed he'd never cheated on her and never told her a lie: not an important, mattering-between-them sort of lie. It served her right, after the way she'd been behaving, if he were being drawn back to Ruth.

Had she tried hard enough with Moscow? She thought she had—didn't know what else she could have done—but she wasn't completely sure. Maybe what she hadn't done was to talk it through enough with Eddie. She thought he'd know, but clearly he hadn't. If she'd talked it out with him, maybe he wouldn't have made the commitment in Washington last time. But he had, and now she had to live with it. Or did she? He'd told her she didn't have to. Which had frightened her, she admitted. The thought of being alone had frightened her and the told-you-it-wouldn't-work attitude of her family frightened her. And her love for Jeremy frightened her. If only he hadn't come to Moscow in the first place! And hadn't been so much fun and been to Cambridge and liked ballet, and if only that night they hadn't. . . . Ann halted, confronting the effort to avoid the responsibility. He had come to Moscow, and he had done all those things, and they had done all those things, and now she loved him too.

Did he love her, as he said he did? She had no way of knowing. He was funnier than Eddie, even when Eddie was trying to be funny, which he didn't very often do any more, and he was more comfortable at dinner parties and more wonderful in bed, but if she were comparing—which was what she had to do, surely?—she felt that Jeremy was the harder of the two.

Ann tried to make the equation in a different way. Given the choice between her and his career, which would Jeremy choose? As she posed the question, she realized she already knew how Eddie would choose and then decided that wasn't being fair. He hadn't completely known how she felt. Jeremy did. Ann suspected it would be his career. But wasn't that how it should be? No. Or maybe yes. She didn't know. Dear God, she thought desperately, why did every hopeful answer produce two more unanswerable questions?

Maybe being alone in Moscow with Eddie would help resolve everything. She was glad he was coming back today, and she was glad that Jeremy was still away so that there wasn't any pressure from him. Maybe she'd have a chance to show Eddie she was sorry and he'd be able to tell her what he had meant by the strange conversation the evening he left.

She made an effort for Franklin's homecoming, arranging fresh flowers and timing the meal by his airport call so it was ready by the time he arrived. She kissed him, trying to show him how she felt, and said she'd missed him, which she had. He kissed her back and said he'd missed her too, which in truth he hadn't. He had been too busy.

Having bought her so many gifts from the last trip, he hadn't been able to think of anything better than the sort of chocolates that weren't available in Moscow, and she said she hadn't expected anything and that they were super.

When they sat down to eat, she asked, "So how was Paul?"

"Okay," said Franklin. "He started getting careless, staying out so that his mother didn't know where he was, and so she asked the counselors for help. There was a thought that he'd have to go back before the court but we managed to scare him against doing it again." Practically all true, and it sounded better than last time, he thought.

"Eddie?"

"What?"

"What did you mean the night you went away? About things not being as bad as I thought they were?"

Franklin had guessed she'd come back to it. Christ, she must hate Moscow. "The leadership's settled," he said, prepared for this too. "Chebrakin's in charge and all the indications are that he's a strong man who'll make changes stay there. I talked things through this time and everyone agreed with me. My agreement to stay on stands, if necessary, but the fresh thought is that we won't have to. That we'll leave on time."

Ann's face was set in disappointment. By herself, able to fantasize and conjecture, she'd imagined something far more positive. "So we *could* still stay?"

Franklin shook his head, wishing he could give her more but knowing he'd given her too much. "I told you, there's been a change of mind."

"And could be again?" Stop it, she told herself.

"I don't think there will be," he said, trying to sound as convincing as possible. Knowing the downward spiral of the subject and wanting to change it, he asked, "What happened while I was away?"

"Jeremy's gone back to London."

Franklin looked up from his food, frowning. "Recalled?" She nodded.

"When?"

"Day or two after you went to Washington."

"Did he say why?" It was a ridiculous quesiton, he knew, but the man might have said something.

"Not a thing," said Ann. "Just that it was going to be a quick trip."

"But he's not back yet?"

"Not as far as I know. . . ." She hesitated, smiling.

"Betty Harrison hasn't reported in, so I guess he hasn't returned."

"Not so much of a quick trip then."

"No," Ann agreed. Thank God, she thought. What had she decided: *really* decided? Nothing, she realized.

"It's good to be home," said Franklin, smiling across the table at her.

"It's good to have you home," she said. "I'm sorry."

"What about?" He knew she'd rehearsed an apology and wanted to give her her opportunity.

"For being such a bitch. I know I have been, and I'm really very sorry."

"Let's forget it," he said.

"Can you forget it?"

"For you I can do most things," he said.

That night they made love better than they had for a long time, Ann's passion a part of her saying sorry. She knew she made more demands than she should have, especially because of his tiredness after the flight, and she could have gone on, but finally she let him sleep. She lay awake beside him, wet from his wetness, *knowing* that she loved him. Please, she thought, refusing to confront reality again, please let Jeremy not come back to Moscow.

It was only two days before Friday, but it seemed like a millennium. The unanswerable queries and messages from Langley became an irritation, and at times Franklin let his impatience show. He'd expected them to have more control that they were showing and guessed that he was the shuttlecock in a game of headquarters politics. The advice before the meeting was practically insulting to someone of his experience, and Franklin didn't even bother to acknowledge the messages.

He took the usual precautions, getting to Krasnaya early, taking that day's issue of *Pravda* and settling himself on a different bench than before, hoping he would merge into the surroundings of the park. There was no guarantee that Orlov would be able to make the meeting—which was why they'd made the elastic arrangements they had—but the American knew that if he had to report a nonappearance to Langley, they'd fall out of the tree. He wondered what plans were being made in Washington—plans that he had no need to know—to gain the maximum advantage of Orlov's defection. There'd been someone of Orlov's ambassadorial rank to defect—once—but never someone in the Central Committee. They'd drain it until there was nothing more to get. Franklin hoped that Harriet Johnson was worth it.

He saw the Russian approaching, thinking to himself that Orlov showed just the slightest signs of increased confidence, as though he were becoming accustomed to the subterfuge. It was right that the man shouldn't be quite so nervous as he had been, but Franklin hoped he didn't become overconfident.

Orlov seated himself and started to read from his own *Pravda*. Franklin closed and folded his.

"Is everything arranged?" demanded Orlov, always the first edgy question.

"Yes," replied Franklin.

"When? How?"

The American set out the contingencies in detail, wanting to impress Orlov with the importance they attached to his defection and the care they were taking to ensure its success.

"I do not like the idea of trying to make the crossing into Finland," said Orlov.

"Neither do we. It's the fallback if it can't be done any other way."

"To form part of an overseas delegation would be best," agreed Orlov.

"Is it possible for you to arrange that?"

"I don't know," admitted the Russian. "It would have to be done carefully, not hurried. So it would mean a greater delay than I wanted."

"Surely the important thing is to make the crossing safely," said Franklin. "We don't gain anything by trying to hurry and risking interception." Franklin was conscious of the other man physically shuddering beside him at the prospect of arrest.

"Yes," said Orlov. "The important thing is to make the crossing safely."

"So you will try to get on an overseas delegation?"

"Yes," said Orlov.

Sensing the doubt in Orlov's voice, Franklin said, "If it looks difficult . . ." remembering Langley's anxiety, he added ". . . or as if it will take too long, then maybe we should consider a border crossing."

"That would be very dangerous, wouldn't it?"

"Yes," replied Franklin honestly.

"It must be a delegation," said Orlov, more to himself than to the American. He looked briefly sideways at the American. "Nothing has been done to involve Harriet?"

Franklin was glad it was Orlov who had raised the subject of the girl. He said, "No, we're doing exactly as you asked. But why? Tell me why you are so adamant against our putting her under some kind of protection."

"At the end, toward the very end, I suspected that I was under some sort of surveillance; that our relationship had become known." Orlov looked quickly sideways again.

"You know how the Soviet delegations are watched, of course?"

"Yes, I know how they're watched." Shit, he thought. Why hadn't the damned man told him this before? But then, why hadn't he asked?

"If they did suspect—and Harriet were to unaccountably disappear from where she should be—I might be put under surveillance here. So nothing would work."

Automatically Franklin gazed around the park. He said, "If there had been any reason to doubt you, you would not have had the immediate promotion. Would you?"

"I try to convince myself by the same reasoning," replied Orlov. "As I said, I only suspected from occasional remarks. Once a strange conversation with a man whom I knew to be KGB. Maybe it was nothing. I just don't want to take the slightest chance."

His own people would have detected any Soviet surveillance on the woman, Franklin thought. And would the Soviets have considered it necessary anyway, with Orlov back in Moscow? It created an uncertainty. Definitely one about which Langley should be warned. It would make the temperature go up a few more degrees. He said, "There isn't a risk. We've made no approach to her."

"What happens now?" asked Orlov.

"That depends on you," said Franklin. "You must try to get on a delegation."

Orlov nodded as though reminded. "We will keep these meetings?"

"Yes," said Franklin. They'd have to change the venue soon, but he guessed Krasnaya was safe for the moment.

"I'll risk Finland if it looks like things are taking too long. I don't think I can go on indefinitely," confessed Orlov.

Franklin looked worriedly at the Russian, aware for the first time of the strain etched around his eyes. He might appear more confident but the veneer was egg shell thin. "Don't worry," he said, trying to soothe the man. "It's all going to work out. Finland won't be as easy as a delegation, but there's a huge backup. We'll get you out."

"I so much want that," said Orlov. "I so much want to get out."

When Orlov returned to his office that afternoon, the consignment of books he was allowed from the West, as part of his privileges, was unpacked and arranged neatly on the side table beside his desk. There was one he hadn't ordered.

CHAPTER THIRTY

Maxwell was chain-smoking, punctuating the conversation with sudden coughs and fogging the room with smoke and smell. Brinkman thought he was repulsive. Once, he remembered, he had liked the man.

"Fantastic!" enthused Maxwell. "Absolutely fantastic. I knew it was going to work."

Asshole, thought Brinkman. He hadn't done all that he had to have an asshole like Maxwell take the credit. He'd make bloody sure it didn't happen. He said, "Nothing's worked yet. He still has to make contact, and we still have to get him across."

Maxwell lit another cigarette from the butt of the first and agreed, "There's a lot to be done. You'll need help."

"Not in Moscow," said Brinkman at once. The credit was going to be all his, unshared by anyone. He wondered

301

if Franklin had been put under the same sort of pressure. But Maxwell wasn't so easily dissuaded.

"It may be necessary," he insisted. "We'll start the formalities, as a precaution. Then if the need arises, we'll be in a position to move."

He couldn't dispute the common sense of that, Brinkman realized. He said, "I'll want full backup outside."

"I'll see you get it," said Maxwell.

And ensure that he would be seen by everyone to be providing it, thought Brinkman. He said, "What?"

"Depends how it goes between you and Orlov," pointed out Maxwell. "SAS snatch squads, I would have thought. Full logistical support. I'll do a full memorandum to the chief today. He'll probably want to raise it before the Security Committee. Maybe the Cabinet."

"Do you want me to stay?" asked Brinkman. Maxwell's name would be on every damned thing, he knew: initiator, planner, organizer and genius. Bloody asshole.

"No, no," said Maxwell quickly. "The message might be quite rapid in reaching Orlov. It's one of the uncertainties. I want you back there as soon as possible. Tonight."

"I was thinking of seeing my father," said Brinkman. The reminder might curb some of the other man's more extravagant claims.

"No time for social meetings. Come on, Jeremy! Don't you realize how important this is?"

If he hadn't witnessed it himself, he would have had difficulty believing the transformation in the man's attitude. "All right," he said. He'd made no plans to see the old man anyway.

Maxwell had smiled a lot, in anticipation, but now he became serious-faced. "You're going to be at the sharp end all the time," he warned. "We'll do everything we can, of course, but it all depends on you. . . ." The division chief paused for the familiar injunction. "So be careful. Be very, very careful. Don't forget what I said before. If anything goes wrong, we've got a major international incident."

Maybe Maxwell wouldn't try to take everything for himself; not at this stage anyway. Brinkman guessed the man would lay the groundwork for later credit but involve him too in case there were the need to apportion blame. "I understand," he said.

"Get back there, Jeremy," said Maxwell like the rugby cheerleader Brinkman suspected him of being on a Saturday afternoon. "Get back there and make it all work for all of us."

Maxwell wasn't a serious threat, Brinkman reasoned on the flight back to Moscow. He'd try for the credit of course—although taking out the necessary insurance—but he wouldn't be able to disguise who it was who had *made* it work. As Maxwell himself had said, there was going to be only one man at the sharp end taking all the risks. Him. And everyone—the important ones at least—would recognize that soon enough. Maybe better to let Maxwell make the effort, laying out sufficient rope with which to hang himself. Brinkman wouldn't be able to stay in Moscow afterward. So why not head of London's Moscow desk? He'd proved himself able a dozen times over. Getting Orlov out would be the culmination—and confirmation—of brilliant Soviet expertise. He hadn't imagined headquarters quite so soon; traditionally he was much too young. But what else was there? Washington was a recognized stepping stone, but he certainly wouldn't be acceptable there if it all worked out. And there was nowhere else that particularly attracted him. Anywhere else would be marking time, and Brinkman had no intention of marking time.

Washington might be out of the question for other reasons too, he thought. Ann had had enough time to decide. And he knew she loved him. As much as he loved her. Oh, he remembered her agonized outburst about loving both him and Franklin, but Brinkman was sure she didn't love the other man. What she felt for Franklin was a mixture of loyalty and kindness and dependence; and a reluctance too to break everything apart, having gone through his traumatic divorce. But not love. Brinkman knew how to tilt the balance, to make her reach the right decision. When he got Orlov out, the leadership after Chebrakin would become the biggest guessing game in town. Franklin would be kept in Moscow for years, sticking pins in lists of names. Brinkman was convinced it wouldn't take Ann more than minutes to make up her mind when he told her how long she was likely to remain there if she stayed with Franklin.

He wanted to call her the moment he got back to his own apartment but he controlled the impatience, not knowing if Franklin was back from Washington and unwilling to get involved in a conversation with the man should he answer the telephone. Instead he waited until the following day, reaching Franklin at the embassy and arranging to have lunch with him there. Having placed Franklin at the embassy and knowing he would remain there to keep their appointment, Brinkman called Ann and said he wanted to see her. Her objection, that she was going out, surprised him but he bulldozed over her, insisting that it was important and that he could remain for only a few moments anyway.

She kissed him when he entered but Brinkman thought he detected a reservation.

"What's so important?" she asked.

"I thought you would have known."

"Please!" she said. "Let's have a rest from that for a moment."

"There isn't time."

Ann had been looking away, refusing to meet his gaze. She turned to him now, curious. "Why not?"

"I might be leaving Moscow; being withdrawn."

Ann felt relief move through her. Without him here everything would be so much easier. There would be only one problem—the big problem—if Jeremy weren't here. "Wonderful!" she said, a reaction to her own feelings.

"I want you to come with me."

Ann shook her head. "I can't. I've thought about it and I can't."

"You can," insisted Brinkman, refusing her refusal. "I know how you feel about Eddie and what it would mean to you. But in the end, when it was all over, you know you'd be happier with me."

"No." Why wouldn't he just go away? Go away before she weakened and changed her mind and ended up as confused as she'd been before both men had left on their trips.

Should he tell her about Moscow? Not yet, Brinkman decided. He hadn't got Orlov yet and still had a lot to do. He'd have to let her know—hint at least—something of what might be happening to convince her that he was telling the truth. It was inevitable she'd challenge Franklin about not going back, and it would all become confused. And, more important, dangerous. "Think about it some more," he urged. "Think about what it would be like."

"I have."

Misunderstanding, he said, "So you know it would work out."

"Give me more time," she pleaded again, her well-worn retreat.

"I've told you," reminded Brinkman, "there isn't much time. I'm leaving here and I don't want to go without you."

Brinkman was slightly late in arriving at the American Embassy.

"How was London?" asked Franklin.

"Good to be back after so long," said Brinkman. "I had to go before a promotion board and there was some discussion about the next posting."

"Must be pleased about the way things have turned out here then?"

"Seems like it," said Brinkman. "How was Washington?"

"It was a personal thing. My first wife is having some problems with our eldest boy."

"Sorry to hear that," said Brinkman automatically.

"It'll work out."

"Wonder how long it'll be before things start moving here again."

"There's no way of telling," said the American.

Harriet had considered disobeying the Englishman's instructions about adding to the message, knowing there was nothing he could do to stop her, but then she remembered the threat and the way he had looked when he made it. So she'd done what she was told. Bastard, she thought.

As the days passed, however, she rationalized her attitude.

At least something—the most important thing—was happening. Pietr was coming! He'd gotten the divorce to protect Natalia, and the promotions and the acclaim hadn't meant as much to him as she did, and so he was coming! Which made it all right. Everything the same as the Americans would give you, the bastard had said. America had seemed obvious because she was there and because Pietr was familiar with it, but he'd adjust easily enough to England. They both would. The most important thing was that they would be together, and to be with him, she'd happily live in a tent in the middle of a jungle. Coming! She *knew* he was coming.

She should be patient—God, hadn't she been patient enough already?—but now that she was sure, it was more difficult than ever. Coming! she thought, her mind blocked by the word. She loved him so much.

CHAPTER THIRTY-ONE

The performance was a revival of *Don Quixote*, created in the specialized Soviet narrative form, and Brinkman had particularly wanted to see it. He supposed he could always apply for tickets through the embassy if Orlov didn't make the meeting and there was a need to come again. But Brinkman was reluctant to draw any attention to himself or the ballet, and he knew that all official applications were monitored. Reluctantly he decided that *Don Quixote* would have to go on tilting at windmills without his appreciation.

The choice of the Bolshoi had been a hurried decision in the Manhattan apartment, but Brinkman was pleased with it. It was the peak of arrival time, people ebbing and eddying throughout the expansive, ornate foyer, creating a swirl of concealment. He moved with the tide, always remaining near the north side but not standing around.

Brinkman realized he would be fortunate if it happened

so soon. If it happened at all. He frowned at the doubt. If Orlov had received the book, it *would* happen. He was sure the message was in it. Because of the CIA surveillance, he had not been able to actually go through the procedure with her, or to even be seen around the UN again, but he'd made her the same sort of confident visit the second night as he had the first, and Brinkman was convinced she had done what he'd told her to do, precisely as he'd told her to do it. So Orlov would definitely come if he'd received the book. But what if he hadn't?

It was now a waiting game to see whether the Americans could get their escape organized before he—through Harriet—had time to screw it all up. Except that at the pace he was working and the pace he knew the Americans were working, it could hardly be described as waiting. Which was what he was doing now. Hopefully.

The tide of people began to flow into the theater, taking away his cover. Brinkman moved over near a pillar. There was still quite a crowd around but he felt naked and exposed. Perhaps this wasn't as good a plan as he had thought. In fifteen minutes everyone else would be inside and he would be entirely obvious, an actual object of attention, the reverse of what he wanted to be.

Then Orlov came through the foyer, his coat over his arm, program already purchased and thoughtfully—cleverly—in his hand. It would have been difficult to imagine the Russian as anything other than a genuine ballet lover, even if he were under surveillance.

Orlov had no reason to know—or imagine—why he was there, remembered Brinkman. He moved out through the rapidly thinning crowd, not to intercept the Russian but to move parallel and just slightly ahead of him so that Orlov would see him approach. The man gave no sign of recognition until just before Brinkman spoke, a frown of half-recollection deepening to full memory as soon as he heard the words.

"The American Embassy," said Brinkman. With only seconds to snare the other man, he went on. "The night you made the approach to Franklin. I've seen Harriet, Comrade Orlov. I spoke to her a few days ago in New York. She's very anxious to see you again. I've promised her I'll make that possible."

Brinkman broke away without waiting for a reaction, moving not toward the body of the theater, the direction in which the latecomers were going, but through the last exit door out onto Sverdlova, startled at the sudden darkness. It should have worked, but he didn't know if it had. He'd been quite certain until the actual moment of approach, but now he wasn't. He didn't know what he would do—what he could do—if Orlov didn't follow.

But he did.

Brinkman was conscious of the footsteps—if it were an arrest, there would be more than one man, surely—and then the Russian drew level and reached out to stop him.

"What is it? What does it mean?" demanded the Russian.

He'd made the catch, thought Brinkman. Was this exhausted but triumphant feeling the sensation that fishermen felt at landing a tarpon after a battle that seemed as though it would never end? It was an intrusive, overly dramatic thought and Brinkman put it aside irritably, knowing that he had to establish control from the outset. "We're going toward Red Square," he pointed out. "I think we should walk the other way, don't you?"

Obediently Orlov turned. Practically gaffed, thought Brinkman. "It means that the British want to offer you everything that the Americans have," he said. "I know all about it. Why you want to defect . . . that you intend to defect. We want you to change your plans. Come with us. Not the Americans.''

"That is not possible. There are plans . . ." started Orlov, but Brinkman cut him off, determined for control. "It is possible. The plans must be broken. If they're not, then you won't see Harriet again.''

"Explain yourself," said the Russian.

Brinkman knew the words now; after all, he'd set them out to Maxwell and to Harriet and then to Maxwell a second time. Orlov listened in silence, so it did not take very long. Brinkman concluded, "I'm not interested in your telling me what you think of me," he said, his voice even. "Harriet called me a bastard, a fucking bastard actually, and I agreed with her. It's just the way it has to be.''

Orlov didn't waste his time on anger and Brinkman was grateful. "Who says it's the way it has to be?" he asked.

"We do," said Brinkman. "Please don't be resentful. I know it's going to be difficult at first. But I mean what I say. We'll provide everything that the Americans would have provided. Maybe more. You will be safe, and Harriet will be safe. Eventually, if you decide you don't like England, it would probably be possible for you to go on to America.''

"After you think you've got everything from me that it's possible to get?"

"Yes," said Brinkman, maintaining brutal honesty. "After we think we've got every last thing it's possible to get from you. I've been utterly and completely truthful with you. I don't know or care what the Americans have told you. You know what you're doing and you know what we want for helping you . . . for making it possible.

I want you to believe me. And I want you to believe me when I say that if you don't come with me, you won't go with anyone.''

"Do you enjoy what you do, Mr. Brinkman?''

"I'm prepared to argue philosophy and morals if you want to,'' said Brinkman easily. "Would you like to argue the morality of the Soviet occupation of Afghanistan? Or the psychiatric prisons in which you incarcerate and make mindless your dissidents? Or the Siberian gulags? All right, you are not personally involved. Governments and members of those governments never are. In America there's even an accepted phrase freeing the president from any culpability for anything that goes wrong and becomes public knowledge. It's called plausible denial. I'm the sort of person who's denied and cast aside if anything *does* go wrong. Despite knowing which, yes, I like it. I'm not doing you any harm, Comrade Orlov. You want to cross to the West to be with someone you love and I'm making that possible for you. I don't see anything to be ashamed of in that.''

"You evaded the criticism and you know it,'' said Orlov. "I was talking about your threats if I don't agree to cooperate with you.''

"What are you prepared to do to get to the West?'' demanded Brinkman.

Orlov considered the question. "Anything,'' he said finally. "I am quite determined.''

"Which is what I am, professionally determined,'' said Brinkman. "So I am prepared to do what needs to be done to achieve the objective.''

"Do you know what would happen to me if you exposed me to the authorities?''

The last time he'd walked along this road it had been

with Ann, Brinkman remembered. He said, "Yes, I know what would happen to you. And so do you. Which is why I know, after you've made the protests and the arguments, you'll do exactly as I say."

"Yes," conceded Orlov, suddenly sag-shouldered. "I suppose I will, won't I? There's really no alternative, is there?"

"Not now, no," said Brinkman. "But it isn't as though you aren't achieving what you want, is it?"

"Should I be comforted by that?"

"I don't see why not."

"What do you want me to do?"

"Tell me all the arrangements you've reached so far with the Americans. All the plans that have been made."

It took a long time and before Orlov had finished, they had walked a considerable distance from the center of the city and turned back again. When Orlov ended, Brinkman asked, "What about a delegation?"

"It hasn't been possible, not yet. The occasion hasn't occurred to make even discussing it possible."

"It's the best way, so try for that if you can," said Brinkman. "Somewhere in the East if actually getting out into Western Europe isn't possible. I'll ensure that London creates an incursion operation to get you out if a delegation is not possible."

"You are so similar to the American," said Orlov.

We even share the same wife, thought Brinkman. He said, "You must break all contact, of course. No more meetings."

"What if his response is what yours would have been?"

"It won't be," said Brinkman confidently. "He won't know you're with me. He'll imagine some internal difficulty."

"Which could arise," said Orlov.

"What do you mean?" asked Brinkman sharply.

Orlov recounted his fear that his affair with Harriet might have been suspected and the danger that would arise from Brinkman's contact. In the darkness Brinkman smiled; the reason why the Americans had not put the woman under agreed protection finally explained. He wasn't behind in the race any more, he thought. Now he was way out ahead and could actually see the finish line, the white tape stretched out invitingly. He said, "No one was aware of my approaching her. If the KGB had known, they wouldn't have let the book reach you. And if they had, we'd have been arrested by now."

Abruptly Orlov stared around him. "Yes," he said. "Yes, I suppose you are right."

"So there's no danger to Harriet and there's no danger to you. You're going to get out."

"I suppose you'll want to maintain this sort of contact," said Orlov wearily.

They were near the theater now and Brinkman paused, remembering how quickly the protectively filled foyer had emptied. "Not inside," he said. There was an alley next to a building almost a block from the theater, a service entry to an area behind the main building. "There," said Brinkman, pointing. "Every Tuesday I shall walk past that alley at precisely seven-thirty in the direction of the Bolshoi. You approach from the other direction. You can rely on me to have arranged everything outside. There's no need for us to talk about that, not until the very end. I only want to hear from you if you've succeeded in getting on a delegation. If we've nothing to say to each other, we make no contact."

Orlov sighed. "I understand."

"It's going to be all right," said Brinkman.

Orlov turned to confront the Englishman. "I'm sick of hearing that," he said, "and phrases like it. Shall I tell you something, Mr. Brinkman? I know I'm trapped now. Trapped without any possibility of going back. But if I had that opportunity, I think I would. I think I'd abandon Harriet and stay in Russia."

Franklin waited until two o'clock on the first Friday. In his later message to Langley he explained that there could be a dozen perfectly normal explanations for why Orlov had failed to keep the appointment. But the excuses didn't succeed. There was a flurry of questions, a lot of which he couldn't answer, and with growing impatience he pointed out the impossibility of his knowing the answers. Aware, even from so far away, of how the inquest appeared to be growing, he repeated Orlov's concern about Harriet and asked for categoric assurance that no KGB watch squad could have become aware of their surveillance. It came but it was muted and Franklin felt he'd made a telling point. He scoured every newspaper and publication in the intervening week for any mention of Orlov. There was none.

Franklin arrived earlier on the second Friday, burning with anger at the futile instruction cables that had been sent to him. He satisfied himself that Krasnaya wasn't under surveillance—accepting as he did so that the fact diminished his point about any possible KGB action against Orlov beause of CIA interest in Harriet Johnson. He positioned himself half an hour early at the bench where they had met before; he waited until two-thirty.

He could provide no fresh answers this time but the questions came anyway, three signed by the director himself, demanding a personal explanation.

When Orlov failed to show up on the third Friday, one of the first cables from Washington said they had succeeded in getting visas for two men who would be arriving before the fourth Friday. There was nothing whatsoever for them to do—less now that Orlov had severed contact—but it enabled Langley once more to imagine they were doing something positive. It also, he realized, was a positive indication of his inability to continue successfully with the operation. Fuck them, he thought.

Orlov was sure he had completely recovered in Sevin's estimation. It had taken extreme will power and concentration—all he had—but he'd succeeded in clearing his mind of everything but the agricultural policy. He'd entirely rewritten the offending pages. Sevin had accepted them practically without correction and complimented him upon the improvement, just as he had complimented him on those that had followed.

And it was through the farm project that Orlov saw his chance. He had evolved a system from the beginning of monitoring everything that was happening elsewhere the work of other committees and groups—and it was two weeks after the encounter with Brinkman at the Bolshoi that he saw the memorandum from the central working committee concerning the delegation visit to Europe. He felt shaken by the initial flood of excitement. For a moment the paper positively trembled in his hand so that he had difficulty in reading the words. France first—the inviting country—and then Denmark, to study that country's dairy system. A full fifteen days. Starting in just three and a half weeks' time.

Orlov prepared his approach to Sevin with the care that he had used over the embassy visit, getting approval for his latest section of the report first and then letting the conversation between them ramble into generalities before he mentioned, in an apparent aside, the proposed European visit.

When Sevin seized upon it, as Orlov guessed he would, the younger Russian said, more direct than before, ''I thought I should be part of the delegation.'' He nodded toward the papers on Sevin's desk. ''All that is written from previous reports and statistics. I'd be better able to argue innovations if I'd personally seen some.'' What right had he had to question morality with Brinkman? thought Orlov.

''The names will have already been selected,'' pointed out Sevin.

''I realize that,'' said Orlov. ''I wonder why the visit wasn't made generally known in the first place.''

The reaction of Sevin, who had lived through a lifetime of plot and counterplot, was predictable. ''You think it was deliberately kept from us?''

''I've no way of knowing that,'' said Orlov honestly. ''Was it ever brought up at any meeting you attended?''

''No,'' said the old man.

''Nor any which I've sat,'' said Orlov. Playing the best card last, he said, ''Comrade Didenko is on the central Working Committee.''

Sevin smiled in appreciation. ''You think he is excluding us?''

''I do not know,'' said Orlov.

Four days later Sevin announced to Orlov that he would be part of the Soviet delegation to France and Denmark.

CHAPTER THIRTY-TWO

It was perfect. Brinkman couldn't believe how perfect. There was an intervening Tuesday after Orlov whispered the details of the delegation agreement in the alley near the Bolshoi, which enabled London to make and then double-check every conceivable part of their snatch plan and actually discuss it with Brinkman before he made his final meeting with the Russian. The plan was perfect too because it was so simple.

Orlov was more nervous than Brinkman had ever seen him, the apprehension vibrating through him so that he visibly shook. This was something Brinkman had not properly considered; he hoped the Russian could last it out.

"Only two more days," he said urgently, pulled into the shadows alongside the Russian. "This time on Thursday it'll all be over. You'll be safe."

"It'll be all right," assured Orlov, knowing the reason for Brinkman's concern. He still shook.

He would be calmed by hearing how good the arrangements were, thought Brinkman. The Soviet delegation was going direct to the Charles de Gaulle Airport on a scheduled Aeroflot flight, departing Sheremetyevo at seven in the evening. Orlov was not to bother about anything; it was all being done for him. London was sending a complete contingent to Paris well in advance of the Moscow flight, all briefed from the photographs. Some of them would be lingering within the baggage-claim and immigration areas, and more outside. The delegation would probably be spared normal procedures. Orlov was to follow whatever routine the French wanted, and nothing else—until the moment he emerged into the public part of the airport. At the moment of his emergence, the diversion would occur, an incendiary explosion in a washroom, which would create an instant fire.

Orlov would be aware of men around him, hurrying him away. He was to go unprotesting with them, no matter what was happening behind with the rest of the Russian party. There would be a car waiting. After three switches of vehicle, they'd reach the military airfield near Orly. A British military aircraft would be waiting there, its flight already cleared and with a flight plan filed to the military airfield of Northolt, near London. The passenger manifest would have Orlov listed under the name of the British passport he would be given during the drive to the airfield, his photograph and forged signature already affixed.

"You will not be with me?" asked Orlov. He was constantly looking around as though expecting arrest at any moment.

They had recognized Orlov's need for someone he knew,

even though they hadn't guessed he would be in such bad shape.

"Not on that flight," said Brinkman. "The men who are going to snatch you are experts. There's no need—no need at all—for you to think everything won't go as I've said it will. An hour after the Aeroflot flight, there's a British Airways service to London. I shall be on it. By the time you get to Northolt, I'll be there to meet you."

"You promise?" demanded Orlov, gripping Brinkman's arm.

"I promise," assured Brinkman. "I'll be there to meet you and I'll stay with you." That hadn't been part of the planning but Brinkman couldn't imagine Maxwell objecting.

"What about Harriet?" asked Orlov.

"We're doing exactly as you asked," said Brinkman. "The moment you're safe, people already in New York will bring her to you in England. Everything's been thought of."

"I wish there weren't so long to wait."

"Only two more days," repeated Brinkman. "You've waited a long time. You can wait two more days."

"You mean what you say? You won't try to cheat or trick me?"

He deserved the question, Brinkman knew, unoffended. "No," he said, "I'll not cheat you. Everything will happen as I've promised it will."

"We will not see each other again until London?"

Brinkman realized Orlov's fear of being left alone but there was nothing he could do to help him. "Not until London," he said. Now he took the Russian's arm. "You can do it!" he said as though he were trying physically to transmit the confidence. "You can do it."

"I hope I can," said Orlov honestly.

Brinkman decided against advising London of Orlov's nervousness. It was only natural—although Brinkman wished it weren't quite so bad—and there was nothing they could do about it if they'd wanted to.

Now for Ann. There had been only one proper meeting since his return from London, and she'd been reluctant to make love. It had been obvious, and it had been awful, and afterward they'd had their first real argument, but Brinkman wasn't sorry about it. She'd admitted that she thought she did love him and repeated it several times.

He was thinking of Ann after the meeting with Orlov. When he suddenly saw a danger he hadn't thought of before—the danger of Franklin's learning that the Russian was leaving the country. He went to bed still thinking it over.

On Wednesday morning he immersed himself in back copies of *Pravda* and *Izvestia* and the smaller publications and the *Tass* tapes, alert for any mention of the delegation. He found it in an issue of *Pravda* eight days earlier, his apprehension intense until he read it through. It was an announcement of the delegation's existence and the countries it was visiting but contained no names. With a date as a guide, Brinkman checked the *Tass* wires for that day. They'd carried it as a story but again omitted names. Lucky, he decided. He'd been very lucky.

Although Brinkman was satisfied that no danger existed, the possibility that one *might* have arisen unsettled him. It was an oversight and a stupid one, certainly one he should have considered. Careful, he thought. He was letting the tension get to him, as it had already gotten to Orlov. But it wasn't entirely Orlov and what was going to happen. It was Ann as well.

He risked the call to her apartment and, intent upon

omens, decided from the tone of her voice that she was
pleased to hear from him.

"I'm leaving," he said.

"What!"

There couldn't be any mistaking the feeling in her voice
that time, thought Brinkman. "Tomorrow," he said. "It's
all very sudden."

"For good?"

"Yes."

It was what she wanted, thought Ann at the other end of
the telephone. Or what she *imagined* she wanted. Now that
it was happening—happening the way she'd prayed it
would when he was last in London—she wasn't so sure.
"Will I see you again?"

"That's the decision I've been asking you to make for
weeks."

"I didn't mean that."

"I'm not going until tomorrow night."

"I think Eddie is going to be at the embassy all day. I
could telephone."

"I'll wait for your call. And, Ann?"

"Yes."

"I want the right decision."

And he knew how to get it, Brinkman decided. He'd
held back until now, but he couldn't any longer. He'd
spell out to her how long she'd have to stay in Moscow—
exaggerate even. He'd tell her if she doubted him to
challenge Franklin directly, to try to get a definite time.
That would sway it, Brinkman decided. He wished he
hadn't had to use it as the final pressure and that she'd
found it easier to decide between them. But she hadn't, so
there it was. He intended to leave Moscow with everything
he wanted.

* * *

The senior of the two men Langley sent was a supervisor—the same grade as Franklin—named Art Blakey. He and the younger man, whose name was King, were naturally aware of what had happened and the pointlessness of their being sent in, and they were embarrassed by it. Blakey actually apologized on the first day, and Franklin said he understood and that it didn't matter. They'd followed the routine because they'd had to, going separately out to Krasnaya and waiting until it was senseless to wait any longer and then returning to the embassy.

The message continued between Langley and Moscow, equally without point, and on the Wednesday of the week that the Soviet delegation was scheduled to leave for France—while Brinkman was talking on the telephone to Ann, in fact—the instructions came that they were again to go out to Krasnaya on Friday.

"Know what I'd like?" said Blakey. "I'd like Orlov to turn up this week with a perfectly sensible explanation of why he hasn't made the contacts so that all those pricks at headquarters would realize that they've been just that, pricks."

"It would be good," agreed Franklin. "But I can't see it happening, can you?"

"You think it was the watch on the woman in New York?"

"I don't know," said Franklin, "I would have expected our people to have recognized any Soviet surveillance if there'd been any."

"What about an announcement concerning Orlov if they'd scooped him up because of what we were doing in New York?" asked King.

"Not yet," said Franklin. "Maybe not at all. Maybe

just something in a few months' time saying that he had been voted off the committee. He'd have been in jail by then of course.''

"Creepy country," said King, who hadn't been in Russia before.

"You know how it happened, don't you?" Blakey said to Franklin. "How your balls got caught in the vise?"

"How?" asked Franklin.

"Perelmen," said Blakey. "George Bush was a CIA director and made vice-president, and Perelmen thought the pathway looked pretty attractive. Set out to show himself the indispensable foreign-affairs expert, better than State and better than anyone.''

"Sorry I let him down," said Franklin bitterly.

"You didn't," said Blakey. "He let himself down by announcing coups before they happened. This thing should have been kept under wraps so tight an Egyptian mummy would have looked naked.''

"Pity it wasn't," said Franklin.

"Sure is," agreed Blakey. "Now it's blame time and you're right at the end of the line. You know how it works. You're the one who fouled up, according to the book. All the panic and bullshit will be justified, the proper reaction to what seemed to be happening. You're the one left carrying the can.''

"Seems pretty shitty," said King, the man of least experience.

"Believe me," said Blakey. "I'm right."

Just how right was proven late that Wednesday. After further consideration, cabled Hubble, it had been decided that there would be no purpose in Franklin's tour being extended longer than was originally scheduled. In fact, he could start making preparations for an early pull-out. Blakey was to remain as acting resident. Franklin smiled down at the decision, remembering ironically that it was what he'd told Ann after his most recent return from Washington. How quickly things had changed since that trip. Ann would be pleased, he thought.

"I'm sorry," said Blakey when Franklin showed him the cable. "I didn't try for this, you know."

"I know you didn't," said Franklin. "Hope it works out better for you than it did for me."

"He promised," protested Paul. "He promised he'd write and fix the trip."

"Your father's very busy, darling," said Ruth. "If he made a promise, he'll keep it."

"The vacation's now."

"Why not write again, to remind him?"

"I've written twice already. He hasn't bothered to reply."

"That's not fair," said Ruth. "He always replies."

"You know what I think?" asked Paul. "I think he's dumped us, just like before."

CHAPTER THIRTY-THREE

Brinkman had acquired few possessions in Moscow. Wanting to travel light, he took only an overnight shoulder bag—and that more for effect at the airport than for necessity—and left everything else to be shipped out by the embassy as diplomatic luggage. He took particular care in packing the icon that Ann had given him on his birthday, knowing it was going to have special meaning to both of them. He was ready very early in the day, like a child anxious for a long holiday. He remained careful in everything he did. He paid Kabalin, the muttering maid, three weeks' salary and said he looked forward to returning. She thanked him and promised to come in while he was away as she always did, and Brinkman said he would appreciate it, knowing that she was lying. She hadn't stolen as much as he had expected and he decided he'd been lucky. He guessed that she'd come under some severe investigation after everything happened, which was unfortunate but unavoidable.

Brinkman moved aimlessly around the apartment, impatient for Ann's call, idly looking about to impress it on his memory. It would be a good memory, he decided. He'd achieved everything he'd set out to do: more, in fact. And no one could detract from that. He'd proved himself. It didn't matter what credit Maxwell attempted to claim; his reputation had been established before this. What was happening today was just planting the flag on top of the mountain.

He looked at his watch, calculating the time difference. It would have already started by now in London. The aircraft probably would have gone to France overnight. Maybe also the snatch squad that was going to work outside the restricted areas. He wondered where those who were going to be on the inside picked up the international flight, to put them in the right terminal area. There'd be a hell of a row, of course. France protesting—because they had to—about violation and invasion of sovereignty, and Russia denouncing everything and everybody. All because of him, thought Brinkman in private triumph. He pitied everyone he was leaving behind in Moscow. Life was going to be unbearable for a lot of people for a long time after this. He guessed that Russia would insist upon some expulsions from the British Embassy here and wondered who. Someone senior if they tried to equate the action against Orlov's rank. To do that properly would mean the ambassador, he supposed. All because of me, he thought again.

He snatched at the telephone when it rang. It was Ann. He promised to be with her in fifteen minutes. He made it in ten. She didn't hold back when he kissed her and he thought her eyes were wet. He wondered if she'd been crying at the thought of his going.

"I never really thought you meant it," she said. "About leaving, I mean. I just thought it was something you said to try to force me to make up my mind."

"Now you know it wasn't," he said. He paused. "But I do want you to make up your mind."

She shook her head, not in refusal but in uncertainty, looking away from him. If it had to be, it had to be, thought Brinkman. He said, "Eddie lied to you, Ann. About how long you're likely to be here. I can't tell you how I know. All I ask is that you trust me. There are going to be a lot of things happening here. Things that are going to upset a lot of forecasts. Eddie's going to be kept on here not just for months but for years. Which means—if you stay—that you'll be here for years. You're going to become the den mother of the diplomatic wives, like Betty Harrison. You're going to see them come and you're going to see them go, and you'll still be here."

"No!" she cried. "Eddie's never lied to me. He told me that and I believe him. He said it wouldn't be as bad as I first thought."

"What the hell does that mean?" he asked, his anger slipping. "Damn lie, and you know it. He was trying to squeeze out of a corner and so he said something that sounded okay just to get you off his back. But it doesn't *mean* anything. Can't you see that?"

Ann nodded dumbly. It *was* vague, just as he said it was. "I'm not brave enough," she said.

"I'll make you brave," said Brinkman urgently, seeing the crack widen. "Just leave. Just leave Moscow—use whatever excuse you like—and then let him know you're not coming back."

"I couldn't do it like that," she said. "That wouldn't be . . ." she hesitated at the word. ". . . I know it doesn't sound right, but that wouldn't be honest. If I'm going to leave, I'll tell him so to his face."

"Tell him then."

"I don't know that I want to."

"Don't tell me again that you're confused. I'm fed up with hearing it!"

"Don't pressure me!"

"You know what you want to do. So do it!"

"Why did you ever have to come to Moscow? If you hadn't come here, everything would have been all right."

"You know that isn't true."

"I'll decide," she said.

"When? And don't say soon; don't try to run away again."

"A week," she said. "I'll decide in a week. I promise."

If she hadn't intended to do it, she would have refused now, here, on the spot, thought Brinkman. She was going to come with him. He'd known all along she would. He held out his arms and she came to him, her arms tight around him. He wanted to make love to her and knew she wanted it too. There wasn't time; not for how he wanted to make love. He didn't want a snatched, illicit quickie. That was all over. He wanted her to be his wife and now he knew she was going to be. "I must go," he said, seeing at once from her frown of annoyance that he wasn't doing what she expected.

"I thought you'd have more time."

"There'll be all the time in the world later," he said.

"Yes," she said distantly. "All the time in the world."

"A week?"

"That's what I said."

"I'll be waiting. It's going to be wonderful, Ann. Believe me, everything is going to be wonderful." Did Orlov love Harriet as much as he loved Ann? He must, Brinkman supposed.

The moment of actual parting was difficult for them, each holding to the other, reluctant to end the physical contact, but Brinkman knew he had to go. It would be ludicrously stupid to ruin everything by staying here an extra thirty minutes when they had a whole lifetime ahead of them.

"I'll be waiting," he reminded her.

"I know."

"I love you." He waited but she didn't respond, and he smiled and kissed her, unconcerned. She'd pleaded with him not to pressure her, and he wouldn't.

Brinkman didn't take an embassy vehicle to the airport, deciding instead upon one of the officially approved airport taxis. As the vehicle started to clear the Moscow suburbs, his watch showed six o'clock. Orlov would be at Sheremetyevo now, maybe going through the routine of a departure ceremony. Brinkman hoped the man's nerve had held. It was the one uncertainty that remained, whether or not Orlov would actually be able to go through with the plan without someone in the party—and there would be KGB guardians present, as there were on every overseas Russian trips—becoming aware of his anxiety. Maybe he should have gone earlier to the airport to see the man through. But why? There was nothing he could have done. They hadn't arranged that he should be there, so his unexpected appearance might have done the reverse, alarming the man even more.

There was nothing he could do now. Nothing except hope. If Orlov made the plane, everything would be all right. All he had to do then was wait until he arrived in Paris and let himself be spirited away by men who would already be in place now, calm and expert and trained and waiting.

They began leaving the city behind and Brinkman looked back, realizing it would be his last sight of the Soviet capital. A good memory, he thought again. Now it was time to move on. To what? he wondered.

Dusk was falling when Brinkman reached the airport. He remained inside the taxi to pay the driver and then stepped out onto the wide pavement in front of the departure building. The large car-park was filled, as it always appeared to be, and cars and taxis formed a solid line against the curb. Brinkman picked his way through them, heading toward the identifiable insignia of British Airways, which would lead him to the desk inside. It was about five doors ahead and Brinkman thought, in passing, that he should have had the driver bring him nearer.

He'd practically reached it when he heard the shout. At first he didn't react because there was no one who could be shouting for him. And then he heard it again and stared beyond the door into the British Airways area. Orlov had been walking, waving to attract his attention, but suddenly the Russian began to run, and as he did so, Brinkman saw uniformed security guards a long way behind him, and plainclothesmen, much nearer, appeared to be moving with some coordination, fanning out into an embracing movement. Brinkman thought he heard *Stoitye!* but he wasn't certain because ordinary passengers were becoming aware of the scene and there were other shouts. Orlov was only about twenty yards away, and Brinkman knew everything had gone disastrously wrong and that he should feign ignorance of the man, but then Orlov was upon him, clutching at him as he had that last time near the Bolshoi, and he couldn't shake him off.

"What is it?" demanded Orlov. "What's gone wrong?"

Brinkman stared at the man, unable to comprehend what was happening. "The plane!" he shouted. "Why aren't you on the plane?"

"The message," said Orlov. "The message at the desk telling me not to board . . . why did you leave the message? It was madness . . . !"

"But I didn't . . ." tried Brinkman. The security police were much nearer now, ordered by the plainclothesmen. Brinkman heard *Stoitye!* very clearly this time, and Orlov heard it too, but he didn't stop as he was told. All control gone now, fear whimpering from him, the Russian pulled himself away from Brinkman and started through the line of parked cars, beginning to run mindlessly. There were more demands to stop and Orlov's hand thrust out, a seeming gesture of rejection that the later inquiry determined had made the security men imagine that the fleeing Russian had a weapon and intended using it, because for them to start shooting was a mistake, against every order.

Instinctively Brinkman had reached out, trying to hold on to the thrusting-away man, and when he missed, he started going through the cars too, so that they were both running. The initial bullets from the first misunderstanding soldier were wide, warning shots, but other security men imagined they were being fired at now. With the breath groaning from him, Brinkman shouted for Orlov to stop, but the Russian was beyond reach, encompassed and completely driven by the fear he'd tried so hard to control.

Brinkman was the first to be hit when everyone started firing, an agonizing pain tearing into his thigh like a punch that, after the first spurt of agony, took all feeling away, and he screamed. The sound was cut short when the weapons started firing on automatic and he was caught by the first swathe. The same arc caught Orlov too, tipping both men over the lip of the car-park perimeter.

It was about a five-foot drop . . . and each was dead when he reached the bottom.

CHAPTER THIRTY-FOUR

Franklin started moving when he saw they were hit—knowing they were dead—wanting to get out onto the road before the Russians cordoned the airport; it shouldn't have happened like this, and he was shaking with the shock of it and knew he couldn't withstand or pass any examination. He kept just within the speed limit to avoid attracting attention. About a mile in toward Moscow a lot of police and military vehicles hurtled past in the opposite direction, sirens blaring, but no one tried to stop him. It was another five miles before he felt he was safe. The shaking was still as bad. He'd intended going to the embassy anyway, but it was essential now. He needed to recover.

He drove directly to Chaykovskovo. At this time of night the embassy would be deserted except for the skeleton night staff; certainly Art Blakey and King wouldn't be there. He wanted the CIA residency within the embassy to himself. Its innermost room was steel-lined for security, and it was there he went, sitting at the desk and physically holding himself, trying to quiet the reaction. He stared around the room, willing himself back to normality by the familiarity of accustomed surroundings.

There were duplicate cipher machines for direct contact with Langley if necessary, and a radio receiver and transmitter against the far wall. Adjoining that was the special equipment Franklin had created and assembled with his electronic expertise. He'd start to dismantle it tomorrow, thought the American as he recovered; begin packing everything, in fact. They'd said he could pull out early, so why not? Reminded, he called the duty clerk to ensure that the diplomatic pouch hadn't gone yet and said he had a letter to enclose in it and could they wait. The clerk said there was plenty of time; there was some sort of flap out at the airport and all the planes were delayed anyway.

Writing to Paul would help, Franklin decided; something else that was normal. He always typed his correspondence because his handwriting was so bad. He apologized to the boy for not replying earlier to his letters but said he had been extremely busy. The Moscow trip didn't look like happening now because unexpectedly he was being reassigned, but that was great because at the moment it looked like Washington, which meant they could see each other all the time. When he and John got to know Ann—he was sure they were going to like her—they could stay over weekends and things like that. He was sorry about the Moscow vacation but, thinking about it, they might have found it dull after a while. Ann didn't like it all that much herself. To make up for Moscow, why didn't they go away for a vacation in America? His own father had taken him as a kid on horseback through a lot of the Grand Canyon.

Why didn't they do that, go camping out? Something that hadn't been available when he was a boy were the special small-plane flights out of Las Vegas, flying right along the Canyon. They could do that if they preferred it. Why didn't Paul talk it over with John and let him know when he got back? He didn't know exactly when that would be, but it would be soon.

He sent his love to John and Ruth, read the letter through and then sealed it. As a test, to ensure he was all right now, he took it down to the duty clerk. The man repeated there was no hurry. The latest news was that the airport was closed. From the clerk's reaction, Franklin knew he'd passed his own test.

The door leading into the inner top-security room was steel-lined of course, and fitted with a designation window into which colored strips could be displayed from the inside, indicating the degree of security applicable to whatever was going on within. Crimson meant absolute security and excluded even the ambassador. Franklin locked the door—using all the devices—and although the embassy was empty, put up the crimson code. He sat for a long time at the desk, staring at the electrical equipment he had created but not really aware of it, deep in thought. At last, quite recovered now, he stirred, reaching back into the cabinet and taking out a burn bag. He erected it carefully upon its tripod and with even greater care, prepared the phosphorus compound that operated upon contact with air and incinerated whatever was put inside. Satisfied, he went to the safe for which, at the moment, only he had the combination; they'd change it after he left, giving Blakey a new one. There were a lot of tapes because Franklin had installed nine listening devices in the apartment as an

internal precaution and so that he would have detected a
Soviet entry when they were out.

The devices were in those ridiculous *matroyshka* doll
sets that Ann seemed to like and in the light socket by the
bed, and again in the living room; and every telephone was
monitored, not in the instrument itself—which the Russians would have discovered had they attempted a bug—
but back along the actual connecting wire. All were voice-
and noise-activated so that the installation was automatic,
feeding directly into the electronic equipment that Franklin
intended to dismantle the following day.

The tapes were numbered and dated; Franklin was a
methodical man. Tape one was recorded while he had been
in America the first time. Franklin picked it up and was
moving toward the bag when he hesitated, then changed
his mind. Instead he slotted it into the machine and de-
pressed the button, listening to the first dinner party that
Ann and Brinkman had had in the apartment.

"Christ, it hasn't been bloody easy!" he heard Ann say.
And then he heard her tell Brinkman about their meeting
and their love—did she really think of him as all John
Wayne and howdy? *"Anywhere but here! If there were an
embassy at the North Pole, I'd happily swap it for here."*
Franklin ran the tape on, knowing the places to stop. It
was Brinkman's voice. *"It's allowed, for special friends."*
Franklin snapped the tape from the machine and dropped it
into the burn bag. There was a faint skein of black smoke
and a brief acrid smell. The next tape was from the
telephone, where the installation was better and the quality
clearer.

"What are you doing?"

*"Nothing much. Nothing at all, in fact. Just sitting
here, thinking."*

"What about?"

"I would have thought that was obvious."

"Sorry, stupid question."

There'd been a lot of discussion about regret on that tape.

"Sorry?"

"Of course I'm sorry! Aren't you?"

"I don't think so."

"You haven't as much to be sorry about."

"I don't think I would be even if I had."

The quality was slightly less on the second section because Brinkman had been in the apartment then. In the living room first. And then elsewhere. Franklin did not wince at the bedroom sounds. Or at the conversation there.

"Don't you think I'm a whore?"

"What!"

"A whore."

"Of course I don't think you're a whore."

"What then?"

"I think you're very lonely. I think you're very unhappy. I think you're looking for something you haven't got; maybe can't have. I think you are very beautiful. And I think you are a fantastic lover."

There was more. *"No, it isn't a casual fuck. And it isn't Romeo and Juliet either. What's wrong with you?"* And then the quality improved, from her end at least, because it was the telephone again.

"It was Eddie. He's coming home."

Ann had sounded so very upset during that homecoming argument when he'd announced he was staying on. *"You know damned well how I hate it here. How I've always hated it."* But then he'd lost his temper too. *"I don't expect you to stay . . ."* Thank God she had. He loved her so much.

Brinkman had been right in warning her about talking on an open line when she'd called him at the embassy and told him about their row. The man had been very clever in his questioning when he'd come to the apartment. And Ann very honest. *"Oh, darling, I'm so unsure of everything."*

Suddenly impatient, Franklin stopped, tossing the whispered telephone conversations and the bedroom sounds—one tape after the other—into the bag, pausing only at the one he knew best, the one he'd replayed the most.

"Do you love me?"

"I don't know."

"Do you love me?"

"Yes, I suppose so."

"What about Eddie?"

"That's it! I love him too."

"You can't love two people at the same time."

"Who says? Where are the rules that say you can't love two people?"

"You're going to have to make a choice."

"I don't want to. I'm frightened."

Something other than a tape was next in line for destruction. Franklin gazed down at the piece of paper that the poor, nervous Orlov had slipped him in Krasnaya Park, with Harriet Johnson's telephone extension at the United Nations on it. It had been an impromptu decision, to leave the copy openly on the apartment desk, because he had by then decided what to do but didn't quite know how to hook the Englishman. Brinkman must have been as desperate as some of his questions sounded on the tape not to have realized the impossibility of my ever making a mistake like that, thought Franklin. But then, Brinkman had other things to distract him.

Franklin threw Orlov's pitiful note into the bag and the paper was destroyed without even a wisp of smoke.

The American stretched. He had been sitting at the desk for almost two hours and it was getting late. Did he need any more reminders? Surely the need was to forget.

There was only one tape left, the one that had been made that afternoon.

"Don't pressure me!"

"You know what you want. So do it!"

"Why did you ever have to come to Moscow? If you hadn't come here, everything would have been all right."

"You know that isn't true."

"I'll decide."

"When? And don't say soon; don't try to run away again."

"A week. I'll decide in a week. I promise."

Now she wouldn't have to decide, thought Franklin, taking the final tape from the machine and putting it into the bag. The equipment was extremely efficient and there was only a miniscule amount of detritus. He shook it into the special container and sealed it, along with the remaining phosphorus, for collection and disposal the following morning.

Franklin rose, stretching again, and looked at the telephone, unsure of whether to call Ann and tell her he was on his way. He decided against it. There wasn't the need for discretion, not any more.

He collected his solitary car from the pound and eased out onto the near-deserted night streets of Moscow. The recall to Washington was a bonus, something he hadn't anticipated. But everything else had gone exactly as he planned. Until the very end, that is. It had been easy—from the intercepted conversations and Brinkman's hurried return to England—to know the man had interpreted the extension. He wondered if the surveillance team would still be in place in New York and whether they had seen the British make contact.

Franklin had guessed that Orlov had gotten on the agricultural delegation he'd read about in *Pravda*, and Brinkman had confirmed it by the sudden departure all so easily set out upon the last tape. The airport message had been impromptu—like leaving the United Nations number in his apartment—once he'd positively identified Orlov's arrival. But it had worked, like everything else had worked. Except for the shooting. He hadn't expected that. Franklin had imagined an arrest: a trial and imprisonment until an exchange deal was worked out. Long enough for Ann to forget. But not that the man would be killed. Panic, thought Franklin. It was always fatal to panic.

At the apartment building he put his car in the reserved space and climbed slowly to the apartment. Outside, Franklin hesitated, remembering the recall to Washington. He'd tell her tomorrow. Not tonight. Tonight was going to be a shock. She'd need something tomorrow.

He hesitated for a few moments longer, preparing himself, and then went in. Ann was sitting in the main room, very close to the *matroyshka* set he hated. Something else to pack up tomorrow.

"Darling," said Franklin, solemn-voiced. "I've got the most terrible news about Jeremy Brinkman."